THE ST
AND PROPHECY

For twelve years, the British Secret Service ransacked India for General Wedderburn's kidnapped daughter, Evelyn. They found not one trace of her. The General's search eventually led him to the Himalayas, where he found Captain Joicey, hospitalized, delirious, and badly burned. Joicey held the final clue to his daughter's whereabouts—a mysterious lead box inscribed in an ancient language with a huge purple sapphire inside. Armed with this new knowledge, Wedderburn then enlisted the help of an adventurer and his niece for the final leg in his never-ending quest. So to the rim of Earth's last frontier they ventured, searching for a long lost girl and holding the sole key to a long forgotten civilization—a civilization that once knew more about science than any scholar in the modern world.

CAST OF CHARACTERS

CAPTAIN JOICEY

His return quest into Tibet might be his last, and he was sure to get silly rich on sapphires—or was he?

JOHN FORD

His skills as a gem-trader and world-famous pathfinder would soon be tested to the utmost limits.

ROSITA ROWE

She shared her Uncle John's love of adventure and was no slouch when it came to traveling into dangerous country.

GENERAL WEDDERBURN

He swore he would never give up searching for his kidnapped daughter—even after twelve long years.

EVELYN

Kidnapped as a child, raised in the mountains of Tibet, she could only wait and hope she would someday be rescued.

SINGH

Yes, he abducted the general's little girl; yes, his act was heinous, and yes, he was willing to give his life for hers!

THE PURPLE SAPPHIRE

By
JOHN TAINE

Illustrated by Virgil Finlay

ARMCHAIR FICTION
PO Box 4369, Medford, Oregon 97504

For more information about Armchair Books and products, visit our website at…

www.armchairfiction.com

Or email us at…

armchairfiction@yahoo.com

CHAPTER ONE
The Lead Box

"WHY do you come to me, General Wedderburn? My specialty is gems and precious stones, not young ladies who are missing. You see, to put it plainly, my niece and I must first of all make a living. Were it not for this awkward necessity, we should be eager to offer you our sympathy. As it is, undue display of feeling on our parts might raise your hopes, only to disappoint them later. So it seems to me best that we understand one another's points of view a little better before we commit ourselves to any agreement whatsoever." John Ford, gem-trader and world-famous pathfinder through the deserts of Central Asia, turned from his white-haired visitor and resumed the leisurely sorting of a small heap of superb sapphires.

"I have come to you, Mr. Ford, for several reasons. The first is that you are an American."

"And what precisely has that to do with it?"

"A great deal. What you begin, you finish. Moreover, your years of exploring and prospecting in Tibet, Northern India and Turkestan have given you a familiarity with the native dialect and customs that is unique, I believe, for reasons which I will explain fully if you agree to my proposal, that a knowledge of the Tibetan language may be of help in following up an important clue. Now, a man of your experience must see that I cannot explain the grounds of my belief until I feel reasonably sure that you will undertake the search for my daughter.

"For, the fewer persons acquainted with the facts and theories concerning such a case as my daughter's, the better will be our chance of success. That is nothing more than the common sense our secret service men have taught me in the past twelve years. Again, so far as your qualifications are concerned, there is nobody in our entire secret service who compares with you in the art of passing himself off as a native-born Tibetan. Now this particular

The desert for miles around was a vast, intricate tangle of
sapphire blue serpents coiling and uncoiling...

thing may or may not be of use in what I wish you to undertake. I mention it merely as an example of the special kind of ability which certainly will be required in this case. And last, your unique knowledge of obscure Asiatic dialects makes you the one man living who stands a reasonable chance of obtaining the information I wish. How, I will explain presently, if you give me the assurance I desire."

"You will make me vain, General Wedderburn," Ford demurred with a modest smile. "It is true that we finish what we begin, at least in my trade. For if we don't, the other fellow makes a quick end of us so I claim no special credit for my virtues which, after all, are only the necessities of my profession. But," he continued, critically inspecting a flawless stone of the deepest midnight blue, you might have included my niece in your estimate of my tricks."

The studied nonchalance of his manner betrayed less indifference to the General's project than he tried to assume. "Now, my niece," he went on, "is really better at some kinds of deception than I am. Though she scarcely looks the part now, she can get herself up to that the dirtiest Tibetan couldn't tell her from his own grease-and-mud-plastered daughter. She's a peach when she gets on her war filth. And as you say, General, what we start, we finish!"

The General thought he saw his chance and took it.

"I could make it well worth your while," he said off-handedly.

Ford selected another sapphire for inspection. "Are you aware," he asked quietly, without looking up, "that such a search as you propose will be a very costly undertaking?"

"I have thought of that," the General replied calmly.

"And has it occurred to you," Ford continued, "that there must be hundreds of my enterprising countrymen who could break into Tibet—or the Bank of England, for that matter—if you paid them sufficiently well? Right here in Sikkim there are probably scores. You will pardon me, General Wedderburn, for again pointing out that you have not yet convinced me that I am the one man for your job."

"Possibly there are others who could traverse Tibet as natives," the General admitted, "although I doubt whether there is a man in India who could do it with the ease and comparative safety—that you can. However that may be, and after all, as I said, we may not need your ability in that direction; there cannot be two opinions about your mastery of Asiatic dialects. Even the secret service men speak of you with respect. Now, I thought that you as a gem-trader would be particularly interested in the search."

Ford perked up his ears. "But I understood that you wished me to find your daughter, not precious stones."

"The recovery of my daughter is all that I care about," the General assented. "Any further gains of the expedition would be yours."

"Ah, I am beginning to see." Ford smiled. "So my compensation is to be whatever I can pick up on the way?"

"Sapphires, for instance," the General suggested with a significant nod at the little heap on the table.

Ford turned to his niece. "Rosita," he said, "General Wedderburn thinks he knows where to find sapphires, even if he can't find his daughter. Shall we search for her?"

Rosita looked quietly up from the tray of many-colored stones which she was arranging, and for a moment the depths of her brown eyes glowed with the strange luster of the precious stones and the world-old lure of their mystery. But the revelation of her deeper self passed in a flash, and instantly her baffling smile masked her, as moonlight in seeming to make clearer the mystery of the sea but draws over it an intangible veil. She turned her smiling face towards the General, and for the first time he saw her rare beauty. The reply on her lips hesitated and remained unspoken before his puzzled wonder.

It was not so much her brown eyes and closely curled golden hair, for the beautiful alliance is not uncommon, that held his gaze, as it was an indefinable "something" about the shape and carriage of the exquisite head that called to his memory poignant associations of another head that he had never forgotten in its least detail of beauty. The prematurely aged man brushed his hand across his eyes and looked hastily away. His dream had been but a dream. He heard her voice.

"Shall we help you to find your daughter, General Wedderburn?" she asked. "From what I have heard, I think the decision rests with you."

"How so, Miss Rowe?"

"By making plain to us how we can afford to do what you wish. We are not unsympathetic. But neither are we millionaires."

IT WAS evident that Rosita was not drawn to this distinguished officer of His Majesty's Indian forces who persisted in hiding his own hand while endeavoring to make her uncle show his. She suspected the General of distrustfully concealing his most persuasive argument, and she knew that her uncle, although as sharp as his neighbor in business matters, was absolutely trustworthy with another man's secret. Adoring her uncle, she consequently felt a little less than chilly toward the General.

Another defect in the General's technique of approach irritated her even more. He seemed still to think that the services of this American gem-trader and his niece could be purchased for considerably less than the maximum which he was prepared to give. This enraged her. If she must work for a living, she was determined to get all the respect and every cent that she possibly could for her labors. In a flash her whole manner became crisp.

"Is the British Government so poverty stricken and so feeble, General Wedderburn, that it cannot protect its own subjects? Why should my uncle undertake this difficult and probably dangerous search? For the sake of a few compliments and vague prospects of trade? They cost nothing. We want the unvarnished truth, also a statement of the most that you can pay us. Nothing less will gain you anything. A clear statement, please."

"You shall have it. The secret service for twelve years has ransacked India from Sikkim to Ceylon for my daughter, and has found not one trace of her. Only the powerful home influence of my late wife's father has kept the department active in what they long ago declared was a hopeless search. Left to themselves, they would have abandoned it eleven years ago, when their best men gave up my little girl for dead.

"But I knew then, and I know now..." He brought his fist down on the arm of his chair, and the iron of his resolute will for a moment made his careworn race young, "...I know with every fiber of my being that she is living and that I shall see her again. Two months ago my father-in-law died. Within a week of his death the head of the secret service notified me that his department would do nothing more. Directly or indirectly, the Government has spent thousands of pounds in the search and now it is through. The quest ends just when it shows the first promise of success."

He thrust his hand into an inner pocket and drew forth a small flat box of highly polished lead. All six sides of the box were deeply engraved with the minute characters of some oriental script.

"There," he exclaimed, tossing the box between Ford and his niece, "examine what is in that box. All my cards but one are face up on the table, as an American would put it. I have nothing further up my sleeve but an ace. I'll lay it on the table too, later. Will one of you be so kind as to open the box? Press hard on the ends."

Ford unconcernedly picked up the lead box. "I'll risk it," he sighed, pressing firmly with his thumbs on the narrow ends of the box. The top sprung open, and in spite of themselves, Ford and Rosita permitted a low cry of pure astonishment to escape them.

"How much is a stone like that worth?" General Wedderburn asked quietly. Although apparently not watching them, he followed every emotion that flickered across the faces of his companions.

"What is it?" Ford demanded tensely.

"That is for you to say, Mr. Ford. You reminded me a few moments ago that precious stones, rather than mere human lives,

10

are your specialty." The General took a grim pleasure in the irony of the situation.

"It is a sapphire, and yet it isn't," Ford muttered to himself. "No sapphire ever pulsated from blue to purple like this. The thing is alive."

He lifted the scintillating disc of purple fire from its dingy bed, turned it over and over in his palm, and then without a word, handed this wonder of all jewelers to Rosita. She gazed into it, fascinated. Then she pressed it against her cheek and rubbed it softly across her lips. At last she reluctantly placed the stone back in its leaden box.

"It must weigh over two hundred carats, and there's not a flaw in, it." She sighed. "What wouldn't I give to have it for my very own."

The General confirmed her estimate. "Perfect, as you say, and over two hundred carats. Two hundred and fifteen, to be precise."

"The Maharajah of Mypore would give your weight in gold for that stone," Ford exclaimed, forgetting his assumed indifference. "And you're no featherweight. Even little Lemuel Anderson, the loan shark, might forget himself and offer you half what the stone is worth. But you have something else to show us?"

"All in good time." The General held up a huge knotted fist. "How much would an equally brilliant sapphire the size of that be worth?"

"Is it cut?"

"Yes, and the cutting is superb. The sapphire is in the form of a perfect sphere four and a half inches in diameter. It appears to have been hollowed out, although I can find no trace of a cut on the surface. There is not a scratch on it—"

"If the stone is perfect," Ford replied, "its value depends only on what the wealthiest purchaser—say one of the native princes—is able to pay. You can set no fixed price on a jewel such as you describe. If you wish to turn it into cash, the quickest way is to re-cut the single stone into several smaller gems. But if the stone really is hollow as you suspect, the loss by re-cutting is obvious. Have you weighed the stone, or taken its specific gravity? How do you know it is not solid?"

She gazed into it, completely fascinated…

"As a matter of fact, I do not know. I only suspect the stone is hollow because it appears to be impregnated with some foreign substance. This causes the entire jewel to glow and flash like an intense purple flame when it is exposed for varying periods of time to the full sunlight."

Rosita again picked up the sapphire and scrutinized it more closely.

"This stone, too, shows traces of the same thing," she remarked. "But I am sure it is neither hollow nor pitted. We can settle the question in half a minute!" She walked over to the balances and gravimeters by the north window and quickly made the conclusive tests. "Except for its unusual brilliance and rare color," she announced, "this is a true sapphire of 215 and a fraction carats. The sapphire sphere, I presume, is your ace?"

The General shook his head and smiled. "A good player always has reserves," he answered. "No, the sapphire sphere is not my best card, although it is a good one."

"General Wedderburn," Rosita murmured, "we are ready to talk business."

THE General enjoyed his triumph in silence a few moments before following Rosita's lead.

"I am glad to hear that my proposition appeals to you, Miss Rowe," he began. "Will you, Mr. Ford, take up the search for my daughter if I can direct you to the place where sapphires like this and the other of which I spoke can be found?"

"I certainly shall. And what is more," Ford continued with a new conviction, "you shall see your daughter again if she is still alive. If she is dead, I will agree to find out when, where, and how she died, and will bring back definite proofs for each item of my report. Now, will you please let us have once more, the details of your daughter's kidnapping? What bearing on the case have this sapphire and the spherical one you described?"

"The sapphires will come in presently," General Wedderburn replied, "also my remaining fact which I regard as more significant than a sack full of sapphires. First, let us go back to what happened here in Darjeeling, not half a mile from where we are now sitting, nearly thirteen years ago. It was early in June, 1907, that I returned to Darjeeling with my party. We came in early because it was impossible to continue our survey of Northern Sikkim during the monsoon rains."

"I can guess that it would be," Ford laughed. "The rains probably will start next week, just when we do. Pardon my interruption."

"Certainly, Mr. Ford. You have my sympathy through the coming deluge, for I know a little water won't dampen a man with your determination. Well, at the time thirteen years ago, long before the war, I was a Captain in the Royal Engineers and in charge of the party. We had pretty well surveyed the lower ranges and valleys at the base of Katchinjinga, and settled down to write up our field notes and prepare the official report of our expedition. Having no further work that season for our field men and camp servants, we discharged them. That was on the morning of June 2, 1907.

"My own personal servant asked if he might remain a few days longer at our Darjeeling headquarters, as he was expecting a friend from somewhere—I forget where—down in the plains. He wished to return with this man to Pedong where, he said, they both lived. Pedong, I need scarcely remind you, is the first 'station' this side of the frontier for the Tibetan caravans. This fact may be significant, or it may not. At any rate the secret service men never thought so," the General remarked savagely, before continuing his narrative.

"Seeing no objection," he resumed, "I granted the man's request. He had always been a faultless servant in every way, and I had grown quite fond of him. His intelligence was extraordinary for a man in his position, so much so that I suspected him of belonging to a far higher caste than his work indicated. However, it was none of my business, although his manner, his avidity for information regarding the white race—he was almost white himself and his aristocratic bearing piqued my curiosity.

"In spite of his fair skin, he claimed he was a Rajput on his father's side and half Tibetan on his mother's. I believed neither statement. For he joined our party in Darjeeling, and it is unlikely that such a mixture of races should be found here. Further, his personal appearance proved that he was lying. His features were remarkable for both strength and refinement with, I may add, a shade of cruelty at times.

"This may have been my imagination, however, for with the one exception of which I shall tell you presently, he was invariably kind to animals and considerate of men. Now, whatever his nationality, he was a thoroughbred, and I feel sure he was not an Asiatic. Yet it obviously was impossible to set him down as a European, although the shape of his head and the cast of his face were strangely reminiscent of the Caucasian races."

"Did it ever strike you," Ford broke in, "that he might have been an Englishman? Such things do happen, you know. Native women, whiskey pegs and more enticing ways of going to the devil do sometimes work miracles on your erratic countrymen."

"It did occur to me frequently," the General admitted. "There was, however one convincing argument on the other side. The man's pronunciation of the commonest English words was unmistakably foreign. It was too consistently peculiar. In moments of genuine excitement a masquerader inevitably must have betrayed himself, but this man's tongue never tripped. Nevertheless, I was haunted by a feeling that the man was in some way disguised and that he was acting an extremely difficult part. But, as I have said, it was no affair of mine. I, of course, did not pry into his life so long as he did his work well, feeling that if he was anxious to live down some foolish slip he should be allowed to do so in peace.

"HIS weaknesses," the General continued impressively, "have always seemed to me, but not to the secret service, to hold workable clues to the riddle of his identity. The one flaw in his intelligence was a curious streak of superstitions that cropped out unexpectedly from time to time, mostly in the trivialities of camp routine. For instance, he never could be induced to sit with his back to the sun; and he seemed to fear deep shadows as a cat does water. Nothing could force him to enter a cave or to pass under an overhanging rock. Beyond these and similar taboos, he had, so far as I ever discovered, no religion whatever. The point interested me, so without his knowledge, I tested him to see whether he was a Buddhist, a Zoroastrian, a Mahometan, a Confucian or a Christian.

All of his reactions were nil. It was evident that none of these great systems of belief had occupied his thoughts a single moment of his life.

"On the other hand, his scientific aptitudes were remarkable. He soon mastered the details of surveying and map-making, and asked if he might occasionally borrow a book to pass away the evenings. Having kept up my reading, I had taken with me on the expedition about a dozen rather stiff works on modern physics. He went through the lot in four months. Then his questions, always diffident and respectful, began in earnest. I was amazed at his scientific insight. Under his penetrating criticism of our modern speculations seemed in some mysterious way familiar and childish. His merciless analysis dissolved away the tissue of modern theory from the ancient fact, leaving only a bare skeleton of crude beliefs, which I instinctively recognized as the folklore of our race inherited from prehistoric ages. Our modern attempts to break up the atom and supply our industries with inexhaustible sources of power seemed to hold him with a perverse fascination. Although his scorn of our achievements in this direction amounted to contemptuous sarcasm, he constantly recurred to the subject with renewed interest.

"Last, I should mention his uncanny sense of locality. It was impossible for him to get lost, even in the mountains on the darkest night, and as a guide or scout he was unerring. In these respects he was more of an animal than a human being."

General Wedderburn paused and lit a cheroot before continuing. "I give you this minute description of the man so that you may recognize him when you meet him. For I am convinced, that the essential first step in the recovery of my daughter, is the location of my former servant—who called himself plain Singh, an obviously assumed name.

"On the third of June, 1907, the day after Singh had asked me if he might remain, my wife and little girl, then just eight years old, came up from Simla and joined me here in Darjeeling. Naturally, I saw nothing of Singh that day or the next. At four o'clock on the fifth, my wife, our little girl, and I were sitting at tea on the veranda of our bungalow, when Evelyn—my little daughter—asked me if she might run across the road to pick some bright yellow begonias which had caught her eye. Her mother assented and Evelyn left us. Having gathered her posy, she turned round and smiled across the road. Then she called out (I can hear her yet), asking if she might go through the hedge. There were some fine scarlet begonias just beyond, not over a foot from the tamarisks, she said. We nodded, and she was gone. That was the last glimpse my wife and I ever had of her, and the last that my wife was ever to have. She died five years later, an old woman at thirty-three."

The General tossed away his cheroot. "After fifteen minutes had passed and no Evelyn reappeared through the tamarisks. My wife became uneasy and sent the servants to look for her. They returned in half an hour empty-handed. In the meantime I had remembered Singh. He, with his extraordinary instincts for all kinds of scouting, would certainly be able to find our little daughter in a very few minutes. On going to his quarters I found him out. Tea had just been prepared, and a large bowl of rice, evidently cooked up for the next day, was still faintly steaming where it had been lifted off the fire. Thinking he must be somewhere nearby I shouted his name. There was no answer. I hurried out madly to look for him."

"You did not find him?" Rosita asked.

"No, nor did the best men of the India Secret Service in all the twelve years of their search."

"Surely, you found some trace—footprints, trodden grass, or something of the sort." Ford suggested.

"Of course. A man cannot vanish from the face of the earth without leaving some record of his going. The servants first found, in a grassy glade about a hundred feet from the hedge where we last saw our little girl, the handful of yellow begonias which she had picked. Twenty yards farther on I came across a shred of her pongee pinafore and a chain and locket with a four-leafed clover that she used to wear about her neck. The chain had been snapped; evidently she had struggled."

It was some moments before the General continued, and when he did, it was in a disciplined voice. "A few feet farther on I found fresh signs of her desperate fight. A yard of Singh's tunic had been ripped from him, and his turban lay under a datura nearby."

"And that was all?"

"There was nothing more that we could find in a month of searching. But when my first distress had passed and I had courage to examine the evidence, I noticed at once the peculiar weight of the scrap of Singh's tunic. It was part of the garment into which several pockets had been worked and completely sewn over. All but one of the pockets were empty. In that last I found that infernal sapphire in its lead box."

THE General flung out his arm at the incomparable gem as though to accuse it, and his companions looked hastily away. Then Rosita broke the painful silence.

"The abduction was premeditated," she said. "Singh waited patiently for his chance and seized the first that came."

"How do you know that?" General Wedderburn asked.

"He could observe your veranda from his quarters where he cooked the rice?"

"Yes, it must have been easily possible through the tamarisk hedge in front of the coolies' compound. The hedge was only a few feet from him, but at least fifty yards from us."

"Well, then," Rosita continued, "he spied on you all day, and when he saw Evelyn cross the road, he slipped out and ran round to the hedge to be ready in case she should go through it. He seized and gagged her the instant she did so."

"You generally know what you are talking about, Rosita," her uncle remarked, "though I'm hanged if I follow you now."

"It is perfectly simple. General Wedderburn found the yellow begonias which Evelyn had picked. Did he find any scarlet ones?"

"No," Ford admitted, and the General nodded.

"Then she had picked none," Rosita concluded, "and they were less than a yard beyond the hedge. So Singh must have seized her as I said. By the way, General Wedderburn, did you ever talk to Singh of your little girl?"

"Often, in the evenings."

"And you described her to him?"

"Yes. She was very beautiful."

"Did he ever see a picture of her?"

"I showed him her miniature several times," the General replied. "You will pardon me if I do not show it to you just now."

"Certainly. I understand." Rosita's businesslike preoccupation had softened as she spoke, and for a moment her face assumed the winsome tenderness of a little girl's. Again the puzzled look crept into the General's eyes, and he studied her with furtive interest.

"Are you by any chance of English descent, Miss Rowe?" he asked.

"Hardly," she replied with a smile, "unless you care to go as far back as the *Mayflower* and the Pilgrim Fathers. My mother traced her ancestry that far. But since then all manner of nationalities have been melted down to make me the plain American I am. My hair," she laughed, "may be Swedish for all I know, and my eyes Tibetan. Why do you ask?"

"Because, in some intangible way you remind me of Evelyn."

"Had she my hair and eyes? Coloring often is the basis of such resemblances, mine is common enough."

"Not exactly, yet it was similar—the same general shades. But it isn't that. I can't explain my feeling very well, but it is the way you carry your head and its somewhat Grecian lines that make me think of my little girl. Your facial expression, of course, is entirely different. Yours is vivid, if you will pardon my being personal. Evelyn was rather of the poetic, dreamy type."

Rosita laughed. "So may I have been when I was eight. Since then there has been little time for dreams. When night comes I am so tired, as a rule, that I dream of nothing but having made enough money to take a long vacation, with lots of stunning gowns and innumerable balls. Then the alarm clock goes off, my fortune vanishes, and I crawl into my working clothes."

"Environment," the General remarked dryly, "is an important factor in evolution after all."

Ford had been absorbed in thought. "Granting," he said slowly, "that the abduction was premeditated, what was Singh's motive? It cannot have been money, for he made no attempt to extort a ransom. And from your description, General, I gather that this man Singh was in no ordinary sense a criminal or a degenerate? Pardon me if I ask painful questions, but I must have something to go on."

"Assuredly, he was neither criminal, as we usually understand the term, nor degenerate. His intelligence was far too high for anything of that sort. As to his motive, I know no more than you. But I feel certain that when we do solve this twelve years' mystery, we shall find that Singh's motives were those of no ordinary adventurer."

Ford picked up the lead box and examined it narrowly. "This writing," he said, when he had finished his inspection, "is very peculiar. I thought I was at least acquainted with the scripts of the principal Asiatic languages, but I can make out only one short sentence on this. There are, I should judge, no less than seven different dialects represented in these engraved characters. The one which I can read is in ancient Tibetan. It is not particularly to my credit," he added modestly, "that I can make out even this one. A venerable and exceedingly filthy Lama taught me the older script and the rudiments of the ancient language on our last expedition after carved jade. I submitted to his instructions merely to keep from being bored to death in the endless evenings. This line says…" He indicated a narrow strip of the engraving on the box, *"…I will keep the jewel in this box, that it may not lose the life of its fire, and that I may have health and happiness.* That is a literal translation. It probably has some talismanic significance, but I am not up on such things. Have you had the rest of this read, General?"

"Not yet. The secret service submitted photographs of all the inscriptions on the box to the best orientalists in the world. Beyond what you have just translated, none of them could decipher so much as a single character. They agree, however, that the rest of the writing is in languages unrelated to any of the parent stocks of Asiatic or European tongues spoken within the last ten thousand years—since the earliest Sumerian and Chinese. So that gate is barred to us. There remains one more."

"Which?" Ford demanded. "Personally, I see nothing yet but— a blank wall."

"The one that our penny-wise, pound-foolish service refuses to enter. The one that would take them to within a few steps of success after twelve years of futile wanderings through every hamlet and city throughout all India. If you will come with me presently, I will show this other thing to you."

"Is it the other sapphire—the sphere?" Rosita asked eagerly.

"Yes, Miss Rowe, and better. Jewels by themselves are worthless trash. It is only when a gem has some human significance that it becomes interesting and valuable."

HAVING sat on this money-making young woman to his own taste, the General freely forgave her and even favored her with a genial smile, which she ignored.

"I shall now play my ace," the General resumed, evidently well pleased with himself. "When you have seen it, you will agree with me. I think that you have as excellent a prospect of getting your sapphires as I have of recovering my daughter. To me, the facts I am about to lay before you are as good as a guarantee of the success of our search. First, I saw the owner of the sapphire sphere less than three hours ago."

"What!" they exclaimed together.

"Just as I say. I left him to come directly to your bungalow."

"Has he told you anything?" Ford asked tensely.

"Yes, an immense amount. In fact, he has talked almost incessantly for three days."

"What did he say?" Rosita demanded.

"Blest if I know," the General ruefully admitted. "I only understood one word, and that was at second hand."

"Do you mean to say," Ford asked incredulously, "that you have talked with this man for three days and haven't wormed out of him where he got the sapphire sphere?"

"That isn't what I said. He did all the talking. I merely listened until I had to give it up as a hopeless job. Then after a short exchange of telegrams with the secret service, I came to you."

"Ah," said Ford with a knowing smile, "I see. He's some native who is trying to interest you, as the most important Mogul in this province, in his find of sapphires. And you can't understand his lingo. If he's from anywhere near Tibet, I should be able to act as interpreter!"

"Not a bad guess," the General admitted condescendingly. He seemed to be testing out the astuteness of this gem trader who was to be his agent in the search. "Not bad," he repeated, "except that it's wrong. Miss Rowe, what do you say? A keen young business woman like you should be shrewd enough to see through such an obvious paradox."

"And I do," Rosita exclaimed. "For I cannot imagine you letting any human being talk to you three days on end if you had the power to shut him up. So it follows that you were powerless."

"Right so far," the General assented with a grudging nod. "What next? Why couldn't I make him hold his tongue—provided, of course, that I really wished to do so?"

"Because he was delirious."

The General's crestfallen air proclaimed the correctness of Rosita's solution.

"And he is still raving, for all I know," the General added. "Poor fellow, he is in a terrible condition."

"Fever?" Ford hazarded.

"Not according to the doctors at the sanitarium where he is. They say it's more like a severe case of prolonged drug poisoning than anything else, but what drug could have produced such distressing effects they can't guess. As you will see for yourselves, he has also been injured in a peculiar way."

"He's an Asiatic, I suppose?" Ford, asked.

"His complexion is that of a hillsman. His features, however, are anything but Asiatic."

"Does he resemble Singh?" Rosita asked.

"Not in the least, except that he is a thoroughbred."

"Then who and what can he be?"

"That," the General replied, "is what I hope your uncle will be able to tell me. I am convinced that he is English, or at any rate a high-class European. But that really tells me nothing of value about the man. Either he has been away from civilization so long that he has forgotten his own language and now must speak the jargon that has become as second nature to him, or more probably he is still living over in his delirium the hardships of his travels. From his appearance he must have gone through hell.

"Although I can understand nothing of what he says, I know he is suffering the intensest mental agony. If only he would break into some recognizable language or dialect, we might be able to help him. Of all the flood of words he has uttered the hospital interpreters have understood only one. They say he has repeatedly used the Tibetan equivalent of 'yak.'"

"Have the doctors tried suggestion on him?" Ford asked. "It frequently works in cases of delirium, and is a common way of easing the patient."

"One of the younger interns did try it several times. But it was useless, for the physician had no clue as to what is tormenting the man, so he could make no reasonable suggestion to calm him. There will be no hope of doing anything for him that way until we learn in what language he is thinking. The interpreters and I tried all we know and got nothing."

"Then you came to us?" Ford queried.

"Not directly. The man's use of the Tibetan word for 'yak' first gave me the idea. Before that, however, I had telegraphed the facts of the case to the secret service, with what result I have told you. They courteously refused to reopen the matter, and mentioned your name, which had already occurred to me. Is it not the apex of their stupidity," the General burst out, "to refuse now to follow a sure clue after having wasted thousands of pounds on futilities? It is no longer a gamble that we are on the right track, it is an absolute certainty!

"Just consider the facts. Singh, the abductor of my little girl, leaves behind him a sapphire of unique size and quality. You as a gem-trader, and the secret service men as investigators of this case for twelve years, know that nowhere in the civilized world is there another sapphire of the same peculiar brilliance as Singh's, nowhere, I say, except in the sanitarium here at Darjeeling. And the companion to Singh's stone is this broken-minded man's sphere. Isn't the conclusion obvious? Singh and this delirious patient have visited the same place. Singh has returned to it, this other man has left it.

"NOW mark what I say," the General continued after an impressive pause, "and you will see the inevitable logic of my theory. This other man turns up twelve years after Singh's disappearance with my daughter. In all probability Singh made straight for his own country, which without a doubt must be the place where these peculiar sapphires are found. If this place is in

Asia at all—and where on earth could it be but in Asia?—it cannot have taken Singh more than three years at the very most to reach it. By the same argument the other man has not been more than three years on the road from there to here.

"To be safe, however, let us give him seven. He may not have been as familiar with the route as Singh. That leaves two years in which he could have wandered about Singh's country while Singh was there. In those two years, wouldn't he have heard at least some rumors of the strange young white girl whom Singh had brought back with him? I say that he must. It is against all probability that he could penetrate the place where Singh got his sapphire and remain ignorant of an event which must have made an impression on the people. To me it is inconceivable that this man can have travelled the country successfully enough to come back with a huge fortune and not have heard something at least suspicious. That man knows where my daughter is."

"Even if we pass over the possibility that Evelyn may have died on the way," Rosita quietly interposed, "there is still a serious flaw in your argument."

The General's face went white. "Don't tell me," he begged, and then, "out with it!"

"You have allowed this man seven years in which to return from Singh's country. How long do you suppose it took him to get there?"

The General groaned. "I see," he said. "This man may have left the country before Singh returned to it."

"In which case, he will never have heard of Evelyn. For all we know, he may have been ten years on the road there. If he did not know the way, it seems likely that the journey there must have taken longer than the journey back. You allow him seven years to return, I think it equally probable that he reached Singh's country as long ago as seventeen years. If so, and if it took him as much as five years to get his sapphire sphere, he left Singh's country just twelve years ago. So unless they met on the road, this man never heard of either Singh or Evelyn. It seems to me that your kind of arithmetic is too fluky. By changing the possible figures a little we can make it prove either case. Perhaps we may get at it in another way. How old is this man?"

"About thirty, I should judge."

"And you feel sure he is English or a European?"

"Certain."

"Then it is unlikely that he started on his travels before he was twenty-one. That gives us, say, ten years at the outside during which he was on the road. Your theory begins to look better. If your guess of his age is near the truth, he must have been in Singh's country at sometime within the past ten years. Evelyn disappeared twelve years ago."

"After all, then," the General exclaimed triumphantly, "the odds are in our favor. It is even better than I thought. This man must certainly have heard of Evelyn."

"Provided Singh met with no accident on his return journey," Rosita quietly objected.

"I'll chance that." The General laughed. "Wouldn't you, Ford?"

"It's a surer bet," Ford agreed, "than many that we have taken with my life and Rosita's as our stakes. This much is probable: Singh and your man have both been to the place where the sapphires are, and that's where I'm going if I can learn the way from the man who knows it. And I shall use all means in my power to find out. If, as seems more than probable, your daughter is being held a prisoner, that alone is sufficient justification for anything I may have to do to get this man's secret."

The General nodded. "So I felt when I set the interpreters onto his delirious monologue. Such a thing is, of course, contemptible, but this is not a case for the usual decencies of etiquette."

"If we do learn anything," Ford warned him, "we mustn't expect the poor devil to welcome our interference. I shouldn't, myself, in his case, if I knew where to find such sapphires. Well, General Wedderburn, hadn't we better be visiting your friend? The sooner we get to work the better."

The General rose. "I'll take you to him at once." His eyes hungered for a little encouragement. "It's not a forlorn hope, is it?"

"I should say not! Remember, we are as keen after this as you are."

CHAPTER TWO
The Man with the Scorched Hands

IT WAS but a few steps from Ford's bungalow to the sanitarium toward which General Wedderburn conducted the party. In answer to the General's request, the white-uniformed orderly saluted and led the visitors to the private ward at the cooler end of the building.

"Still unconscious, I presume?" the General asked.

"Yes, sir. The delirium this morning has been more violent, if anything, than yesterday. He quieted down half an hour ago. I think he is resting a trifle easier now." The orderly opened a door and stood aside for the visitors to enter. They found themselves in an immaculate white room. Closing the door, the orderly left them alone with the patient.

The silent figure on the cot was that of a man of perhaps thirty, strongly built, but now terribly emaciated from either disease or long starvation. He lay flat on his back on a narrow cot, his arms straight and rigid at his sides on the single sheet which covered him. The palms of the hands were pressed close against his thighs. In some curious way his motionless form gave the impression of a soldier standing at attention. Evidently from long exposure to the tropical sun, the face and arms were almost black. But for his features he might at first glance have been mistaken for a native. From where they stood, Ford and Rosita saw his finely cut face in profile.

"He reminds me of a Roman sentinel on duty," she whispered.

"Yes," Ford assented. "Julius Caesar must have looked like that when he was a young man. It is the face of a born soldier."

"You may talk aloud," General Wedderburn said; "he hears nothing."

"And he has been like this all the time?" Rosita asked, bending over the still form on the cot.

"Almost. He was semi-conscious when a company of pioneers discovered him almost naked in the hills, twenty miles from a road. At first they thought he was a native hillsman," the General chuckled. "Then they noticed, of all things on earth, a monocle screwed into his left eye. That, mind you, when the man had nothing but a filthy half yard of some sort of cloth about his middle, and the last remains of what looked like scraps of yak hide bound on with twisted grass to the soles of his feet. You may imagine that his monocle and lofty though unconscious superiority made those pioneers gape. They treated him with respect. The sergeant, I hear, even offered to lend the unfortunate man his trousers, but he was too far gone to bother about trifles."

"Poor fellow," said Rosita softly.

"Oh, I don't know about being so poor," the General demurred. "They had the very deuce of a time bringing him in. There was a dirty bundle of rags in his hands which he simply could not be forced to give up, even in his semi-conscious condition. That naturally made him very difficult to carry over the twenty miles of steep trails and slippery rocks. His body for the whole distance lay as rigid as a petrified tree. Every muscle, they said, strained like steel to make a locked vise of his arms and hands."

"I can guess what he was carrying in that bundle of rags," said Ford. "The sapphire sphere."

"So the nurse found, with the aid of some soap, and an expert way of going at things. Look, see his hands? He will show them in a moment."

Even as the General spoke, the tense figure on the cot relaxed slightly, and the stern features by almost imperceptible degrees lost something of their simple, commanding nobility. With the slow return of consciousness the clear-cut profile became that of a different man. A new spirit, more subtle and reserved, animated the face and interposed an impenetrable barrier between the mind of the man and the external world. He seemed to withdraw farther within himself, and deliberately to conceal the true man whom complete unconsciousness had betrayed. The change became more rapid. Presently arms twitched convulsively. Then very slowly the palms of the hands released their pressure against his sides and turned outward on the sheet.

Ford and his niece tried to look away from the sight which met their gaze, but something stronger than their wills compelled them to stare in fascination at those terrible hands. The flesh of the palms was seared and scorched as if by a white-hot branding iron, and deep fissures cleft through the excoriated flesh to the bleached bones. Only a dull, highly glazed tissue, like the dried skin of a snake, covered the nakedness of the bones on the inner sides of the fingers, which now closed slowly over the cracked palms.

"Do you suppose he has been tortured?" Ford asked. "Only a red-hot iron could do that."

"The doctor says not," General Wedderburn replied. "At least so far as hot iron is concerned. Those are not ordinary burns. The doctor has no idea what caused them. At first he thought they resembled burns from an over-exposure to radium. He soon decided, however, that these are radically different."

"Oh, I wish I could help him," Rosita exclaimed, recoiling in pity from the scorched hands. "Can't we do something for him?"

"Apparently not. As I told you, the interpreters say he has several times used the Tibetan word for 'yak.' Taking this and the fact that the scraps of stuff bound onto the soles of his feet looked like yak hide, the doctors thought that perhaps his feet also were paining him. Beyond being badly calloused, however, his feet seem to be in good shape. It is only his hands that are injured."

"I wish he would talk," Ford muttered.

"You will probably have a chance to test your knowledge of outlandish dialects in a moment," the General replied. "His is unlike any the interpreters have ever heard. This showing of his hands is usually the prelude to delirium. He seems to be struggling to make us understand what he wants done to them."

"Poor fellow," Rosita sighed.

"IF HE has been in Central Asia," Ford asserted confidently, "I am almost sure to place the dialect."

"We have tried all we know, but nothing pacifies him. There— he's beginning."

At the first word, spoken rapidly and incisively, Ford started in surprise and leaned over the cot. The sufferer spoke one sentence; each word distinctly, paused a few moments and then repeated what he had said. His eyes remained closed. The words were automatic, uttered subconsciously.

Ford straightened up. "Let me see that box again, General." He took the lead case containing the sapphire and again translated aloud the single line of ancient Tibetan. Then he pronounced it slowly, giving the words as nearly as possible the same intonations as those of the man with the seared hands. "Does that sound like what he said?"

The General nodded, but Rosita seemed doubtful. "It does, and yet it does not," she said. "Your accent is entirely different. His was alive, yours is dead. It is just as if a modern Italian was to express himself in Latin—you see what I mean. He might come somewhere near the sounds, but they would be meaningless to an old Roman."

"I noticed a difference, too," General Wedderburn agreed. "Still, if I know anything about Asiatic dialects, the two sentences express the same idea, whatever its real significance."

"Of course," Ford added, "my accent is second or third hand. I tried to reproduce exactly the sounds as the Lama taught me, but the ancient Tibetan is much more difficult than the modern, to pronounce accurately. This man may have learned the ancient language from a Lama connected with some other monastery. Indeed, it is probable that he did. And besides, we do not yet know this man's nationality, in spite of his monocle. If he is French, say, his tongue would make quite a different job of the ancient language than mine in trying to overcome its natural English. Wait a minute; I'll try him out. In his present state he should be open to suggestion." Putting his lips to the patient's ear Ford whispered rapidly in English:

"I understand what you want. I will keep the jewel in its box, that it may not lose the life fire, and that you may have health and happiness. I shall see to it for you, old fellow. Don't worry. That was it, wasn't it?"

A shadow of doubt, then a gleam of profound peace flickered for an instant over the drawn face on the pillow, and the lips moved. The man began to speak in the purest English with a characteristic drawl.

"Right, old chap. I don't know who you are. You may be another of those bally dreams. The blue flames cooked my brain. That's what's the matter with me. I know I'm talking, and I know I shouldn't, but I can't stop it. At least *I* can't stop *me*. I'm dotty, don't you know, with the heat and tramping about in that confounded desert—and all that sort of thing, don't you know. Damn the compass. It's a greater liar than I am."

"You're all right," Ford said reassuringly. "It must be your compass. Which way does it point?"

"All ways. Bally thing has no choice. South just the same to it as Northeast. Beastly bore. Can't find my way out. Know I'm making an awful ass of myself, but can't help it. Know I'm dreaming, or unconscious, or something like that. Can't make it out. I say, old chap, what have I in my hands?"

"Nothing," Ford answered.

"There is nothing there? You're sure?"

"Positively nothing."

"Then what did I do with the bally thing?"

"What thing?"

"The big lead box weighed about thirty pounds. But I never funked it. Hung onto it till I reached the desert. No, not that far. The box, you know. All covered over with queer writing. Got hot as the devil coming up over the pass. No shade, you see. Just those everlasting blue rocks and the snow. I say, I must be as black as coal, what?"

"Blacker. What did you do with the box?"

"Chucked it away. Too heavy. Got so infernally hot I couldn't hold it. I remember now. It must be on the other side of the pass from the desert. But I say, I didn't throw away the stone, you know. I carried it in my hands alone for two hundred and sixty-eight days before—no, it must have been after—I hid it. I don't know when it was. Two hundred and sixty-eight. Kept count, don't you know, to keep from losing my baby mind."

"Then you were foolhardy enough," Ford suggested, venturing a random shot, "to disregard the warning on the box? You took the stone out of its lead casing and carried it in your bare hands?"

"What was a chap to do? All silly rot about any warning. The priests just put that on the box to frighten away the children. The kids might have used it to play ball with, and smashed it. Awful liars, those ignorant old priests. I say, old fellow, where is the stone?"

"It is here," General Wedderburn interposed. "Would you care to have it given to you?"

"Thanks awfully, old chap. But I say, you aren't the chap who asked me about the box. Who the devil are you?"

"Never mind now. I'll fetch the stone for you." General Wedderburn hurried from the room, and Rosita approached the cot.

"CAN'T I do something for your hands?" she murmured.

"Ah, pardon me, but are you a lady?"

"Of course I am!"

"Then I must be in heaven... There are no ladies in this forsaken hole. I shall never see Sikkim again, and the rhododendrons."

"Yes, you shall. You are in Darjeeling now."

"What a refreshing change after hell." He sighed wearily, and seemed to sink into a deeper coma.

"Can't I do something for your hands?" Rosita insisted.

Was it an illusion, or did the ghost of a smile flicker about his lips? "You may hold them," he replied. The words were barely audible. Rosita crimsoned but made no attempt to execute his wish. The emaciated figure modified its request. "That is, if you are a lady and not an angel. Wouldn't allow an angel to touch me with her tongs."

"I don't believe you are nearly so far gone as you pretend," Rosita retorted with some heat.

"But I am. Much farther. I am walking somewhere, but I can look back and see myself lying face down in the desert. There are two—no three—of me. One is here, wherever this is, and the other two are out there. And there is another of us that babbles like a brainless fool, and I can't make him hold his silly tongue. This is all a dream, but it is as clear as water. Hope I never wake up. I say, you haven't taken hold of my hands yet. I know yours are cool."

"Better do it to humor him," Ford advised. "That man isn't shamming; he's getting rapidly worse. I'll bet a dollar he kicks the bucket before midnight."

But Rosita would not take the bet. A moment later the General, entering with a small wooden box, found Rosita administering first aid, and for once in her life looking painfully self-conscious and uncomfortable.

"Ah," said the General. "I see you hold jewels at their right value, Miss Rowe. You must be half-human, after all. Pity is akin to—what?"

"I don't know and I don't care," she answered shortly. "I'm doing this to humor him."

"They always say that. Well, he probably won't want his stone now. I needn't bother taking it out," and he carefully deposited the box at the foot of the cot. "Has he said anything more?"

"Too much," Rosita said, "for comfort. He is less distressing when all four of him are asleep."

The still figure never moved. If it heard, it gave no sign. Once more the lines of the face grew sterner, and the sheer nobility and indomitable courage of the true man reasserted their reign over the unconscious body. Ford picked up the box.

"May we see the sapphire?"

"Certainly," the General responded. "It is at its best, for I have had it in the full sunlight all morning."

Ford slid back the cover and almost dropped the box in his astonishment. "Great Scott!" he exclaimed. "The thing is on fire. Lord, what a stone."

"Take it out," the General suggested. "It's as cold as a lump of ice."

And so it proved. Forgetting her patient, Rosita caressed this blazing king of all jewels in her two hands, loath to let another touch it. She fondled and spoke to it as a mother speaks to her first-born. And what woman would not? Here was a sapphire, perfectly spherical, and over four inches in diameter, that coruscated with a dazzling, scintillating purple fire.

It seemed to have soaked up all the sunshine of India only to yield it back again intensified and wonderfully changed. Beside this incomparable gem the super-best of opals would have been but dingy clay. It was a dream of millions of flashing stars in a sapphire sky, and like the purest flame, it lived and pulsated from one shape of beauty to another. One human being had all but sacrificed his hands to possess this gem. Rosita in the madness of the moment felt that she could give her arms for it.

A sharp, commanding voice from the cot cut short her ecstasies. The man evidently was delirious, for he continued to speak rapidly in a broken mélange of languages. So rapid was his ghostly monologue that Ford was unable to follow its drift. His tones alternated between command and entreaty, finally subsiding in a short succession of despairing monosyllables. Then he resumed, calmly and distinctly, in the language which they had first heard him use, and which Ford now recognized, in spite of the unaccustomed accent, as being beyond doubt the ancient Tibetan which his Lama had taught him.

He held up a hand for silence from the other listeners, and strained every sense to catch the meaning. As the long recital proceeded in a clear, high-pitched monotone, Ford showed signs of intense and increasing excitement. His companions understood nothing. At last the voice ceased, and again the strained features relaxed. The man sank into natural sleep, breathing regularly and easily. His long illness had passed the crisis. The three crept from the room, leaving him in peace.

"THAT settles it," said Ford as they sat down in the shade of the deodars opposite the sanitarium. "I hate to be an eavesdropper—for anyone who consciously listens to the confessions of delirium is no better than that—but in this case the end justifies the means. General Wedderburn, if that man on the cot lives, I shall find your daughter and bring her back to you alive, or failing that, I will find out what happened to her."

Ford's excitement was so great that he had difficulty in speaking. His diffidence had vanished; he was a new man, with all the self-confidence of an assured though as yet unrealized success. "Without himself knowing the significance of what he has revealed," he continued, "that poor beggar with the scorched hands has unconsciously given away enough to make our gamble a practical certainty. I shall get my sapphires—of that I'm sure, and your end of it is so nearly certain that I would stake all my own gains on your probable success. Of course, much that the man said no doubt can be dismissed as the delusions of a disordered mind.

"Nevertheless, knowing what I do of Singh's case, I believe it possible to make sense out of an apparently meaningless mystery. His main revelation—it has to do with his search for the sapphires—must be substantially true. But let me say in self-defense that, without his sapphire sphere as tangible corroboration of your theory and his extraordinary disclosures, I should have believed nothing. The whole story is incredible but true. You were right in your guess. He is living over again in his delirium fragments of a terrible experience.

"We can see that he has suffered physically. It is not pain that torments him, I should judge, but the mental anguish of a great failure. Now, as I piece together your problem and his, I can see that his failure is to be our chance of success. At least, that is all that I have to gamble on. If I'm wrong, we shall all lose. It is our one chance. Therefore, we must take it. And I thought," he concluded with a laugh, "that I knew my way about Asia."

"Do you mean to say," General Wedderburn exploded, when at last he was able to speak, "do you mean to tell me that black scoundrel had a hand in the abduction of my daughter?"

"Easy, General, easy. Keep your shirt on. You may need it when the monsoon starts, for you're coming with us as far as Jelapla, and no further, I may add. Now don't get excited. It's dangerous in this heat. This man never set eyes on your daughter. In fact, he wouldn't believe that she exists if you were to swear to the fact on a stack of Bibles as high as Mount Everest. He has told me nothing *directly* about Evelyn."

"Then how in…" the General burst out, but Ford stopped him.

"Remember, General, that my niece is present. We Americans do not swear before our women unless they drive us to it. I repeat that our sun-baked friend knows nothing of the abduction. But he knows a great many other things that are just as important, and he has given away the whole show. I have put two and two together, your story and his, and now I know twice as much as both of you together. You naturally want your daughter; he wants something quite different. And the best of it is that I'm the one man who can get both of you what you want. Incidentally, I shall make a fair profit out of the deal for Rosita and myself. You and the other fellow haven't got a pair of deuces between you. I've got a royal flush. Are you on?"

"I'm on," the General ventured, not quite sure that he wasn't off.

"Then, first of all, you must give me entire charge of operations."

The General stiffened. "I am not in the habit of going blindly into things. So I must ask you to explain what you have learned from this man's story."

"I shall do nothing of the sort. To begin with, it would take a year. You shall have all the explanations necessary as they develop. In fact, my whole life for the next year is likely to be a sort of modest little footnote to our friend's revelations. If your eyes are good, you will be able to read my notes as we get on. But in all seriousness, General, I must go into this in my own way, or stay out. Disclosure of my half-formed plans now might very easily wreck the whole project."

"IF THIS man dies," the General asked suspiciously, "will you be able to find your way into Singh's country?"

"Let us climb no mountains till we see them. I am assuming that he will recover. But if he dies I shall attempt to take up his work where he drops it. I'm going after these sapphires…"

"What good will that do me?"

"Have you forgotten your own argument? Singh returned to the place where the sapphires are to be found, this man has come from it. If Evelyn is still alive, where is she to be sought? Obviously, where the sapphires are."

"Yet you say this man knows nothing of Evelyn."

"And I mean exactly what I say. Nevertheless, knowing that Singh abducted your daughter, I am justified in guessing an entirely different interpretation for the facts which this man has learned of Singh's country—facts which were the cause of his great failure and which he has totally misunderstood. In all this I am assuming that I am not crazy in believing the gist of his ravings. There is such a thing as being too rational, and that, I think, is at the root of our friend's trouble.

"Now, I may be going wrong in the opposite direction. If so, I should be able to judge from his behavior when we attach ourselves to him—if he recovers. If I am right, he will finally accept our interference. That is my guess. If I am wrong, he will treat us as lunatics, and we can begin to think up another theory. In either case, he will not receive us cordially, I predict, for probably he alone of all white men knows where those sapphires are.

"My first job will be to convince him of our discretion and straightness. His conduct will indicate how he must be handled. Personally, I incline to putting everything on a rock-bottom business basis. He will stand from me, an American, what he would never tolerate for an instant from you, a fellow Englishman—provided, of course, that he is English, as you suspect. If that fails, I'll acknowledge myself incompetent and let you, General Wedderburn, with your ignorance of Tibetan, take over the management and try to talk him around in very plain English."

"I have half a mind to try it," the General snapped.

"Then," said Ford earnestly, "let me offer you one piece of gratuitous advice. I had hoped you would not drive me to say what I now must, but it is for your own good. Don't assume that Evelyn reached Singh's country alive. Don't assume that she reached it at all. I am only taking your odds in believing that we have a gambler's chance of finding her."

The General's face changed. "You have formed no theory?"

"I did not mean that. Yes, I have a theory, but it is nothing more. And let me emphasize what I have already tried to make plain to you. Even if that man with the scorched hands were to hear your whole story, it is my opinion that he could tell you not one word more than I regarding the actual fate of your daughter. That is my calmly considered conclusion, based on what fragments of his unconscious self-betrayal I understood."

"But he could guess?"

"Anybody can do that. Now, General Wedderburn, be reasonable. Obstinacy is becoming only in a government mule. Do you go blindly, or do you stay out, as wise as an owl and as far-seeing as a bat?"

By a supreme effort the General corked his yeasty emotions and answered quite calmly. "I'll go in blindly. What am I to do?"

"Work the India Government to a Pan-American finish for permission for two men and one woman to cross the frontier into Tibet. Also for twelve ponies broken both to pack and saddle and thoroughly acclimated to hard work at altitudes from ten to seventeen thousand feet. Incidentally, too, you might get supplies out of them for a year. Use all the pull you have. But don't boggle over the money. I can raise enough for a small army from a certain source."

"How?" the General incautiously asked.

"Hand over your sapphire—box and all. Thank you, General. This is merely to supply the commissariat and distribute bribes— pardon me, gifts—if necessary. I'll give you a receipt."

"Much obliged," said the General ironically. "Is there anything else?"

"Yes. A jug full. The two men in the expedition will be myself and our friend with the scorched hands. You stay behind."

"I'm dashed if I do! What kind of a hound do you think I am, to let you and another man risk your lives to find my daughter, while I sit around and drivel at gymkhanas in Simla?"

"Then you most certainly will be dashed. For you can't go. Every member—and there are to be three and no more—of this expedition must speak Tibetan like a native. You can't manage a single word of it. Why, you didn't even recognize the Tibetan for 'yak' when you heard it, and that's one of their commonest everyday words. Rosita I would gladly leave behind if I dared, but I don't know where to find another white girl who speaks the language fluently and who knows Asiatics as well as I do. She must come. We may not need her. But if we do, it will be badly."

"I refuse to let you go unless I go too. Two men and a young woman, risking their lives to help my own flesh and blood while I stand by—it's preposterous!"

"LISTEN to me, General Wedderburn," Rosita quietly interrupted, laying a hand on his arm. "It is only natural that you should feel that way about it. If I were in your place, I should be just as unreasonable. But you don't know my uncle. He has never yet made a mistake in planning for any of his expeditions, and he has carried through dozens. He knows Tibet and the natives better than you do. And he has trained me since I was six years old. Ever since my parents died I have been with him, and I'm no dummy. Do you realize that I learned to jabber the dialects of Northern India before I ever spoke English? Or that I spoke Tibetan before I knew enough English to read Hans Andersen's fairy tales?

"As for any danger to me, you're mistaken. When I really set my mind to it, I can make myself from my yellow hair to my heels as black and filthy-looking as a pig, and the Tibetan girls just fall on my neck—only that isn't exactly what they do—and greet me as the long lost little sister of their childhood. I could spend a month alone in Lassa with greater safety than I could an evening after ten in your dear Piccadilly. Now, do be sensible and stay behind gracefully. You will have to, anyway, whether you like it or not. My uncle means business."

"Very well, I'll stay," he agreed. But he muttered something to himself that sounded suspiciously like "I'm dashed if I do."

"What did you say?" Rosita asked sweetly.

"Oh nothing. I was just wondering who our friend is—the other member of your expedition."

"We can be pretty sure as to his identity, I think," said Ford. "He did not mention his name in his ravings, of course. But from his story I gather that he must be Captain Montague Joicey, given up for dead by the India Survey about eight years ago."

"By Jove!" the General exclaimed. "I wonder if he is. Let us go and have a look at him. I knew him quite well," he continued as they hastened back to the sanitarium. "Joicey was in charge of the party working to the northeast of where I surveyed twelve years ago—right in the heart of the Himalayas. I used to supervise his reports after I took up the office work, and saw him often. Some years later he slipped into a crevasse and was killed. At any rate his body was never recovered. If it's Joicey, where the deuce has he been all these years?"

"His own version as to that," said Ford as he followed the General into the patient's room, "is that he spent most of his absence without leave in hell. Is this Joicey?"

"Gad," the General exclaimed, peering into the emaciated face. "I believe it is. No," he said looking closer, "this can't be Joicey. Joicey always seemed such a perfect ass."

" 'Things are not what they seem,' as our dear old Longfellow discovered," Rosita reminded him. "Shall we leave him now to have his sleep out? If you will pardon me for differing from you, General Wedderburn, I should say that if Captain Joicey ever appeared foolish to you, it was for an excellent reason of his own."

"What?" the General demanded.

"I had rather not say," Rosita replied with an enigmatic smile into the General's not very intelligent countenance. "Anyway, he won't deceive either my uncle or me if he tries it on us when he wakes up."

"What do you mean, Miss Rowe?" the General asked, flushing uncomfortably.

"Oh, just that he might try to disguise himself. Here, don't forget your sapphire again, or rather his. It is losing some of its fire already. Perhaps you had better put it back in the sun before he asks for it again. Good afternoon. No, please don't trouble to escort us home. We shall see you tomorrow evening and talk over our plans—perhaps."

"WELL, Captain Joicey, how soon will you be able to travel?" Ford asked genially when the orderly had closed the door, leaving him and Rosita alone with the convalescent. It was now three weeks since they had seen the invalid. General Wedderburn, acting on Ford's advice, had not been near the room during this time, and he had given strict orders that Joicey be told nothing about himself or his sapphire sphere. Long sleep, excellent food, and the best of nursing had wrought a marvelous transformation in the man. His seared hands, they thankfully noted, were now gloved. His face was filled out, the haggard look had given way to a mask of guarded restraint, and in place of the dominating mien of the born commander there was now only the calm reserve of the typical well-bred Englishman.

Nevertheless, his features, do what he might to efface his personality, still betrayed now and then the carefully concealed mind of the man. He might successfully act the minor part of the indifferent gentleman, but he could not convincingly play the commonplace. He now raised himself on one elbow and favored his visitors with a hostile stare. Rosita smiled back bewitchingly. Ford returned the ill-mannered stare with compound interest. It was a duel of rudeness between the two men. Ford won easily, forcing his weakened opponent to overstep the line of common decency.

"Who the deuce are you?" Joicey blurted out. Then, remembering his assumed part, he drawled wearily, "I fear I have not had the pleasure of your acquaintance."

"Then let me introduce myself. My name is John Ford. My business, trader in gems and incidentally explorer of certain parts of Asia. Ah, I see that you have heard of me. I regret that my maps were of no value to you in your recent travels. This lady is my niece and constant travelling companion, Miss Rosita Rowe. She speaks Tibetan—the modern variety—as well as I do, and probably much better than you. Now you should be able to talk business intelligently."

"American, I presume?"

"Isn't it a bore?" Rosita laughed, and her brown eyes sparkled with delight over this perfect jewel of an Englishman. "But really, Captain Joicey, we can be quite decent when we try. Now, won't you please get used to our outrageous manners at once? It will make it so much easier for all of us. You see, we shall be together for a long time, several months probably, with the Himalayas between us and the nearest Englishman."

Joicey's only immediate reply was a callous appraisal of Rosita's radiant beauty, from the supple lines of her trim figure, buoyant with youth and perfect health, to the exquisite face, alive with humor and intelligence that shone softly, but clearly, from her brown eyes, and the clustering curls of pure, shining gold. She was of a rare type. The flawless beauty of the features and her glorious coloring would attract any man; the womanliness, and above all, the vivacity and intelligence of her face, mostly certainly would repel fools. It appeared to make not the slightest impression, favorably or otherwise, upon Captain Montague Joicey. Suddenly he shot at her in Tibetan, "Who told you my name?"

"You," she replied instantly in the same tongue. "At least you told us so much that we guessed the rest. You were not killed when you fell into that crevasse in Northern Sikkim in 1913. I do not know how you escaped, where you have been in the meantime, or what you have been doing, but I suspect my uncle does. Nevertheless, I do know your name."

If her fluent command of the difficult language impressed him, he studiously concealed the fact. Turning to Ford, he asked in British, "And what do you know?"

"Let me tell you frankly what I don't know. I have no idea of the exact route to the desert, the way across it, or how to reach the caves. These details I shall learn from you later."

"I don't follow you, sir…"

"You will presently," Ford replied with perfect good humor. Then his manner changed. He bent down and whispered a few sentences in the ancient Tibetan. Joicey's face betrayed nothing. Ford said:

"So it is agreed, Captain, that you are to accompany us on a short trip into the hills to recuperate? General Wedderburn has arranged the necessary formalities about your leave, and so on."

"Wedderburn? Stuffy old ass. Used to mess up my reports. So they've made him a general, have they? Couldn't arrange his father's funeral. When do we start for the hills?"

"The day after tomorrow. We can travel easily the first week. You are quite able to make the first stages without tiring yourself. I hear you have been promenading regularly six hours a day this past week. You're better. By the way, have you heard that there was a European war while you were buried?"

"O Lord, yes. The orderly jaws about it all the blessed day when I want to sleep. Comforting chap, I must say. I shall be court-martialed—desertion in face of the enemy and all that sort of rot."

"No fear. Thanks to the General, you were officially killed eight years ago and officially raised from the dead, as innocent as a babe, last Thursday. They have begun asking questions about you in Parliament, so you had better clear out before you fall into sin again."

"I prefer sin to one of those beastly crevasses," he remarked with the sage gravity of a bronze Buddha. "Don't you, Miss Rowe?"

"IT DEPENDS," she said. "I'll wait until I've seen the crevasse. Now slip into your clothes and we'll meet you outside. We have an important engagement at eleven o'clock."

"I have no clothes," he said gloomily. "They destroyed my toga, and my evening dress is somewhere in Simla. Pajamas wouldn't do, I suppose, or the hospital slops I've been wearing?"

"That's all right," Ford reassured him. "The orderly will bring you an outfit in a moment. I had you measured before you came to."

"Confounded cheek! Thanks awfully, just the same, old chap."

"Don't be long," Ford admonished him. "There is something for you in a box at the office. We'll take it outside."

Within fifteen minutes he joined them under the deodars, strolling up unconcernedly smoking a cigarette. In his perfectly fitting white duck and soft silk shirt he looked the typical sun-browned chappy out for a jaunt to see the other chappies risk their silly necks at polo. He had dressed with extreme care, even to the cigarette, which dangled from one corner of his mouth as if the languid smoker were too weary to enjoy it. How he had accomplished the miracle was a mystery, but his whole expression was one of tenderly nourished banality. Even his aquiline profile was softened to a putty imitation of a well-rubbed Roman coin. Civilization had worked wonders on him. Rosita critically inspected the apparition.

"It isn't quite perfect yet," she decided. "Something is lacking, and I don't know what."

"I fear I scarcely follow you." He gave her a cold stare and turned to her uncle. "Mr. Ford, you have a box or something of mine?"

"Right here. Sorry it isn't lead, but as you will probably want to sell the contents it makes little difference."

Joicey accepted the box, and in spite of his languid manner his immaculately gloved hands trembled. "Pardon me," he said, and turned aside. The sound of the cover sliding back was followed by a low exc Lamation of gratified surprise.

"By Jove, old fellow, this is awfully decent of you," he murmured, facing Ford. "I thought I had lost the bally thing."

He began fishing about in the box. They waited for him to bring out the great sapphire sphere. All morning it had soaked up the sunlight and now it seethed with every hue of violet and purple. It was the General's kindly idea to have the stone at its best, as a pleasant surprise for the poor fellow, who doubtless, thought he had lost his treasure forever. Joicey continued to fish awkwardly with one gloved hand, and presently caught the elusive and slippery thing he was after. With a subtle smile of the completest self-satisfaction, he drew forth a large monocle which he proceeded to screw into his left eye.

"Ah," he sighed. "I thought I had lost the bally thing in those beastly hills. Can't see without it, you know." And closing the box without further comment he carelessly stuck it under his arm.

Ford gazed at him in open-mouthed admiration. "You'll do," he said. "You beat the Dutch. Let's go."

Rosita for some moments found no words to clothe her emotions. She just filled her eyes with him, unashamed. Then she sighed. "Now you are perfect," she said. "It is the finishing touch. I understand now what the General meant. Only…" she added doubtfully, "…I always thought they were born that way, not made."

"What way, Miss Rowe, may I ask?"

"The way you look now. Oh, please don't spoil it by trying to look intelligent. You don't do that part of it at all well. It's too much like the real thing. Your disguise is absolutely perfect."

He stalked on by her side in bored silence, his face a blank. The miracle was accomplished. At last he was the complete gentleman; not the softest zephyr of a thought ruffled the placid mirror of his countenance. No wonder the General had been deceived.

CHAPTER THREE
To Hell via Eden

"I SAY," Joicey expostulated presently, "where are we going?"

"We have an appointment at eleven with Lemuel Anderson to negotiate a loan," Rosita informed him. "It is only a step from here."

"Sort of pawnbroker chap, eh?"

"Precisely," Ford replied. "A great and miscellaneous collector of precious stones, carved jade and ivory, estates, IOUs, and in fact, of anything that can be melted down to cash. In one way he is scrupulously fair; he skins all comers alike. I always expect to be done when I go to him, and just charge the difference to over-head."

"His specialty," Rosita added, "is dashing young army officers who worship sport in your fine English way, and who are waiting for inconvenient brothers or fathers to shuffle off. His collection of younger sons is said to be the most extensive and noblest in existence."

"I shall add myself to his cabinet."

Rosita laughed. "Well, see that he sticks you into his box with a pin of pure gold. We regret having to use him this time but we must, and that's all there is about it. He is the one man in India who commands sufficient cash to buy us out."

"Why sell?" Joicey drawled.

"Because," Ford explained, "it is a gamble whether we shall come out of this business alive. We always convert our assets into cash before quitting civilization. Then by a simple piece of legal machinery we leave the money in trust for ourselves when we return, or for the right people if we don't come back after a reasonable time. We take all precautions possible against being done out of our money. I needn't bore you with the details. The point is that if we don't come back, the lawyers get nothing and our friends everything. See?"

"Simple," he answered curtly. Something in Ford's manner had aroused his suspicions. They walked on in silence for a few moments. Then Joicey turned to Ford and gave him a keen look. "You are taking too much for granted," he said shortly. "I see no reason why I should not bid you good morning." He raised his hat to Rosita and stalked off.

"Just a moment, if you please, Captain Joicey," Ford called after him. Joicey turned. Ford spoke, first a few rapid sentences in the ancient Tibetan, continuing then in English. "It is immaterial to us whether you join us, go by yourself, or stay here. We're going. Only, if we all go together, we individually stand a hundred to one better chance of getting there and back alive. You've made up your mind to go back and get the rest of those sapphires. Any fool could see that, and we're not fools.

"When you return, you will be by all odds the richest white man in India, or in all Asia for that matter. We mean to have our legitimate share in the profits. Legitimate, I say, because incidentally we have another commission to carry through for General Wedderburn. I'll tell you something. The General's little eight-year-old daughter was kidnapped by a man of unknown nationality twelve years ago. Does that throw any light on the past two weeks? If it doesn't, I'll tell you when I get good and ready to do so. Just now, I see, and so do you, in spite of your dumb-blind look, that the success or failure of either mission—getting the sapphires or the General's daughter—entails that of the other. I know more about the situation than you do, and I don't care to reveal my plans, even to my niece, until we're well under way. Now let me ask you a question. Did you ever come within a thousand to one chance of getting into the caves? Take your time to answer."

Joicey stood silent. His face betrayed nothing of what was passing in his mind.

"I am not obliged to satisfy the curiosity of casual acquaintances," he said frigidly. He stood hesitant, idly fingering his precious monocle. "But you were so jolly decent about this bally thing, old chap, that I'll meet you halfway. Can't see without it, you know," he remarked, screwing in the monocle so as to get a microscopic view of Ford's face. "I'll ask you a question. Could *you* get into the caves?"

"No!" Ford snapped. "But my niece could."

"I must have chatted in my sleep like a female chimpanzee," he said with an air of intense disgust.

"You did," Ford assured him. "And it will turn out to be the most profitable speech you ever made. Rosita, do you think the Captain could pass himself off as a beautiful woman?"

Joicey blushed under Rosita's discomforting inspection. "I don't think it would be possible," she said judicially. "Especially if he were thrown much with other beautiful young women—real ones, I mean. They would penetrate his disguise instantly. He is so very masculine. Again, it is extremely, difficult for a man who likes women as well as Captain Joicey does to masquerade in anything but very masculine roles. I don't believe you appreciate how excellent his present disguise really is." She glanced diffidently at his broad chest and athletic build, permitting her eyes for just an instant to flicker over his slim hips. "I can't see anything the least feminine about his figure," she concluded.

Joicey collapsed. "You will have to learn the ancient language," he grudgingly admitted.

"Then you shall teach me," she smiled. "It should be comparatively easy on the top of the modern Tibetan. The grammar can't be so very different. You won't find me incurably stupid after we get better acquainted." Joicey did not kindle at the prospect. In fact, he seemed chilled.

THEY walked on in constrained silence, Joicey now and then glancing suspiciously at his companions.

"What color—" he began. Then, thinking better of his intention, he abruptly checked himself.

"What color was what?" Ford demanded.

Joicey withdrew within his reserve. It was plain that he distrusted the gem traders. He was not yet ready to commit himself and his secret to the cooperation of this pushing American and his businesslike niece.

"Pardon me," he said, "but it really doesn't matter now."

"You mean what color was Singh's sapphire?" Rosita interrogated sweetly. "Why, similar to yours. Purple, I should say. You wouldn't call yours blue, would you?"

"Blue?" he repeated after her suspiciously. "Either you know too much," he said acidly, "or you are guessing too little." As he spoke, his face changed. The carefree gentleman vanished for an instant in the true man.

"Don't be so suspicious!" she replied with some asperity. "Can't you see that I am trying to help you?"

"And yourselves," he added.

"Well, why not? Must we risk our lives for nothing?"

"I am sure I don't know." He gave her a searching look. Failing to find in her open face either the confirmation or the denial of the suspicion that was haunting him he walked on without another word. For the moment, at any rate, he seemed resigned to follow his companions' lead. But they could not be sure of him. His cold, reserve effectively masked his thoughts, which his apparent acquiescence in their immediate purpose made but the more difficult to read.

"Well," said Ford, "here's our destination. Prepare to be skinned and well salted."

Anderson made his welcome just a trifle too cordial. He was a pudgy, effusive little man with a close-cropped black mustache, jet-black oily hair and a noticeable lisp. The foxiness of his small black eyes was coyly and not altogether successfully sophisticated by a huge pair of tortoise-shell-rimmed glasses of a rich amber hue.

"And now my dear friendth," he breathed when his visitors were comfortably seated, "what can I do for you?" His manner had all the slick suavity of the more expensive brands of scented olive soap.

"You have done so much for me already," Ford began, "that I feel it is now my turn to do something handsome for you. One good turn deserves another, you know."

"Yeth, yeth. We live by helping one another."

"Well, Lem, if it's how you live, here's where I give you a boost that should lift you half way to immortality." Ford took the General's small lead box from his breast pocket and tapped it significantly. "Anderson, a man of your genius and unrivalled opportunities for helping the needy should be able to get at least three hundred thousand pounds for what is in this box. You have done me so many good turns in the past that I'll let you have the contents of this box for two hundred and twenty-five thousand. I'll keep the box itself as a souvenir. You wouldn't be interested in it. It's only lead."

"Deah me. Two hundred and twenty-five thousand dollars is a conthiderable thum of money." Anderson sighed, taking the box but not opening it.

"You bet it is," Ford agreed. "And at the present rate of exchange two hundred and twenty-five thousand pounds is a little better than four and a half times as considerable a sum. I spoke in pounds, not dollars."

Anderson opened the box. "Yeth," he lisped, "it ith more money than I have at present. Thith ith a pretty thapphire, Mr. Ford. May I write you a check for fifty thousand poundth?"

"Don't bother, Lem. Save your tips for the office boy. He needs them, I don't. I'll trouble you for the box and the stone."

Anderson, ignoring Ford's outstretched hand, continued toying with the sapphire disc. Where will you dithpothe of it, Mr. Ford?"

"Well, since you're an old friend, Lem, I'll whisper it to you. I shall offer that unique sapphire to the Maharajah of Mypore."

"Why didn't you go to him before you thaw me?" All this time, although apparently indifferent to the jewel, Anderson was slyly appraising its value. Under pretext of rubbing his eyes, he now removed his amber glasses.

"I came to you first, Lem, because you will buy anything under the sun without asking where the seller got it. The Maharajah would meet my terms without haggling. But I should have to fool and fiddle about his court a month, and I haven't the time to waste. We're off tomorrow morning on another trip."

"I should like to oblige an old friend, Mr. Ford, but weally, I haven't got that much money."

"No, but you could borrow it. Just think of all the friends you have helped who would be glad to lend you fifty times the amount on your personal note."

"I'll thee about it," he said, rising.

He soapily excused himself. Just as he was about to close the door softly behind him, Ford called after him, "Our usual cash basis, you know. Bank of England notes; thousand or five hundred pound denominations will do. No checks or other monkey business. Hurry back."

Anderson did not deign to reply.

"He seemed to be a decent enough chap," Joicey disingenuously remarked. "Shouldn't wonder if he'd take this bally thing off my hands. Too deuced heavy to carry all the way back, you know."

"Oh, he will take it, right enough. Your wisdom teeth, too, if you let him see them."

THEY sat silently admiring Anderson's art treasures for several minutes. Joicey began to fidget. "Takes the beggar an infernal time to make the arrangements," he complained. "I want my lunch," he prevaricated, and all but grinned as he caught Rosita's intelligent, understanding eye.

"Lem has the notes in his safe. If he is telephoning it is to the Maharajah's bankers. When he comes back, he will know to the nearest farthing how much he can squeeze out of his customer."

The door opened, and Lem sidled in with a fistful of crackly white Bank of England notes. "Thorry I kept you waiting," he apologized, "but they thent a thlow methenger." He began methodically counting out the notes on the green baize.

Joicey's face grew blanker and blanker.

"Much obliged, Lem," said Ford, pocketing the fortune. "The stone's yours for what it's worth. Hope I can do you a favor someday, in return. Kindly give me back the box. It's of no intrinsic value. Thanks."

"Pray don't mention it," Anderson rejoined, with a smile that was smooth as oil and strained honey. "I'm alwayth glad to oblige a friend. Now, gentlemen and lady, ith there thomething more I can do for you?"

In a flash Joicey sized up his man. "Don't know, yet," he drawled. He placed his wooden box on the table, slid back the cover, and nonchalantly rolled the huge sapphire sphere, alive with violet light, out on the green baize. Anderson stood speechless. Then he found his tongue.

"Thith ith a thwindle!" he almost screamed, crimson with rage.

"You are mistaken," Joicey sighed. "How can you be so dense? It is a sapphire."

"Tho I thee, tho I thee! Thith ith a fine way to treat a friend," he spluttered at Ford. "I thought you were a gentleman!"

"Well, I try to be, provided it doesn't interfere too much with my business. But what's eating you, Lem? What have I done?"

"Done? Everything! Me! If I had theen thith first I wouldn't have given you thixthpenth for thith rotten little thing." He contemptuously tossed his two hundred and twenty-five thousand pounds worth of sapphire down on the table beside the incomparable sphere. The disc was out-classed, there could be no doubt of that. Anderson almost cried with rage.

"I don't want it, I don't want it!"

"All right, old man. Don't shriek. You don't have to take the bally thing unless you can't be happy without it." Joicey returned the king of sapphires to its plebeian box. "If you change your mind before I get outside you may have it for five million pounds cash. Otherwise I shall leave it at my bankers and sell it for something like its true value when we return."

His hand was on the doorknob when Anderson capitulated. He was shrewd enough to see that Joicey meant exactly what he said.

"All right," he snapped. "Come to the bank. I shall have to cable London and Paris."

"That is agreeable to me. Now, Mr. Anderson, it will be much more satisfactory to all parties if we have this thing examined and certified by an expert who is more than a mere dealer in precious, stones. Then you will know precisely what you are buying. I am selling you a sapphire of unusually fine quality. Its shape and weight, of course, put it in a class by itself.

"To avoid possible misunderstandings later, I want you to realize very clearly that this sphere increases greatly in brilliance when it is exposed for even a few minutes to the pure sunlight. It retains this greater brilliance and fire for varying periods. Sometimes it will blaze away at top fire for several days, sometimes for only half an hour. The stone as you now see it is in its normal, dullest state. Put it in the sun for twenty minutes and you'll see wonders.

"Now, if you agree to pay me five million pounds cash for this sphere in its present state I'll call it a bargain. But if you think you are buying a stone that will always be exactly as it is now, I refuse to sell. Mr. Ford's stone is of the same general kind as this. Perhaps you had better make your receipt and quit-claim, for any reconsideration of these transactions cover both his stone and mine. And you had better include explicitly in the quit-claim that it has special reference to any change in the stones from the condition as certified by the expert at the exact time of delivery to you."

Anderson's foxy little eyes gleamed with cupidity. Here he was getting at least ten times as much as he had bargained for, and this immaculate young fop with the monocle—a first-class polo player and possibly a tennis champion, to judge by his bronzed skin and athletic build—was actually trying to talk him out of buying. But, then, it was only natural that Joicey should do this idiotic and gentlemanly thing; he looked the part.

"Come on, then," Anderson said. "I know an expert who can convinthe all partleth that you are weally thelling me a thapphire. I'll leave you with him while I go to the bank. We can meet there in the Directors' room at thix o'clock. Bring the thertificate with you, and the other thing, and I'll thign them both. You need them, I don't," he concluded with an undisguised sneer.

They passed out and separated, Ford and Rosita to return to their bungalow, Lem and Joicey to go about their lawful business. "Shall we see you this evening, Captain Joicey?" Rosita asked. Her eyes held a warm, but not too warm, invitation.

"Delighted. I'll drop in on my way to the hotel. Not going back to that beastly sanitarium." Had they quieted his suspicions? His easy courtesy might mean anything.

ABOUT eight o'clock that evening Joicey appeared. "I shan't come in," he said. "Just wanted to show you these." He exhibited photographic duplicates of the expert's reports on the sapphires and of Anderson's receipts. In these the buyer declared himself satisfied with the quality of the stones and waived all claims to reconsideration of the purchase price should either of the stones at any future time prove to be other than as certified that day by the expert. "The originals are deposited at the bank in our names jointly. By the way, I presume you have made all the arrangements you spoke of about your money? We are not going on a picnic, you know."

"Yes. And you?"

"Mine is deposited to my credit in the strongest banks of England, France, and America. Between us, Anderson and I kept the cables hot for seven hours this afternoon. If I don't come back, the banks can do what they like with my money. But I have tried to arrange that it shall go for a particular exploration of a certain crevasse in the Himalayas," he added with a laugh. "My people are all dead, so it is either champagne or science so far as my fortune goes if I don't return."

"Then everything is ready. We start tomorrow morning at five sharp. All the bothersome details of the caravan are attended to, so you can sleep soundly. The pack train has already gone ahead. Be prepared to meet General Wedderburn in the morning."

"Stuffy old boy, what?"

"Not when you really know him," Rosita demurred. "We have learned to like him immensely this past week. When you hear all his story, you'll pity the poor old fellow. Now, good night."

"Good night, Miss Rowe. Tomorrow we start to break our necks or make our sillier fortunes. Queer, isn't it, that some chaps would be content with a rotten five million pounds?"

"Evidently you are not."

"Not while there is more where the five million came from, to be had for the taking."

"Even if you have to go through hell to reach it?" she asked, before she had thought what she was saying.

"What do you know?" he demanded fiercely. "Who has been talking to you?" His face almost frightened her. It was again the face of the man whom she had first seen; the well-nurtured nobody had vanished.

"It was only a chance remark," she stammered, "from something—really it was nothing definite—my uncle dropped."

He peered into her face. "You are telling the truth," he said. His features again lapsed into a mask of carefree indifference. "Well, good night, and pleasant dreams," he said, and left her to her thoughts.

"We parted on good terms, anyway," she said with a sigh of relief, as for the last time for many a month she turned the cat out to enjoy the moonlight.

IT WAS a sober little party that assembled before Ford's bungalow early the next morning. The mists still clung to the hills, and the valley yet slumbered a mile beneath the sleepy little town.

"Where's the General?" Rosita fretted. "He's ten minutes late already."

"I shouldn't be surprised," Joicey hazarded, "if he were in the throes of an exciting correspondence by cable with His Majesty the

King. You impressed upon him the necessity for passports, I hope?"

"Naturally," Ford replied. "He would have burst ten days ago unless we had given him something to do. Well, he'll be along presently. We should do twenty-five miles today. The pack ponies are a march ahead of us by now; we can pick them up at Pashoke tonight. Joicey, you get four meals today, the rest of us two."

"Thanks awfully old chap. Four meals a day is better than four days a meal. Hullo, here's the sluggard. Where have you been, General? Buckingham Palace?"

General Wedderburn was in no mood for frivolity. "It's no use, Ford," he groaned. "I have moved heaven and earth, in fact every blessed thing except the British Government. Look at this."

It was the climax of his endeavor. All the past fortnight he had maintained a lively and expensive correspondence by cable with his "home influence." The cablegram which he now waved like a banner was the last of several dozen. It was a curt refusal of all his requests. Under no circumstances would the Americans, Mr. John Ford, Miss Rosita Rowe, and the Englishmen, General Lindsay Wedderburn and Captain Montague Joicey, be permitted to cross the frontier into Tibet. Should they attempt to do so, they were to be forcibly prevented. Instructions to that effect had been cabled the Commander-in-Chief of His Majesty's Army in India.

"Ah," said Captain Montague Joicey. Neither Ford nor his niece made any comment. The General went crimson and exploded in the immediate vicinity of Joicey.

"Our project is nipped in the bud, and all you can say is 'Ah,'" he sputtered. "'Ah,' why don't you say something sensible?"

"Ah, really now, I couldn't say." He screwed in his monocle a little tighter and stared blankly at the General. "Why don't you?"

"Now, you two," Rosita broke in, "please keep your compliments on ice till they cool off. The rest of this town wants to sleep. What are you going to do, Captain Joicey?"

"Go."

"Without a passport?" the General queried.

"Bring a bale of them if you like. The ponies might like some when we run out of barley. Personally, I never cared much for them."

The General turned sadly a way. "Perfect fool," were the inaudible words that his lips framed.

"Ready, Ford?" Joicey called. "Very well then, give the word. You're conducting this show. I'm off."

He climbed onto his pony and trotted briskly up the sleepy-looking road. Without a word Ford sprang into his saddle. Rosita was already mounted. Joicey turned his head.

"Coming with us, General? You can tell them at the Home Office that you saw us tumbling down a crevasse."

"I'll be dashed if I do," the General snorted as he fell across his pony and started in pursuit of Joicey. "I'll tell the Government to go…"

Luckily, his pony just then indulged a penchant for ruts, so the General's remarks ceased for lack of wind. The four soon joined and trotted on in silence. Each felt that this perhaps was the last time that he or she might drink in to the utter most, all the magical tropical beauty at the Sikkim valleys and forests and the unsurpassable wonder of the mountains. The heaving mists parted. Out flashed the incredible blue of the morning sky, and range upon range of forest-clad hills billowed up in turquoise and indigo to the last sublime range of an white, calm and infinitely remote, ethereally suspended in the clear azure. And above the sharp white line that cut the main range from the blue of heaven gleamed the supreme peak, the marvelous height of Kinchinjinga. On their left towered the eternal silences of the hills; on their right and all about them the luxuriant beauty of the tropical forest resounded to the varied din of innumerable crickets and strident insects, the distant booming of waterfalls, and the boiling rush of cataracts that foamed down the hillsides to the river.

The splendors of the forest moved past their eyes like the landscapes of a dream. Late flowering rhododendrons here and there shone through the giant palms and tree-ferns in vivid splashes of crimson and orange; every tree trunk was a many-colored bower of maidenhair, festooned vines and mosses and rich orchids of all hues from white to lavender and scarlet, and solitary white, golden-hearted lilies rose gigantically up, heavy with fragrance in the shady glades.

Great cables of flowering climbers, of morning glories, and ropes of vegetation, robinias and bauhinias, matted over with orchids and the most brilliant begonias wove the forest together into one transcendent robe of ever-changing beauty that Nature herself might wear at her bridal feast. And it was sweet-scented; the huge magnolia trees from their creams white blossoms, each like an alabaster loving cup, poured out fragrance on the air.

AS THE road dipped steeply down three thousand feet or more the forest changed; as it climbed again up rocky ledges, new trees and shrubs, or more luxuriant masses of perennials seemed to flame into flower to wave the travelers farewell. All shades of green, from the glossy emerald of the young hollies, the chrysoprase of the maples and Himalayan birches to the bright, clearer hue of the banana leaves and massed bamboos, shone on the steep hillsides or along the ravines in a perfect harmony, and the roadside was a symphony of many-colored caladiums.

The road now descended to the Teesta valley, the hothouse of the world, with its rushing chocolate-covered river and its steamy, perfume-laden atmosphere.

"Up there among the orchids and ferns," Rosita observed to Joicey who rode by her side, "I was wondering why human beings are such fools as to leave a paradise like this deliberately to court misery in outlandish places. Take those tea planters up there in the hillside, for instance. Can you conceive of a lot happier at the lives they live? Look at their neat plantations, high up on the ridge out of this steaming heat, with every imaginable flower that their hearts could long for blossoming in their gardens. Don't you envy them their lack of ambition, if nothing else? Why on earth are we forever wandering into forsaken deserts?"

"I don't know, I'm sure. Suppose it must be a disease of the white race. Now I, for instance, only begin to enjoy life when I get cooked through in the middle of some desert, or frozen stiff on the plateaus of Tibet. Extremes keep a chap moving, make him expand and contract, don't you know. Beastly bore, growing tea. Stuffier than surveying and having some old fool mess up your reports. Annangnisskeh!"

"What did you say?"

"I was talking to the gnats. Thought I had better not say it in English. A camel-driving Mussulman from Turkestan, whom I used to pump for geographical information, used to say that when a gnat stung him on the back of the neck. I offered him soda, but he preferred his own remedy. Kaper!"

"Where did that one sting you?"

"Couldn't tell you, I'm sure. Kissingnisskeh! I shall be jolly glad when we get out of this infernal paradise of yours, Miss Rowe. Look at those beastly leeches waving their heads at us. They make me sick. Just look at the beggars—millions and millions of them. It must have rained last night down here. Every blessed leaf and blade of grass is draped with the bloodthirsty little brutes. Shouldn't care to take a nap in the open."

"Yes, but see the butterflies!" she exclaimed. "They shine as if their wings were thin gold or beaten copper—oh, do look at that beauty—the big iridescent blue one. I've counted fifty-four different kinds in the last two miles."

"That's nothing. I've counted over a hundred new species of gnats and mosquitoes in the last fifty yards. The midgets are infinite. Ha! Look at our friend the General. His arms are going like a bally semaphore. I say, General Wedderburn," he shouted, "they don't understand signaling. Why don't you converse with them?"

Turning like a weathercock in his saddle, the General vociferated. The gist of his remarks seemed to be an unsympathetic estimate of Joicey's mentality.

"He shouldn't do that, you know," Joicey expostulated to Rosita. "Someday he will burst like a hot sausage. Can't you calm him?"

"It's the humidity. I feel stifled. It is worse than a Turkish bath down here."

"Really now? That's interesting." He eyed her with admiration. "I spent two weeks in Constantinople once, and never got a bath all the time I was there. How did you manage it?"

"Oh, this was in New York."

"I shall pay it a visit when we return. A chap needs something drastic after a sojourn with the Tibetans."

"I know," she agreed. "When we came back from our last trip it was a month before either of us looked like a human being. But you are thinking of something?"

His face had revealed a flash of the iron will behind the bland mask of banality. For a moment he looked as when she had first seen him, rigid and unconscious, on his cot in the sanitarium. He started slightly and gave her a keen look.

"I was," he admitted. Then he went straight to the point. "General Wedderburn cannot possibly come with us."

"MY uncle has already told him so. But he is more obstinate than a mule. Outwardly he agreed to follow my uncle's instructions and remain on this side of the frontier. Yet both of us know that he is planning to outwit and join our party on the Tibet side of the pass."

"It would not be difficult for a man who knows the hills as he does. I dare say he has surveyed all through that district, and what he doesn't know from personal experience he could easily pick up from his subordinates. Has your uncle any definite plan for getting rid of him?"

"Not that I know. We are to hold a council in camp tonight. The General is to explain his situation to you. Of course, you understood long ago, that our expedition has a double objective?"

"Your uncle rubbed it in while you were present, if you remember. Well, let us not cross our bridges till we come to them. Ah, the General is dismounting. This must be near our camp. Have we a relay of fresh ponies?"

"Yes. Including the pack ponies, there are twelve in all. They are all first-class mountain beasts thoroughly hardened to climbing and long marches at high altitudes."

"Good. I must have a few minutes with your uncle."

"Do you plan to flit by moonlight and leave the General with the leeches?"

"No. I always prefer to work when the sun is up. Now, be very careful what you say tonight."

"I shall. Good luck." The proposed council was abandoned. All that Rosita could get out of her uncle was a warning to keep a close guard on her tongue, both at night and during the long marches to follow, whenever the General might be within hearing.

"Where's Monty?" she asked. "He should be in bed by now, and I haven't seen him since supper."

"Perhaps he is," said Ford. "It is more probable, however, that he's off in some dirty native village buying more supplies. Most of the things I had stocked didn't seem to suit his fastidious taste."

"You might tell me something now." She pouted. "We're less than a week's journey from the frontier."

"Honestly, Rosita, I don't know myself. Joicey is as close as a clam. I sometimes think he is planning to skip out and leave us to our own devices."

"He shan't if I have anything to say about it," she said firmly. "After this, he doesn't get out of my sight for more than five minutes. Then I'll be on his trail."

"Fascinate him, Rosita," her uncle said.

"I may have to," she replied, "though goodness knows I don't want the job. Leave him to me."

ALL through the trying marches of the next five days, with their sharp ascents and drops of anything from two to four-thousand feet, Joicey and Wedderburn were as thick as a pair of sixteen-year-old sweethearts. Possibly their mutual interests as old surveyors lent this roughest part of Sikkim a sentimental charm which the others missed. Rosita's guess was perhaps nearer the truth.

Her intuitions told her that the sudden friendship between the two men was one-sided. She guessed that Joicey was slowly but exhaustively pumping the General dry. She admired his staying qualities, and certainly Joicey did stick to the older man like one of his abominable leeches.

Overjoyed at first to find a new ear into which he might pour all the story of his little girl's abduction, the General soon wearied, and now desired nothing so much as the moral courage to punch that sympathetic ear turned so persistently toward him. Occasionally, seeing his friend's neck swell ominously, Ford cantered up to the General's relief. Joicey on these occasions dropped back and rode with Rosita. Ostensibly, he was charmed with her society, but she had an uneasy feeling that she was not making him out as completely as she could have wished.

In the evenings he was sociability itself. The General retired early, being older and more easily done in than the others. Joicey then would labor for three hours or more instructing Ford and Rosita in the ancient Tibetan. This looked promising. If he intended deserting them, he surely would not go to all this trouble. There were easier ways of deceiving them. Yet when in the morning they found the packs tampered with, and Joicey's sleeping bag suspiciously fresh looking, they wondered.

Rosita obviously could not follow him about all night. For one thing, she lacked a suitable chaperon. Ford once accompanied her a hundred yards or so, and made so much noise that they decided to return to camp. The lack of a chaperon did not seriously bother her however; she could take care of herself anywhere, and up here on the roof of the world there were no cats to gossip about her. But the ease with which Joicey gave her the slip was decidedly annoying. He would be standing talking to his favorite pony one minute, and the next, night had swallowed him without a sound. Worst of all, he showed a willingness to meet her halfway in her attempts to interest him.

That she honestly liked him, she was too candid to conceal from herself. Now, she knew well enough that if he were in the least interested in her, he would shy like a frightened horse at the first sign of interest in him, when, of course, she would immediately treat him as so much invisible air.

Unfortunately, he never shied, so she missed her chance to play the indifferent. She regretted this, for she imagined it to be one of her most effective roles. Had anyone hinted this to her, she would undoubtedly have lost her head; for like all young women suffering from the same malady she was entirely unconscious of her ailment. She was just being as natural and as miserable as nature intended that she should be under the circumstances. Behind it all lurked the fear that he distrusted both her uncle and her, and that he was secretly planning to leave them in the lurch.

The long march to the frontier was now all but ended. Tomorrow they must either cross it or turn back, beaten. They sat around the campfire discussing their prospects, and presently

Joicey, for the hundredth time, began cross-questioning the General. Briefly and irritably the General recounted again the incidents of his little daughter's abduction twelve years previously. "Ford," he concluded, "is confident he can find and bring her back. That she is alive I have not the slightest doubt." He paused and glanced shrewdly from Joicey's frankly interested countenance to Ford's non-committal poker face. "I suspect," he said, "that you two oysters could be quite eloquent if you chose. Joicey, what do you know?"

"Nothing. But I am always ready to learn. What color was this chap Singh's hair?"

"Brown—no, it must have been black. Blest if I could say now." The General subsided in evident confusion.

"Sure it wasn't blue, General?"

The General's only reply was a silent version of "perfect fool," a sort of song without words or music. Joicey, however, to the astonishment of the others, persisted in his idiotic question. "Did you ever see your impeccable servant without his turban?" he queried. His tone had suddenly become perfectly serious.

"Now that you mention it, I don't believe I ever did."

"But you found his turban on the grass where your little girl had knocked it off in her struggles? Do you happen to remember the exact color?"

"Sapphire blue," the General admitted testily. He began to grow restless under the persistent questioning.

"IF I recall your description," Joicey continued mercilessly, "you remarked the unusually fine shape of Singh's head. It was rather Caucasian than Asiatic, you observed, although the general molding and carriage were finer—nobler, if I may put it so—than either. You also commented on the refinement of his features, on his extraordinary intelligence, his superstitious abhorrence of caves and overhanging rocks, and his curious reluctance to sit with his back to the sun.

"But what astonishes me," he drawled, screwing in his eyeglass and inspecting the General's face with flattering interest, "is the remarkable fact that you often saw Singh without his turban and yet never noticed the color of his hair. He must have dyed it before—I speak literality—he entered your service. I won't ask you whether he had a glass eye."

"Why not?" Rosita interposed, to avert the threatened explosion.

"Because he probably hadn't. Only one unfortunate man in several hundred thousand has."

The General exploded. "Look here! Do you see anything ludicrous in the abduction of a helpless eight-year-old child?"

"No," Joicey rejoined imperturbably. "I see something much more important. After five weary days it finally has burst upon my vision." He screwed up his eyeglass.

"What are you staring at?" the General demanded. He was now irritated to the point of exasperation.

"A great light. General Wedderburn, I shall have something to say to you in a moment. First I wish to apologize to Mr. Ford and Miss Rowe for certain unworthy suspicions which I have spent the past week in fighting, and which a chance expression of astonishment upon their faces a few moments ago finally dispelled. You will pardon me, Ford, for having set you down as a common adventurer. Beyond your excellent maps, which unfortunately were of no use to me, I know nothing whatever about you. I take no man on trust. Therefore, during the past week, I have made little expeditions of my own to the nearest telegraph stations while you and your charming niece were fast asleep.

"At Kalimpong, you may remember, I was absent several hours. When not telegraphing at night or going ahead to get replies to my last dispatches, I have made a thorough search of all our luggage. What I learned by telegraph, cable and the inspection of our supplies almost convinced me that you were playing a straight game. But not quite."

"May I ask what did finally convince you that we are on the square?" Ford interrupted. "Mind, I'm not blaming you for looking us up. I should do exactly the same myself in a like case. I really am curious."

"The fact that neither you, nor your niece knew the color of Singh's hair."

"But how in thunder could we have known? We never set eyes on the man."

"That is the point. Without knowing the color of this man's hair, you stand not the ghost of a chance of reaching your goal. Now I never saw Singh—that is, not to know him. Nevertheless, I know to half a shade's difference the color of his hair. And I told you so much in my delirium that I thought possibly I had given away that essential detail along with others of less importance.

"A thorough search of our joint effects convinced me that one of two things was true: either you were honestly ignorant of the essential detail, or you were dishonestly concealing your knowledge of it. If latter, then you were playing a double game with me, and I should have to watch you like a cat to see that you and your niece did not give me the slip. For, you two knowing that essential detail, would stand a chance of success where I stand none. That much is certain. By myself, as you pointed out when we were on our way to Anderson's, I could expect nothing but failure and perhaps death. But without searching your persons I could not be sure that you really were ignorant of the color of Singh's hair. The omissions of certain useful articles from the packs—omissions which I have now supplied—might have been due either to honest ignorance on your part or really clever deceit. They were of just that kind which a man would make who wished to appear ignorant of the true nature of the difficulties which his caravan must surmount.

"On the other hand, they tallied with what a delirious man would forget in his ravings as things of no consequence beside the compelling importance of his fixed idea. In that case you would be acting honestly. The thing that finally convinced me of your absolute squareness was the look which passed over your faces when I began asking the General silly questions. Now, before we start on the serious business of our expedition, I want to set things right. Henceforth I agree to be open and above board with you, Ford, and with you, Miss Rowe, in everything connected with our undertaking. I agree to this provided you give me a like assurance."

"We do," they assented.

"Then that's settled, and you needn't try to shadow me anymore, Miss Rowe. You will pardon my over-sensitiveness to certain defects of human nature, I know, for both of you have dealt with Asiatics. Like me, you must find it difficult not to attribute second, third and even fourth motives to men whose actions are as simple and regular as clockwork if taken at their face value."

"WE KNOW," said Ford. "A man gets so into the habit of husking the hulls off fat oriental lies to get at the few grains of truth inside, that he comes in time to suspect the multiplication table of lying elaborately and ingeniously. What is worse, he catches the disease himself."

"I haven't," said Joicey with a grin, "except to priests who have no religion. Now, General Wedderburn, for your end of it. Before you leave us to spend anxious months waiting for our return, I want you to know one thing. Your daughter was alive and unharmed the last time I heard of her. That was about seven years ago."

"Then you have seen her?" the General exclaimed, springing to his feet.

"No. I never came within a mile of her. Until half an hour ago I seriously doubted her existence. I thought she was a lying, oriental myth. One difficulty was to find a motive for Singh's abduction of her; I need not trouble you at present with the other grounds of my disbelief. It is enough to say now that I had what seemed good reasons, based on my distrust of the oriental character for truthfulness, to doubt her existence. The chance that you had lost a daughter who might possibly but improbably be the substance of truth behind the mist of lies seemed too slight for serious consideration. I preferred to trust my judgment that all Orientals are born disguisers of the truth. But your last account brought out one or two details of Singh's character that have given me a clue to his motive. You emphasized his extraordinary intelligence and his sudden interest when you spoke of your little girl to him. His rather minute questions about her personal appearance which he seems to have put to you piecemeal were evidently well spaced, for you never resented his wholesale, unwarranted curiosity.

"A stupid man would have asked you everything at once. Singh's procedure bears out your estimate of his intelligence. This removed one difficulty: the man must have been really intelligent, and therefore a rare exception to his race as I know it. They are civilized, but not at present on a level of intelligence approaching that of the better Europeans. Being an exception, he would be urged by great motives. Now what could tempt him to an act that at first sight seems wanton folly?

"If your daughter had been say, twenty-five, and highly educated, I could easily enough have imagined a possible though foolhardy motive behind Singh's act. I need not go into this now; you will most probably learn it from your daughter's lips. But she was only a child, just eight years old. It suddenly dawned on me, Singh was a schemer and a shifty politician of the first order. His whole probable plan of action lay before me like a map of lying Asia drawn by the champion liar of all time."

"What was it?" Rosita asked, when Joicey paused to light a cigarette.

"I have only guessed it," he replied, "and so must ask you to let me off. For if I'm wrong, I shall feel like a fool when we learn the truth. I'll bet you a sapphire, though, that Singh has been dead at least ten years. We can verify that, at any rate, when we rescue Evelyn."

"Take me to her!"

"Impossible, General Wedderburn. No man on earth could take you to your daughter." He slowly drew off his left glove, exposing the cracked and withered flesh of his hand. "Take a good close look at that. It isn't very painful now; that's the curious thing about these burns. How would you like to have every shred of flesh on your body first cracked like my palms and then withered up like the dry skin on those finger joints?"

They said nothing, gazing fascinated in spite of themselves at that terrible hand. Joicey drew on his glove again. "That," he said, "is what would happen to the man who should try to see your daughter. And it would happen to his whole body."

"Then how are we ever to rescue her?"

"We?" Joicey repeated. "That doesn't include you, remember. As to your daughter, Miss Rowe will find a way. A mouse can go where a cat can't. Now, General, if you will excuse us, we shall leave you to get a good night's rest. It's a long steep climb tomorrow, and there's worse to come. The monsoon can't hold out forever. Early tomorrow morning I must meet a messenger who is coming after us with an essential piece of luggage which Ford omitted, and for which I telegraphed." He shot Ford a significant look. Ford took the hint.

"I think I had better make a tour of inspection before turning in," he said. "Some of the animals seemed restless."

"Very well," said Joicey. "In the meantime, I'll give your niece a short drill in the ancient Tibetan. You pronounce it fairly well now, so you're excused from your lesson this evening. Now, Miss Rowe, shall we stroll over to that hedge of daturas?"

"That will be delightful. I can smell them even here. The moonlight always seems to make their strange fragrance sweeter, just as it brings out the soft glow on their long, white trumpets."

They had taken a few steps when she whispered, "When do we give him the slip?"

"Tomorrow, about noon," he replied. "It's a dirty trick, but unless a chap is willing once in a while to mess himself up, he'll never accomplish very much, good or bad. Charming evening, isn't it?"

"Beautiful— Oh! There's a man behind the daturas."

"So I suspected," he drawled. "My messenger must have confused this evening with tomorrow morning." He approached the man, and without a word gave him a piece of money, receiving in exchange a small package. The man immediately vanished. "Pardon me a moment. I must give this to your uncle to pack with the rest of our truck. I shall be right back."

His "moment" was an hour and fifteen minutes long, but Rosita waited. Curiosity got the better of her natural anger.

"Awfully sorry," he apologized sincerely, when at last he hurried breathlessly to her side. "Your uncle was having the very deuce of a time finding places for all my comforts, and I had to show him where to squeeze them in."

"That's all right," she said. "I hardly noticed your absence."

"Oh? Shall we start your lesson?"

CHAPTER FOUR
The Forgotten Highway

ABOUT three o'clock the next morning Ford was busy by the light of lanterns with the pack animals and their attendants—a polyglot crew of hillsmen and hardened dwellers in high altitudes. With the skill of an old campaigner he got his apparently absurd orders executed instantly without a word of protest or argument, although more than once, the tried veterans of many expeditions glanced at him uneasily as though doubting his sanity.

Was the man mad, to be saddling up at this unearthly hour? His proceedings were certainly those of a lunatic. Many articles from the packs were discarded and thrust into obscure corners where prying eyes would be least likely to look, and the loads of all the animals were eased and readjusted. Giving his labors a last thorough inspection, Ford passed from one animal to the next, tightening a girth here, and loosening a strap there, until he came to the end of the pack train.

"How many torches did you pack?" he asked the head man. He already knew, but wished to see whether the master of the caravan was alive.

"Eighty, sahib," the man replied with evident pride. He was not to be caught thus easily.

"Then align the train in marching order."

The leader quickly executed the command, fastening the halter of the last pony to the pack of the one before him, and so on up the train, until all were a linked unit. Ford then did something that no commander of an expedition should ever do. He called the men together and made them a short speech, complimenting them on their efficiency and endurance through the long stiff climb from tropical heat to Alpine temperatures.

This of itself might not have ruined the men for future usefulness. But considering that the real difficulties had not yet begun, the caravan leader's belief in his commander's sanity vanished utterly when Ford put his hand into his pocket, drew forth a number of large gold coins, and presented one to each man.

Naturally the men accepted the money. But they could not conceal their contempt for this generous greenhorn.

"Some of you," said Ford, "have wives and children in Pedong. It is our last halt this side of the frontier. When we cross over Jelep La into Tibet, we leave wives and children behind us, perhaps never to see them again. All but your leader, who will take charge of the caravan until further orders, are dismissed for the rest of the day. Hasten on to Pedong, enjoy yourselves, make your farewells, and be ready at sundown to receive my commands. Keep sober; don't spend all your money. If you have wives, give your money to them. Travel fast. This is your one free day for many a month. Away with you."

Overjoyed, contemptuous, and amazed, the little band scurried off through the dark in the direction of Pedong. Ford turned to the caravan leader. "Keep strictly to the way I told you to follow. Be sure to branch off from the main caravan route in plenty of time to avoid meeting anyone. Ready? Then go."

The man stepped quietly to the head of the string, grasped the first pony's halter, and led the sturdy animals off at a brisk walk. The first lap of the expedition proper was begun. How would it end? Ford glanced at his watch. Then he strolled over to the saddle ponies and killed two hours petting them. Finally, just before sunrise, he went to rouse the sleepers. They crawled out of their sleeping bags like sluggish larvae awakened in midwinter.

"Coffee ready?" the General asked some minutes later.

"Great Scott!" Ford exclaimed. "I never thought of breakfast. The caravan has gone ahead." Then he explained it all.

"Beastly bore," Joicey commented. "Hate to ride on an empty stomach."

"Then walk," the General snapped as he climbed disgustedly into his saddle.

Rosita had not yet rolled up her sleeping bag. "Wait a moment," she said, giving the bag a vigorous shake. Four large cakes of chocolate tumbled out. "My private stock," she explained, handing each of the men a cake.

"You carried that off quite well," Joicey whispered, taking his. "I admire a girl who can lie in a good cause without winking."

"You put me up to it," she retorted. "Last night at about a quarter to twelve under the daturas, if you have forgotten. If you behave I'll give you a thick sandwich and a cup of steaming hot coffee when the General gets out of sight." She exhibited a large thermos bottle snugly reposing in an inner pocket of her sleeping bag. "I kept a firm grip on it while I did the shaking."

Joicey removed his eyeglass. "Ah, thanks awfully, Miss Rowe. A breakfast without coffee is like an Eden without its Eve."

"Are you sure you can see to drink without your monocle?" she asked solicitously, offering him the cap of the bottle full of steaming, fragrant coffee.

"Probably I shall spill it down my neck," he replied, taking a sip. "But sometimes it is better not to see too much at once. Especially when one is about to enter Tibet. I'm blind."

She flushed slightly. "I understand," she murmured. "We'll say no more about it until we see Darjeeling again." Evidently last night's romantic moonlight had brought out more than the sweet fragrance of the daturas.

"I shan't, at any rate," he promised. And when he calmly proceeded to screw in his monocle once more she could have flung the thermos bottle at his too cool head. "Ah, jolly sandwich, this," he remarked gratefully. He did not catch her reply distinctly, but thought it sounded like, "I hope it gives you indigestion."

HAVING finished their breakfast they mounted and rode on leisurely. "We have plenty of time to overtake the caravan before noon," Joicey remarked. "Let us enjoy the scenery. We shan't see rhododendrons like these for many a long day."

"I thought you didn't care much for flowers?"

"A chap can't care for two things at once when one of them is a host of sociable gnats," he explained. "Up here it is too cool for the beggars. Did you ever see anything more beautiful than those hillsides down there?" He pointed to the great rounded hilltops and spurs beneath them, ablaze with the vivid orange and scarlet of vast patches of rhododendrons in full blossom.

"No," she said, "unless it is those higher slopes with their great fields of white and purple splashed here and there against the background of crimson and bright gold. It is so wonderful," she sighed, "that like Keats— we 'cannot see what flowers are at our feet.' "

"That meadow of primulas is rather gorgeous," he admitted. "Makes a chap think of home, don't you know."

"Yes, and so do the geraniums. Just look at that hill," she exclaimed. "It takes Nature to make a proper garden. See how those gentians and ground orchids are flung down with just the right touch, of carelessness between the light blue delphiniums and campanulas, and how exquisitely she has arranged those stunted junipers. No human being could make a flawless work of art like that."

"No," he agreed, "nor could any mere mortal give us such a deuce of a drenching as we shall get in about five minutes. Our luck has turned at last. Here comes the monsoon."

He pointed ahead to the pass revealed by a sudden turn in the road. Down the pass marched the gigantic clouds bearing their millions of tons of water to dump without ceasing for week after week upon the precipitous hills and narrow valleys of Sikkim. They almost fancied they could hear the earth-shaking tread of that advancing host as it swept toward them in league-long paces. "By Jove, won't the General get a ducking," he chuckled.

"That's all very well," she said; "and no doubt it will do his temper good. But what about ourselves?"

"Oh, we shall be comfortably lost, I hope, long before it breaks. I wish that caravan would show up," he added anxiously.

The road made another detour to avoid a steep hill, and the pass was again hidden from view. Rounding the hill, they came upon a wonderful sloping meadow about five miles broad, carpeted with soft, low growing grass, and bluer than the steel blue sky above with the innumerable widespread chalices of dark blue Himalayan poppies. At their first glimpse the strange beauty of the scene was absolutely still, as if vast clouds of sapphire-winged butterflies had just alit upon the mossy emerald of the meadow. Then almost instantly the blue of the poppies on the farther side, where it sloped steeply up to the snow line, darkened. The deeper blue seemed to hesitate a moment before it swept down the slope toward them in a perfect crescent, and before they realized that the meadow was alive, the first cool breath of the advancing storm had kissed their faces. Under the light feet of this first swift messenger of the coming deluge the whole meadow whirred and shimmered with living sapphire.

For a few seconds Rosita and Joicey sat entranced. Then Joicey broke the spell. "Come," he said. "That will be something to remember in the desert. Do you see the caravan?"

She scanned the glistening snowfields some five miles across the meadow. High up the dazzling white to the left, the green-blue mass of a broad glacier coiled down the mountainside like a huge serpent, disappearing farther to the left behind a sheer, towering wall of jagged red rock. "It should be there," she said, pointing toward the foot of an immense pillar of red rock at the base of the snow line. "That is, if the caravan leader followed your directions. Lend me your glasses. Ah…" she exclaimed after a moment's search, "there go my uncle and General Wedderburn. They are bearing toward the head of the glacier, so the caravan must have gone right. I've spotted it—just at the snow line by the extreme right of the lower wall of rocks. We can head off the men before they reach it." She spoke to her pony, and the pursuers were off at a brisk canter.

Coming up with the others, Joicey contrived to attach himself to the General and sent Rosita ahead with Ford to intercept the caravan. In the few minutes' ride before they overtook the pack animals, Joicey for the last time, obtained a minute description of the General's little daughter Evelyn, as she had been when she disappeared. The purity of the features, the dark brown and unusually big, luminous eyes, the clear, delicately tinted skin and the warm gold of her curls made a picture that no father could forget in twelve years or forty, and she had been the sun of the General's existence.

"Let me see that miniature again?" Joicey requested, just as they caught up with the caravan. The General handed over the gold locket containing his daughter's likeness, and proceeded to study the unearthly grandeur of his surroundings while Joicey scrutinized the exquisite miniature.

The caravan had halted at the base of a titanic crag of red rock which jutted squarely out from the main labyrinth of which it formed the extreme right portal. For twenty miles or more to the left of this outpost of rock stretched a maze of fantastically elaborate citadels and buttresses of the same peculiar bright red stone, as if the whole had been hewn by a race of giants from the living rock when the mountains were young. Colossal square pillars, a hundred yards broad at the base, towered sheer up a thousand or twelve hundred feet at irregular intervals, and between the stupendous masses of this vast maze of natural fortresses and temples ran broad stone causeways as level as the avenues of New York. Behind this labyrinth towered the main unbroken mass from which the whole had been hewn, the sheer wall of red rock behind which the glacier cut and crawled its slow way down to some strange and unknown moraine.

JOICEY was studying every detail of the lovely eight-year-old face with the intensest concentration. "I have a mental photograph of it now," he said, closing the locket and returning it to the General. "It is the face of a poetess."

The General started. "How odd that you should remark that. Evelyn, since she was four years old, was passionately fond of anything with a beautiful rhythm, and her mother—later I—used to teach her whole books of poetry by heart. I can hear her now," he said, brushing his hand across his eyes, "lilting through Scott's 'Lay of the Last Minstrel.' It was her favorite when she was seven years old."

Joicey's face betrayed more than polite interest, but he made no comment. "By the way," he said in a low tone, "has it ever struck you that Miss Rowe's coloring resembles that of your daughter?"

"It struck me the first time I got a square look at her face," the General admitted, "and all this past week I have been watching her surreptitiously. My daughter and Rosita must be about the same age." He stole a glance at her now where she stood beside her uncle talking to the caravan leader. "I see now that her coloring, although similar to Evelyn's, is distinct. It isn't her hair and eyes or complexion that account for the resemblance. And her expression, her—" the General hesitated for the word, "her soul, is not like Evelyn's. I think it must be the way she carries her head, and its beautiful lines. Evelyn's mother used to say that our little girl had the Grecian type of beauty warmed by something of the English."

"I can well believe it from the miniature," Joicey remarked, readjusting his monocle so as to get a precise and critical view of Rosita. Turning just at the right moment she caught him in the act.

"Is there something on my face?" she asked, with truly feminine anxiety.

"A great deal," he laconically informed her.

She made a frantic dive for her handkerchief and began a vigorous rubbing.

"It won't come off for several years," he drawled. "You were born with it."

"You see too much sometimes, with that precious eyeglass of yours," she retorted, reddening. "If you know what's good for you, you'll put it in your innermost pocket until we get back to Darjeeling."

"I think I shall. Capital idea, by Jove." He removed the cause of offense and slipped it into the pocket of his shirt. "Now," he said, "if some beggar of a Tibetan pots me through the heart I shall tinkle like a bally cymbal. In the meantime will one of you lead me by the hand? Can't see, you know."

"Take a torch," Ford suggested significantly.

"Thanks awfully, old chap." He gravely selected one of the largest and stalked ahead. "Coming with me, General? The man can lead our ponies."

"Lunatics!" the General muttered to himself as he started to follow, leading his pony. "One suggests an absurdity, the other does it."

"Which way?" Ford called after them. "The snow to the left of that rock looks like firmer walking."

"Ah, don't know about that, I'm sure. It was in a place like this that I fell into that beastly crevasse. I say, old chap, why not send old what's-his-name, the caravan leader there, up ahead a bit to see how the going is? You and Miss Rowe can look out for the pack train and our saddle ponies. Suppose you follow the General and me up slowly. Then, if we have to turn back, we shan't lose much ground."

"All right," Ford agreed, and ordered the man up the slope to the right.

"This way is good enough for me," the General obstinately insisted. "I'll take care of my own pony."

Now, if anyone had dared to hint to the General that his "free" choice of that particular avalanche-infested slope had been carefully prearranged about twelve o'clock the preceding night, he would have been called a lunatic for his pains. Like many of us who are skillfully led, the General was a steadfast believer in the freedom of the will.

"Not a bad idea," Joicey remarked. "You may want to ride like the devil if the monsoon catches up with you. It will be coming up this way when the valleys get too narrow to hold it all."

They crunched over the snow for some twenty minutes without speaking. "Sure you know the way?" the General at length asked doubtfully. "It seems to me we are heading due south. We can't possibly get into Tibet by going south over that range ahead of us. Besides, it will be impossible to force our heavy pack up a ridge like that. Why, man, the thing's sheer rock. And look at these infernal crevasses everywhere! The first thing you know we shall fall into one and break our silly necks. Come up, confound you!" this said to the pony who evinced a desire to go tobogganing. "You'll start an avalanche, idiot. Come up! There's one up there on those rocks, just ready to slip."

"What's a chap to do?" Joicey rejoined. "We can't go over the pass like Christians. I'll wager there's half a regiment of British soldiers camped on Jelep La at this moment waiting to welcome us. Now, if you had managed the passports we might have been riding down the other side on comfortable yaks, instead of crawling up this white barn like a couple of bally horseflies."

"I did everything I could," the General puffed.

"We know it, old chap. It isn't your fault that we're trying to sneak in at some back door that perhaps doesn't exist, when by all rules of the game the footmen should be kowtowing to us at the front. Phew! Just look at that bunker we've got to hole out of." He waved his torch toward a sheerly precipitous rampart of red rock topping the long steep snow slope of the next range. "It must be at least seven hundred feet high. And there's not a break in it, I'll lay odds, for a hundred miles."

THEY stood disconsolately staring up at the impossible task before them. The vast barrier of rock, as level as a city wall on top and as vertical as a plumb line, was an infinitely more effective "no passport" to the forbidden land beyond than all the perverse obstructiveness of British officialdom. From the base of the snow slope where they had left the caravan this crowning barrier was hidden from view. Now it was only too plainly visible.

"That must be a spur of the same mass of rock that the glacier cuts through lower down," Joicey observed. "The color is the same."

But the General was not interested just then in geology. A small avalanche—a mere trifle the size of a Swiss village—suddenly thundered down the declivity by which they had ascended. Their passing, doubtless, had started the dainty little thing a week or so before its appointed time. The General, wheeling sharply about, went livid.

"Good God," he gasped, "where is the pack train?"

Joicey did not wait to reply. Wildly brandishing his torch to balance himself, he shot down the slope toward the jutting red crag where they had left Ford and Rosita with the caravan. In a flash he turned the sharp corner. That was the last the General saw of him for many a long, anxious month.

Turning the sharp corner of the giant rock, Joicey dashed up the broadest of the stone causeways opening from its base and ran at top speed for half a mile up the echoing corridor. On either side of him the sheer red cliffs rose in an unbroken sweep of a thousand feet to the steel blue sky above, and the clamor of his haste reverberated from wall to wall like muffled thunder. He panted and staggered, all but done under his terrific exertion, but his will urged him on with speed undiminished.

Presently, on his right, he saw the first break in the red wall. In a flash, he had turned into this narrower corridor branching at right angles from the first, but not until he had made six such turns, passing several corridors unentered, did he slacken his pace. Leaning against the stone wall he pressed his hands against his heaving sides. Then he was off again at a brisk march, twisting his way of amazing intricacy through the stone labyrinth. Gradually his sure tread faltered, and glancing irresolutely at his surroundings he came to a dead halt, listening intently. Not even an echo broke the silence of that vast stone mesa.

A sickening doubt made his brain reel. Was he lost? Or had the others taking a wrong turn, vanished into the bowels of the mountains? One false turn meant disaster. The sweat started on his forehead. Strain as he might he could not catch the faintest echo. Surely the noisy clatter of the ponies' hoofs must carry for miles. If Ford had made no mistake, he should now be only a few hundred yards down the narrow corridor to the left. If not? Why, then. It was the end of their journey.

He remembered with a sinking at the pit of the stomach that sound soon loses itself and dies out after many sharp turns round corners. Thinking about to get a grip on his shaken nerves he took out his pocket compass, uttering each word deliberately he said, "If I am not lost, that corridor should run due east from here." Steeling himself, he looked at the compass. The corridor ran due north. "I'm lost," he said, and sat down on the stone floor.

Wisely, he did not at once attempt to straighten himself. "Let us talk this thing over calmly," he said. "There's no use getting panicky. First, I'm a fool. That's clear. Second, Ford will never let me hear the end of this. I jawed him deaf and dumb about not losing his way. Next time, he shall do the memorizing and I'll keep the map." He began going over in his mind each turn that he had taken since entering the labyrinth. "First to the right; passed two on the right, one on the left, took the next on the right," and so on, retracing mentally his whole devious route. "The false turn must have been the fifth from here." he said, rising. "Now to get back to it. If that's wrong, I may as well give up."

He marched back over his route with a firm tread. Emerging from the fifth turn he again consulted his compass. "Next to the right," he said, and made for the side corridor. Reaching it, he gave a glad shout, for far down the dim distance glowed a tiny crimson spark. "They set a torch for me," he cried exultantly, and raced down the echoing corridor toward it. Reaching it he sat down and laughed. "They must have thought me an awful fool—leaving this thing burning. Well, I am a fool. Can't find my way into my own maze." With a deep sigh of relief he rose, stamped out the last embers of the signal and strode down the corridor.

At the next turn, another torch showed him the right way, until finally above a heavier din he caught the distant clatter of the pack train, faint but unmistakable. A little farther on, a deeper echo quivered on the cold air. It was the distant thunder of subterranean torrents rushing through the roots of the Himalayas. Quickening his steps he took the last turn of his devious route, and far down the black distance descried two minute sparks. "There they are," he shouted. Lighting his own torch, he hastened to overtake them.

THE causeway along which he now ran was the highest of several ledges of dark green basalt on the steep side of a vast subterranean chamber or tunnel. The torch flaming high above his head lit the broad stone causeway for perhaps eighty yards ahead and to the right, while overhead the velvety darkness remained as sooty and as impenetrable as ever. At intervals of about thirty feet, with a sheer drop from each ledge to the next lower, eight similar stone causeways ran parallel to the highest, the whole titanic structure giving the impression of a vast stairway hewn from the solid basalt of the tunnel.

Each "step" was the breadth of a modern city street, and the lowest apparently broke sheer off at the black edge of an absolute void. The blazing torch was as powerless to pierce the nether darkness as the upper. This colossal nine-fold system of causeways appeared to hang suspended in a starless abyss, broad roads out of nothing into nothing. Nevertheless, from below rose faint clamor of many rushing waters, and far overhead the steady grinding of a constant thunder rolled and rumbled like the passing of express trains along the invisible roof.

The two sparks ahead of him steadily increased in brilliance as he approached, until presently their motion became plainly visible. They came to rest abruptly; Ford and Rosita had seen his torch.

"Ah, you made good time," he drawled, catching up with the pack train.

"Can't say the same for you," Ford retorted. "Did you have to conduct the General back to Darjeeling, personally? We waited half an hour for you before turning in here."

"The General took a fancy to a bunch of edelweiss for his buttonhole," Joicey lied on the spur of the moment, "and I had to climb up and get it for him."

"Tell that to the General," Rosita laughed. "You got lost. That's what kept you."

"Well, I did," he confessed. "Thanks awfully for the signals. They saved my life."

"Ours too, then," she replied. "For we certainly should be like calves in a butcher shop without you. Shall we go on? We've rearranged the ponies' loads now so that they should be able to make good time."

"Yes. I'll lead the train, and you can walk along with me to see that I don't fall downstairs. Ford, will you walk behind to pick up anything we may drop?"

"That hint, for instance?" He smiled good-naturedly. "All right. You pull, I'll shove."

"Ready? Then we're off. There are twelve or thirteen miles of this, all downhill. One march with no halt will make it in five hours at most."

"How did you get rid of the General?" Rosita asked.

"As we planned, only Nature forestalled me. I kept his attention on what was ahead so that he shouldn't look back to see nobody behind him. I was just planning to look back and discover in great alarm that you and your uncle were not following with the pack train as we had agreed, when an avalanche saved me the trouble of completing our invention. It seemed superfluous, then, to tell the General to wait while I ran back to see what had happened to you."

"Do you suppose he's safe?"

"Perfectly. There is no real danger on that slope if one uses common sense. Our little experience will have taught him not to shout at his pony. He'll get down all right if he has to do it by inches. Don't worry; he's safe."

"I feel mean about it," she said regretfully.

"So do I, but he had to stay behind. He had come as far as we dared take him."

Now that their burdens had been shared with the saddle ponies, the rest recovered their spirits and stepped along at a sharp walk.

Conversation became difficult under that steadily increasing din from the roof of the tunnel, and neither Rosita nor Joicey attempted much. Yet they were sociable enough. The sheer significance of that march by torchlight through the black void made ordinary speech a triviality. But as the second hour passed into the third, Ford could endure his isolation no longer, and made his way to the head of the train.

"Did we drop anything?" Joicey shouted in his ear.

"No," he shouted back; "but some idiot up there keeps dropping mountains about all over the roof. I wish he would quit. The first thing we know we shall be buried alive."

"That's the glacier grinding the boulders and rubbish into mud along the rock above us," Joicey managed to make Ford hear. "Jolly glad we have a roof over our heads. We should be mud, too, if we hadn't."

Ford went back to his post to endure the racket as best he could. Another hour passed, and he again felt the need of human companionship. "What's that new celebration they've started just ahead of us?" he shouted.

"Water."

"Has some fool let the Atlantic Ocean in here too?"

"No, only the Red Sea. We'll reach it in five minutes. All hands light an extra torch. We're going to get damp."

GREAT drops were already pattering down on the glistening stone. Joicey tied the guiding ropes about his waist, carrying his torches high. He waved one toward the blackness on his right. Far out beyond the lowest of the nine stone causeways, the others saw what at first they took to be a huge column of dark red rock, some forty feet in thickness, towering up from the black abyss to support the invisible roof. But a bucketful of muddy water deftly extinguishing one of Ford's torches shed a brilliant light on the situation.

Joicey signaled for double speed, and in four minutes they were out of the shower, drenched to the skin. Not a single torch had survived, and it was impossible just then to relight them or kindle others. For those in the packs also were sopping wet. By mutual understanding they did the obvious thing with the least possible delay. Ford felt his way back, guiding himself by the wall of the tunnel, and stationed himself between it and the last of the ponies. Taking the pony's cheek strap in his right hand, he felt his way along the wall with his left. Rosita did the same for the leading pony and Joicey took hold of the other side of the bridle, walking on the right.

It was a nerve-racking march, and they were relieved some forty minutes later when Joicey, having constantly swung his torch to dry it, pulled up the leader and succeeded in getting a light. The drowsy thunder overhead and the roar of the water far behind them were now much diminished, and it was possible to hear a shout the length of the caravan. The torch flared up, and Rosita nearly fainted. Their own ledge had narrowed to a scant four feet; the remaining eight terraces had vanished utterly in the black abyss below.

Joicey was unconcernedly marching along within two inches of the sheer edge of nothing. He did not seem to mind. But she, with an unbroken wall on her left and a solid little pony on her right, felt suddenly seasick. "I won't. I swear I won't," she kept assuring herself. Exactly what it was that she resolved not to do, she did not say. At any rate she did not do it. Mind overcame mere matter.

"How long have we been walking this giddy tight-rope?" Ford shouted from his end of the caravan.

"Ever since we got past the fountain," Joicey shouted back.

"Have you no imagination?" Rosita demanded indignantly.

"Too much of it. That's why I prefer to take a thing like that in the dark. You don't see me looking down, do you?"

"No—oh, do look where you're going. Walk in front of the pony, can't you?"

"Not safe. Don't know whether this beggar suffers from vertigo. Probably not, but we mustn't take any chances. Where he goes the others must follow. The ledge broadens after a bit."

He continued his even gait along the black edge of the precipice. Rosita suspected him of walking just half an inch closer to destruction than was necessary. The thought enraged her. It made her so angry that she quite forgot her own squeamishness. She spent a blissful ten minutes in daydreaming that she would take it out of him at the earliest possible opportunity. She even pictured him with snow-white hair from the shock of some as yet unimagined mental torture of devilish ingenuity and her own happy devising. She would get even; just wait. Her dreams were at their rosiest when the causeway began to widen. When presently her uncle came up once more for company, she temporarily forgot all anticipation of revenge in thankfulness for their safety.

"Phew," said Ford. "Never again. Next time we'll take the pass. British soldiers notwithstanding."

"They won't stop us coming back," Joicey assured him. "The Government is queer that way. Once you're in Tibet it's all right. You can do what you like and come out any way you please. I shouldn't wonder if they sent a brass band to welcome us back."

"They will if they get wind of the sapphires we're bringing. What do you suppose that fountain affair is, anyway?"

"It seems simple enough if you know the geography of the mountains over our heads as I do. I tramped all over them looking for this tunnel before I found it. About two miles straight overhead is a big lake fed by several large glacial rivers. This lake has no discoverable outlet, so the water must run out of the bottom somehow. Probably ages ago the accumulating pressure of the water burst a hole through the bed of the lake into another subterranean funnel intersecting the floor of this one. This whole range, I imagine, must be honeycombed like a rabbit warren—the skeletons of dead volcanoes."

"Well, whatever it is, I'm glad we're past it."

"There's worse coming," he said gloomily.

"Great Scott! Soon?"

"In about six weeks. Then we shall have reached the rim of the desert, if all goes well and the Tibetans let us make good time. But cheer up, there are some really fascinating sculptures on the wall just before we get out of this tunnel. We should reach them in a minute or two."

Rosita brightened. "I wonder what this whole place is. Don't you think it strange that none of the explorers we read about have discovered it?"

"Oh, as to that, we're not the first to take this passage under the Himalayas. It probably was a great highway long before the British ever saw India."

"Then who traveled this way?"

"The Great Race," he said. "The people whose degraded remnant we are to visit. But as there is lots of time between now and our destination, I'll tell you all that you need to know for safety's sake some night when we're less tired. Since the Great Race passed this way, at least one other man has made the journey."

"You?" she asked.

"Once that I know of," he replied. "But I was thinking of another man. Singh. You shall see why in just another moment or two."

"AH," Joicey exclaimed, "there's the first of the procession."

The sculptured figure on the rock wall was that of a gigantic man striding forward as if to meet the travelers. They held their torches high to throw a good light on this truly wonderful example of a long since perished and forgotten art. The figure was fully thirty feet in height. The flowing lines of the loose robe or mantle which fell from the shoulders to the knees of the marching giant, leaving bare the throat and sinewy arms, recalled the freedom and grace of draperies from the golden age of Greek sculpture, while the bold, lifelike modeling of the muscles on the neck, arms and legs even excelled that of the great masterpieces of Assyrian art. But there played about the whole colossal figure an aura of virility and living, easy motion that neither the Greeks nor the Assyrians ever attained. The giant was alive; he seemed actually to move.

They waved their torches back and forth, endeavoring to throw a better light on the face and head. Succeeding presently, Ford and Rosita nearly dropped their torches in astonishment.

"Well," said Joicey, "what do you think of his taste in hairdressing?"

"It certainly is striking," Rosita admitted, "although personally I should not care to adopt the fashion."

*The gigantic sculptured figure was that of a man, thirty feet high,
who seemed to be striding forward to meet them...*

"That's unfortunate," he laughed. "For our last job after we say good-by to the Tibetans and our first before setting foot on the desert will be just that of imitating him to a hair. We must dye ours blue."

"Anything would be a relief," Ford sighed, "after the past dizzy hour. I'm glad this fellow didn't stain his face pea green. It's a blessing, too, that he didn't wear a beard or mustache."

They stood staring up at the curious apparition. Strangely enough, the effect was neither grotesque nor displeasing. The intense blue curls clustered tightly over the splendidly shaped head, stopping short just at the base of the skull. The giant's feature's, neither Asiatic nor European, radiated intellect as a blazing torch that radiates light. It was not a cold intelligence that played about the noble face, but something warmly human and almost infinitely patient and understanding.

"I should like to meet a man like that," Rosita sighed, "on a smaller scale, of course. He would take the taste of Anderson off my mind. Just think, that odious little turtle is actually a human being, and by mere money one of the most powerful specimens of our exalted race."

"If ever there were beings like this on earth," Ford agreed, "we certainly have taken a long climb down our family tree. Why, the best of the Greeks would be a hod carrier beside this fellow. Hereafter, you may count me among the rabid eugenists."

"And me," Joicey added with a glance at Rosita. "Does either of you know what that thing he is carrying in his right hand is meant to represent?"

"Not I," Ford admitted. "I've been trying to puzzle it out, but can't get the hang of it."

"Isn't it a scientific apparatus of some sort?" Rosita suggested.

"That's obvious," her uncle agreed. "But what? How does it work, and what does it do when it works?"

"One of those physics chaps at the Royal Society in London might see through it," Joicey hazarded. "Sorry now we didn't bring a camera and some flashlight powder. Well, we must leave him to carry it himself, whatever it may be, the rest of eternity. He leads the procession, so probably he and his machine were great guns in their day."

"How many more are there?" Ford asked as the caravan started.

"When I was here before, I counted over four hundred. You'll see them as we go. Sorry we can't stop to examine them all, but we must be getting on. Take a look as you go at the queer things they carry. That chap's machine is the simplest of the lot. In comparison with his, some of the others are like a modern linotype beside a baby's rattle."

They went on slowly and in silence, overawed by the sheer majestic beauty of that procession of colossi which marched out of the darkness to meet them and strode past with an easy, flowing motion into the darkness of the cavern or beyond. The strange complexity of the machines or apparatus which they carried increased rapidly all down the procession to its climax at the end.

Eight colossi brought up the rear, wearing on their shoulders a single contrivance of the most bewildering intricacy. What purpose all these marvels of reasoned complexity may have served in their long-forgotten day of usefulness, it was impossible to guess, for none of the travelers had ever seen any modern apparatus or machine that resembled them even distantly.

"If we ever see Darjeeling again," Ford exclaimed when they halted for a few minutes to scrutinize this last riddle, "I'm coming back with flashlights and a camera. There's a young scientific shark in New York at the Eastern Electric Company who would give his ears for a chance to puzzle out what practical use these things are good for. This beats all the sapphires in Asia."

Joicey agreed. "That fits in with what I planned lying on my back in the sanitarium. Then you two came along and I jumped at the opportunity of beginning from the easier end."

"You didn't seem to jump very far," Ford remarked. "What do you mean by the easier end?"

"Where this procession must have started from years ago," he explained. "It can't be far from where I 'acquired'..." He laughed as he accented the word, "...that precious sapphire sphere of which Anderson so generously relieved me. You shall see for yourself soon enough, I hope."

"Then nobody but just we two shall ever hear an embarrassing word of it," she said sweetly. "Your family secrets shall perish with us."

They pushed on, laboring up a steep ascent of the stone causeway. Presently the tunnel swerved at a sharp angle, and less than a hundred yards away in the arched entrance they beheld the crystal jewel of a great planet scintillating against the deep sapphire of the night and the steely blue of myriads of stars. A keen blast of the night air, blowing down from the distant glaciers and eternal snowfields of the mountains, smote their faces and quickened the tired ponies into new life. Emerging from the tunnel they found themselves in a narrow valley carpeted with soft grass and walled in on three sides by precipitous mountains of snow and sheer ice-cliffs glistening in the starlight.

Far to their right the great glacier under which they had marched shone dim and ghostly for mile after mile against the edge of the valley, where it crawled at last free of the snows to fret itself out on a wilderness of huge white boulders. The distant music of innumerable streams gushing from the foot of the vast glacier filled the valley with a soft lullaby, and from the far, open end came the steady, subdued thunder of a mighty waterfall.

"If this isn't a pony's paradise," Joicey remarked, unloading the leader, "I never saw one. You can enjoy yourselves while we sleep."

"Shall I take the first watch?" Ford suggested when all the animals had been eased.

"No. We can all sleep with perfect safety. Even the most adventurous of the nomads never heard of this place. We have it to ourselves."

They turned in. Two minutes later the Angel Gabriel himself could not have awakened them.

CHAPTER FIVE
A Call from The Past

LONG before the dawn had descended from the mountains they were up and on their way, skirting the right bank of a river which flowed swiftly and without a ripple down the middle of the narrow valley. The boom of falling water steadily increased as they marched rapidly down with the river and when after three hours of devious winding in and out among the huge white boulders of the moraine they at length forded the last of the shallow glacial freshets, the boom rose to a drowsy thunder that seemed to shake the very hills.

Leaving the glacier far behind them, they passed two others which debouched from the opposite range and sent their bright green waters roaming into the river on its farther bank. The sun was now well up in the valley, and the raw cold of morning became a blistering heat of noon. Joicey called a halt.

"We may as well change our togs and faces now," he said. "There is no reason why we should bake ourselves before entering the oven."

Rosita made herself an indescribable hue that might have been compounded from black mud, tobacco juice, coffee grounds, shoe polish and bacon grease. She had rubbed it in well. Nor had she neglected her wonderful golden hair, which now in filthy straight black strings down the sides of her face, and stuck out like a dirty mop on the back of her head. Her expression, too, had undergone an astonishing change. Something, one would think, of the vivacity and pure beauty of her face should have survived even the hideous mistreatment of her complexion. But no; she was as flat-faced and expressionless as an Eskimo or a batch of sour dough. The truth was that she had changed inside as well as out. She was now a young Tibetan girl thinking Tibetan thoughts and dreaming Tibetan daydreams.

She even thought in the Tibetan language, except when she consciously sought to practice herself by mentally naming various objects in the ancient tongue which Joicey was teaching her. The strangest part of it all was that there were actually then living, not thirty miles away, scores of young men who would look upon her as a raging beauty and who might, only given the divine chance, fall rapturously in love with her. The loose, absolutely filthy outer garment, which she wore gracefully as a gunnysack, and her clumping yak boots—not shoes, but honest high boots—should alone have sufficed to paralyze any man in his right mind.

Then she found the others, two unspeakably dirty Tibetan nomads, huddled over a few smoky embers of dried yak dung. As she approached they stuck out their tongues in greeting, and she politely returned the salutation. Not to have done so would have been an unpardonable breach of etiquette.

"You don't smell right," Ford grunted in Tibetan.

"I know," she admitted in a series of similar grunts, "but I thought that part of my toilet might be left until after supper. I didn't want to spoil the Holy Lama's appetite. Do I look all right?"

"You'll do," he said, speaking English.

"Joicey's religious cast of countenance must have given him away to you. He is to pose as a traveling Lama if we meet any nomads."

"Yes," Joicey added, "and I have not yet had the courage to face all of my sacred duties. I'm but half a monk. Like you, I omitted the perfumes—just for tonight."

"You may give us the true story of how you fell into that crevasse, if you like," Rosita told him. "There is still an hour or so before dark."

He began diffidently, for he hated nothing so much as talking about himself. But presently, warming to his story, he seemed to forget his audience, and to live once more the far off days of his boyhood. They sat spellbound, fascinated by this intimate revelation of a boy's dreams and ambitions all too soon sealed up behind the impenetrable reserve of the mature man.

"My people for generations," he began, "were connected with the India Service, through either the military or the civil. They came with Warren Hastings and Wellesley, and later others of the line saw the Mutiny through. There have been judges, doctors, soldiers and plain adventurers—thieves, if you like—among them. The men wore out their livers fighting heat, fever and brandy pegs; the women reared the children at 'home' and in due time sent them out to India to rot as their fathers had rotted before them.

"My father was the last on his side of the family. He died at thirty-four, five years after I was born and his wife died. An uncle on the other side of the family, a retired civil servant nursing a tropical liver on mutton curries, whiskies and sodas, and mango chutney to the limit of a too generous pension, took charge of my upbringing and education. India was his passion and the whole range of his circumscribed outlook. Naturally, he sent me to a crammer to prepare for the India Civil Service exams. I was sixteen at the time.

"The daily, senseless grind of futile Greek prose, dry Latin syntax, and fanciful mathematics irked my nerves. I struck and became as stupid as an ox. My end was gained; the crammer reported me utterly hopeless, and I returned in disgrace to my uncle's house. He was very decent. Although heartbroken over my unaccountable failure—I had given promise at school—he merely expressed a hope that I would read for the easier army exams, and so carry on the family tradition that way.

"THE prospect was not particularly alluring. Familiarity with our history had filled me with a lasting hatred and incurable disgust for all things Indian. My uncle left me to myself. I wasted the idle days in desultory browsing in the family library which he had inherited. Here were stored all the diaries, mementos, books, letters and curios collected by our tribe for generation after generation. So far as I could discover, none of the books except the antiquated atlases, obsolete books and old peerages had ever been read or even opened.

"The English administrator of a province with a population of five million natives need know nothing and think less about their traditions and customs; he is concerned only with the efficient collecting of the taxes. The leaves of most of the books were uncut; all were suspiciously clean and fresh. Finding nothing of interest among these, I began on the diaries and personal journals of our redoubtable family.

"These at first were equally disappointing; dreary annals of plague, famine, and slaughter. Then one morning I chanced upon a journal which from the first faded entry to the last unfinished page, throbbed with the living personality of a man apart from the herd, dead a century and a half ago, but still living in this curiously individual record. I devoured this fascinating journal from cover to cover, not once, but twenty times.

"The writer had dabbled in many things, among others Asiatic exploration. He even traversed Sikkim from end to end when it was an unknown province beyond British influence. One passage relating to these particular travels gripped my imagination as nothing else has before or since. It fixed unalterably the current of my life. I committed the passage to memory and transcribed an accurate copy. Having done this, I went to my uncle and told him I was ready to swat for the army exams. I promised to do my best and try for a high place in the entrance into Woolwich, and later a commission in the Royal Engineers. The poor old man broke into tears; the honor of the family had not perished utterly."

Pausing in his narrative, Joicey reached into the inner pocket of his shirt and drew forth an oilskin case from which he extracted several handmade maps and a number of small, closely written sheets of yellowed paper.

"This," he continued, exhibiting the sheets of writing, "is the story that made me what I am for life. These sheets are the transcribed copy of which I spoke; the maps I made for the most part myself. I need not read all; a few extracts will do. I shall alter the quaint wording of my ancestor as I read, so that you may follow his narrative more readily."

He selected one of the sheets and began reading. " 'Now in those parts I met a traveler'—in Sikkim, that is— 'from beyond the high mountains, whose hair was stained blue, as the ancient Britons are said to have dyed their bodies with woad, which is a blue pigment. This man averred that he was a priest of the Great Race, which I could well believe, he being a man of singular nobility and intelligent aspect.' "

Joicey looked up. "I shall skip my ancestor's long description of this alleged priest," he said. "It tallies fairly well with General Wedderburn's portrait of his servant Singh, and of my own observations of the race to which this man belonged, which, by the way, was not the Great Race. You shall see living specimens your-selves, if you are alive about nine weeks hence. I want to emphasize as strongly as I can, however, that both Singh and the man of my ancestor's narrative were very rare exceptions to the rest of their race. They were the geniuses; all the others are fools. The case is exactly like that of England. You recall, of course, Carlyle's famous estimate of us: 'Fifty million, mostly fools.' "

He continued reading. " 'This priest conversed with me in the Hindustani tongue which he had acquired, he said, in his travels farther south. His own language I could not understand, neither before (nor since) having heard any like it. He boasted that his had been a far higher race than any he had seen on his wanderings. I was much flattered when he complimented me on my features and fair complexion, he saying graciously that I was the first being whom he had met since leaving his own country who resembled a man rather than an ape or a baboon.

" 'I asked him why, then, had he quitted this superior people of which he boasted. Did he prefer the company of monkeys to that of men? Not so, he said. Then why had he suffered thirst in the desert and icy cold on the high mountains to pass over into India? For he had told me of great and strange perils endured that he might cross the desert which shut off his country from the filthy dwellers in certain high regions.'

"Here follows a detailed description of the priest's route across the desert, then an account of his brief sojourn among the Tibetan nomads on the plateau between the desert and this valley where we now are. As we shall follow practically the same route, I can skip the description of this priest's travels over a hundred and fifty years ago. No details, not even the Tibetans, have changed in all the century and a half that has elapsed since this priest confided his troubles to my ancestor.

" 'He thereupon told me a strange story of the past greatness of his race,' the narrative continues, 'and of its present declined state. Their priestly legends, he said, told of a time when the vast country to the north of his own, by which he meant China, was inhabited by a race of savages, naked or clothed only in the skin of animals. At that time, he declared, these savages knew not the art of killing with bow and arrow, but slew their enemies, their food and the wild beasts which preyed upon them with stones hurled from slings.' That," Joicey commented, "must put them at the beginning of the Stone Age. Either this priest was the champion long-distance liar of all time, or his own Great Race was of almost unbelievable antiquity." He went on with his ancestor's narrative.

" 'Yet, this priest asserted, at that very time when the Chinese were not yet human, his own race knew all the arts of meals and many others, some of which I shall recount presently, now lost. And he boasted that while all other men were little higher than the beasts, his own race lived almost without toil like heathen gods, enjoying every pleasant thing at their ease. This, he said, was possible because in the very morning of their history their wise men or "readers of nature's mysteries" had mastered the chief secrets of nature. With this knowledge they bound Nature herself with chains, compelling her to be their slave, while other men then living were in chains to nature and were her most wretched subjects.

" 'Now he told me a very curious thing, which I would not believe were it not that no less a philosopher and alchemist than the great Sir Isaac Newton himself publicly avowed that this thing is possible, and indeed gave forty years of his strongest manhood (but unavailingly) to bring about. This thing is the manner of changing one metal into another, so that the baser metals become the nobler, and vice versa. Thus, this priest asserted the "wise women" of his race in ancient times knew how to change lead into a metal that "lived" and was more precious than gold, and practiced also the higher alchemy of making all metals from a subtle air which, he said, they were wont to draw from the grosser air of our atmosphere. In this more difficult art was great danger, and only the most skillful among the "wise women" of the ancient Great Race were allowed to practice it for the common good. It gave them fire and heat without fuel, light without fire, also food from the air if they so willed, and rich fertility for their fields!

"THE narrative continues with a long enumeration of the wonders which legend asserted this Great Race could accomplish, of the luxury in which they lived, and of their marvelous control over all the forces of nature and, rather strangely, of the extraordinary laws by which they safeguarded marriage and the rearing of children.

"One of the most striking parts of these legends is the part played in them by women. The 'wise women' it seems, were the practical brains of the race; the 'readers of mysteries,' the scientists or theorizers. The 'wise women' at any rate had charge of all the delicate operations connected with the actual changing of the metals into something either more useful or more precious. The men, other than the scientific sect of 'readers of nature's mysteries,' appear to have attended chiefly to government and the planning of new ventures. One detail in regard to the wise women is of the highest importance for us, as you shall see step by step as we approach our goal. I need not stop to explain this now; it will do to state what this fact is. The wise women were not permitted to bear children lest the cares of motherhood distract their minds from their exceedingly dangerous work.

"This ancient law, laid down ages before our race emerged from barbarism, and preserved now only in obscure traditions, has kept Evelyn Wedderburn in physical safety for twelve years, I suspect, and would if necessary keep harm from her for sixty years longer. I only guessed this a very short time ago, as I shall tell you some other night. Now, all these details of the traditional life of the Great Race are interesting enough; but I shall pass on to the priest's version of the legendary migration southward of a part of the Great Race, and the subsequent fall of the remnant."

Joicey lit a cigarette, one of his last, and the last that he should dare smoke for many a weary day, before continuing his narrative.

Joicey shuffled his papers several times before finally selecting the few which he wished.

"These," he resumed, "are like a cry from the dead to us, imploring us to go to their aid and show them the way to life once more. We are not going merely for a few bits of colored stone to tickle some idiot's vanity, nor are we going on this expedition to rescue but one lost member of our own tribe. We are going in obedience to his call, which is that of a whole race clamoring for our help. At least I am. And if that sounds like a piece of priggishness, I'll let the wind out of my own balloon by confessing that nothing but crass, vulgar curiosity has induced me to answer the call."

Ford winked across the campfire to Rosita, who returned the signal. Joicey must think them as "easy" as Anderson, was Ford's meaning. Well, they should see whose hand first grabbed for the sapphires. Rosita's understanding of the situation was that Joicey's perverse modesty prevented him from giving himself due credit for his splendidly unselfish motives. And so these three, mutually misunderstanding one another, understood each other perfectly according to their own rights, which is as near as any human being comes to the hidden mind of another. Joicey continued to read from his ancestor's account of what the priest had told him.

" 'To the north of the regions where the Great Race dwelt rose lofty mountain ranges white with perpetual snow and inaccessible to the savages beyond. To the south was a yet loftier and more rugged barrier which none might cross. This barrier, I take it from the priest's account, was the Himalaya range. Now, as the race prospered and multiplied, a dispute arose. One faction wished to carry the boon of their civilization beyond the southern barrier and in that way extend it over the whole world. The other faction desired to proceed northward.

" 'Failing to agree, each party set about the execution of its own purpose. The southern faction was to migrate first; the northern was to remain until the depleted population again multiplied to its full strength. The southern faction dispatched explorers to discover an easy pass through the barrier. After many trials they succeeded. The beginning of this long journey is at the foot of a waterfall.' "

Joicey looked up. "You shall see it tomorrow. Next is a description of the valley we are in now, and then a long account of the rock tunnel which we traversed, followed by a description of the red rock labyrinth at the other end and the landmark of the glacier. At the time of the migration, all nine causeways ran unbroken the entire length of the tunnel. The break by the waterspout has happened since. There was given also a map of the correct route through the rock maze; it was my copy of this which I gave you, Ford. As you shall not need it again, I should like it as a souvenir."

FORD handed back the carefully drawn map, and Joicey continued to read selections from the narrative.

" 'To commemorate their departure, the priest said, the southern faction left a record of their march in the form of certain sculptures on the rock wall at the entrance of the tunnel under the barrier. This they did, he averred, so that any coming after them, and failing perchance to find them, should nevertheless decipher for themselves from these records the chief arts of the ancient civilization.

" 'Now, according to the priest, in the second generation after the departure of the southern faction, disaster of the most appalling nature all but obliterated the northern faction which was yet living at the home of the race. Wishing to augment their supply of a certain foodstuff obtained from the soil, the wise women made the necessary preparations for imparting fertility to the barren rock in an extensive province as yet uncultivated. All was in readiness for the delicate operation when, owing to a slight error in judgment on part of one woman, "the blue flame—" so the priest described it— which was to have converted the rock into rich soil, leapt from their control. All of the wise women and "readers of nature's mysteries" were annihilated, and of the entire population but one in a hundred thousand escaped destruction. The labor and slowly accumulated knowledge of ages vanished in a withering whirlwind of flame.

" 'But one thing in all that land survived, although practically all that it contained, which indeed was the very nerve of their civilization, was converted instantly into less than ashes. This relic of their destroyed greatness was the elaborate system of lead-lined rock chambers and galleries in the heart of a vast cliff, or mountain, where the wise women did their work. It was from this place that all the life of the race flowed.

" 'And now, said the priest, it was swept clean, save one of the smaller chambers, by the instant, all-consuming fire which had once been the fountain of their life and later the source of their destruction. Except only in the one lesser chamber, the very fire itself had been annihilated. Here, in a block of metal, he declared, it still flames to this day. But none of his race have seen the block; their knowledge is the faith and tradition. For the manner of "causing the flame to leap from the stone," and the beneficent use of the flame itself, alike perished with the wise women. Not one of the survivors was of the sect which dwelt in the city at the base of the mountain, and whose once was the discovery of the laws of nature.

" 'Legend, so the priest declared, related that the few survivors walled up the entrance to the caves and at once tried to communicate with the southern faction of their race. In this they were frustrated. The rocky province which the wise women had sought to convert to fertility was now, as the priest put it, "a writhing wilderness, through and through rotten with cold, poisonous blue fire." None might venture onto it and live. The flame of destruction had but half done its work; only the slow lapse of ages could complete it, extinguishing the poisoned fire and crumbling down the rotten sand and rock to innocuous earth. This impassable wilderness of fire lay between the remnant of the race and the path by which, two generations before, their kindred had departed to the south.

" 'The remnant lived on, millennium after millennium, and of their perished greatness only the dim legend survived. This, and the determination to cross the desert if ever it became possible, alone remained of all the world's golden age. The daily habits of a great and happy people became the legendary dreams of a sweating, degraded race.

" 'The priest claimed that although thousands before him had tried—he had seen the bones of some—he was the first of all his race to win across the desert and see the records of his ancestors. But neither he nor any man of all the tribe, he felt sure, could decipher the meaning of the strange implements which those marching colossi bore. He therefore had pushed on, searching through all the land south of the great barrier for descendants of the ancient race. Not until meeting me, he declared, had he seen any in human form who could possibly have descended from his ancestors, and even I was impossible because my head was wrongly shaped.

" 'He must seek yet again farther south, he said. I tried vainly to dissuade him, saying that the other branch of the race must have perished long since, or through an accident similar to the other have sunk into degradation, for history holds no record of their achievements. Possibly, I hazarded, the bearers of the implements were overwhelmed by avalanches in descending the mountains to the fertile plains. Or, if not that, their delicate implements were rendered useless by the loss of essential parts in the long journey over precipitous snow and ice. But he argued that the Great Race feared neither snow nor ice, and that it might, if it desired, "soar over the mountains on wings" if only there were sufficient air above the great heights. Then I suggested what indeed seems likely; the southern faction succumbed to the sudden fevers of the valleys to which their race had never been acclimated. But after all, I said, it was more probable that they too had perished long ages ago through the mischance of their own dangerous science.

" 'I could not dissuade him from his futile quest. He persisted in his folly, saying that he dare not return without some "child of the Great Race" to teach his people once more the supreme secret of the fire which they knew, by faith and by tradition, still lived in that block of metal fast sealed up in one undestroyed chamber of the mountain. Before departing southward he showed me an inscribed box of lead which he asserted, was his "passport to the intelligence of the Great Race and his key to the land of the remnant." Without such a talisman, none might leave or enter his country. Opening the boxes for my inspection he disclosed a kingly purple sapphire, as large as a silver florin, shining like the sun.'

"The narrative then tells of the unsuccessful attempt of my ancestor to buy the sapphire, and of his successful struggle against the temptation to murder and rob the priest. Now, that's enough to show you why I officially 'fell into a crevasse' while surveying in northern Sikkim. It is scarcely necessary to add the intermediate details that I passed my exams into and out of Woolwich and was transferred through my uncle's influence, from the Royal Engineers to the India Survey. I knew where I was going, and I went.

"Cross-examining natives, consulting old maps, and leading outlandish expeditions, I worked feverishly to locate the landmarks of the glacier and rock labyrinth. Finally, a little over eight years ago, I picked up my first clue at Pedong from a Tibetan caravan leader. He had once lost his way in a snowstorm which continued four days. When it ceased, he saw on the mountains far to the northeast the green of a huge glacier buttressed by sheer, red cliffs. The hint was enough. Five months later I was officially dead."

Ford suddenly reached into his pocket and drew forth the lead case. "Great Scott, Joicey, do you suppose we shall need the sapphire as well as the box? What a chump I was to sell it."

"We shall, or something just as good. And I've got it."

He proudly exhibited an excellent imitation of the sapphire disk, lacking, of course, the superb fire of the original.

"This purple glass cost me just five shillings," he laughed. "I got the lapidary to grind it down to the right size and shape while the expert was testing Anderson's purchase. Of course, almost any shape would have done, but I thought a good job would be more artistic."

"I'll bet that's why you insisted on getting my disk as well as your sphere certified before we sold them," Ford exclaimed. "You can get around without a nurse, I guess."

"Wait till you see it shine." Joicey dived into another recess of his capacious garment and brought out a small phial of luminous paint. He lightly dabbed the purple glass disk with the paint. The effect was really quite good. "It doesn't send up quite such gorgeous fireworks as the real thing," he said critically; "but will do if we're lucky enough to meet a priest who is half blind."

AFTER breaking camp an hour before midnight, they marched eight hours, and finally stood at the verge of a stupendous waterfall which thundered down fifteen hundred feet or more in an unbroken arch of water to the plain below. Speech in that reverberant thunder was impossible. All had been arranged before breaking camp, and they now quickly executed their pre-concerted plan. All but three of the ponies were unburdened of their packs. These they cached among the rocks and stunted poplars beyond the high water mark of the river. Should they be forced to return this way they should have ample provisions for the homeward march.

The unburdened ponies were turned loose to roam at will in this paradise after their own hearts. Should they have to retrace their steps they might possibly catch one or two of the ponies, but failing that they could easily make the march back on short rations after three weeks' recuperation at the cache. Finally the packs of the remaining three ponies were stripped of everything but the barest necessities. Even the poor beasts are grievously overloaded then. The supplies included a dozen water bags of goatskin and a complete change of costume for each member of the party.

Outwardly, everything about the small, compact caravan, from the disguises of Rosita and the two men to the ponies' harness, was distinctly Tibetan. Before starting, Ford had seen to the matter with the minutest care, and during the march through Sikkim he had let slip no opportunity for acquiring further articles of Tibetan workmanship.

Joicey, too, on some of his night expeditions, had secured improved substitutes for several of Ford's originals, in addition to the other necessities for the march after they should have traversed the Tibetan highland. They gazed down on the broad, bleak plains beneath them, confident that when they began their six weeks' journey through this remote hunting and pasture ground of the Tibetan nomads, they should not be sent back as infidel foreigners. They and everything they outwardly possessed were now Tibetan of the Tibetans.

Ford gave the signal that all was ready for the descent, and Joicey, leading his pony, started directly for the great arch of blue water. It shot far clear of the cliff, a glassy, apparently solid mass. Under this arch, down the wall of the sheer cliff, wound a dizzy stone trail, a sort of natural stairway, zigzagging back and forth across the fifteen hundred feet of the precipitous descent. A false step, a slip in clambering from one wet block to the next lower, meant death on the rocks far below.

Reaching the first of these steps, Joicey paused until Rosita, leading her pony, halted immediately behind him. Ford fell into line behind her and tossed one end of a leather rope to Joicey, who made it fast to his pony's saddle. The other end was already secured to Ford's pony. Thus between Rosita and the abyss there was some slight protection, but not much. In the event of a serious slip it would be useless. It was in fact merely a psychological charm against dizziness. The long descent began.

For two breathless hours all went well. Then, in taking a steep six-foot scramble, Ford's pony slipped, hurtling into Rosita's. They were now about five hundred feet above the rock bottom. The middle pony instinctively braced himself on all fours and seemed to make himself heavier. But the impact had been too violent and he slid, snorting with terror, into Joicey's. Ford and Rosita closed their eyes. It was all over but the echo from below. But Joicey's pony, a spirited little beggar, objected to being edged off his right of way. He squatted on his haunches and let the others shove him till they wearied. Then scrambling to his feet he gave himself a shake and proceeded to pick his way daintily to the next ledge. When finally they reached the bottom, trembling but safe, Rosita kissed the hero of her day. He did not seem to enjoy it, possibly because he was a clean beast and Rosita's Tibetan toilet was now complete to its last fragrant detail.

A hundred yards from where they stood the blue arch of the waterfall plunged into the depths of a huge basin worn in the solid rock. Of the three, only Joicey had ever before seen falls of such stupendous volume as these, which shot over the precipice in one unbroken sweep three miles broad. They stood gazing up a few minutes at the massive arch or greenish-blue crystal. It seemed always on the point of crashing down on their heads; yet it never fell, but swept sublimely over them, blue and unbroken, into the basin of the river. They had started across a far, all but deserted arm of the Tibetan highlands.

All that day and the next they saw no signs of human life. Then in the evening they met their first Tibetan, and thereafter for six weeks they lived the life of drifting nomads, working always steadily to the north. Their identity was never questioned, and the simple hunters and lonely shepherds, accepting them at their own valuation, shared with the travelers their humble food and drink. In the evenings, and every hour of the day when they were alone, the three conversed incessantly in the ancient Tibetan, until at the end of six weeks, Joicey pronounced himself satisfied with the proficiency of his pupils. All so far had gone without a slip. But then, they reflected, when three experienced travelers set their minds to the performance of a task within their powers, it is strange indeed if they fail.

At last, as the seventh week of their uneventful march began, they met no more Tibetans for a stretch of two days. They seemed to have passed beyond the limits of the nomads' farther-most wanderings to the north in that locality. The ground over which they now tramped was stony and almost barren. The precious barley was broached for the ponies, who were not sorry for the change.

"Well," said Joicey, "tomorrow morning we should get our first glimpse of the desert that we have come all this way to see."

"How long should it take us to cross this precious desert of yours?" Rosita asked.

"A day and the best part of two nights, if we go the limit of our pace and don't get lost."

"Did you?"

"Well," he equivocated, "the weird scenery so fascinated me that I spent considerable time enjoying it."

"I don't see any signs of nomads," Ford remarked. "We seem to have got beyond their extreme range in this direction. What do you say to pitching camp and cleaning up? There's an abundance of fuel and water, if nothing else. Come, let us boil ourselves."

"Second the motion," said Rosita. "Six weeks of Tibetan beauty is enough for one spell. More might make me vain."

Joicey demurred. "Let us wait till dark. Then if we see no fires anywhere on the plain it will be safe to change our makeup. There probably isn't a Tibetan within fifty miles of us, for we are getting quite near to the beginning of the desert, and neither grass nor game thrives very well in the vicinity. But we can't be too sure, so let us wait awhile. It would be a pity to call out the soldiers from the nearest jong to escort us back now that we got this far."

It was well that they followed his advice. Their own fire had barely started when another, about three miles to their left, flared redly up in answer.

"Prepare for company," Ford said in Tibetan. "Rosita, look your best."

"I'll do my darnedest and my dirtiest," she replied in her mother tongue. "Hand me that bowl of rancid butter that I may make myself desirable."

The thud of galloping hoofs on the sand was heard in the distance, and presently a lone rider loomed up in the dusky twilight. The first square look by the light of their campfire showed that he was friendly. Indeed, his good nature had overflowed in hospitality; for the entire carcass of a sheep draped the shoulders of his horse.

He was a young man, apparently not over twenty-five, of the nomad type, and remarkably handsome for a Tibetan. A haircut and a month in a steam bath undoubtedly would have improved his appearance; but such as he was, he was not unattractive. His evident joy at meeting human beings in this out-of-the-way corner, and his ready laughter at everything they said or did, won their hearts immediately. Joicey, as befitted his character of a traveling Lama, bore himself with proper dignity. Only occasionally did he permit himself the relaxation of a grave smile at the simple, childlike humor of their visitor.

The greetings over, and acquaintance established, they set about preparing the feast, somehow or another they must dispose of that sheep. But how? It chanced that none of the travelers on previous expeditions had been called upon to prepare mutton in the Tibetan manner. If they broiled parts of the sheep like Christians, or barbecued it whole like Americans, they must inevitably give themselves away. Rosita solved the puzzle in truly feminine fashion. She offered the young nomad a sandwich, as it were, of a thick chunk of ardent admiration between two thin slices of maidenly reserve buttered over with coy flattery. Before the guileless a young man knew what he was about, he was cooking his own sheep.

During the interminable meal that followed the travelers casually pumped their guest dry. Between over-eating and violent love at first sight he was completely anaesthetized. They might have removed his appendix without any disturbance. There were no other nomads in the district as far as he knew. He, his horse, and his dogs, which he had left to look after his two remaining sheep, were the only intelligent beings within a radius of twenty miles.

So far, so good. But was it possible that a human skin could hold yet more tea, more mutton, and all-filling rice? It was. Hour after hour passed, and still he continued to eat. He ate in relays. First he would gorge, then he would lose half an hour in making sheep's eyes at Rosita. Her unlovely attractions had bewitched him. Henceforth he was hers, and he would not be jealous if, in the manner of Tibetan girls, she took two or three husbands who were as dirty as he along with him.

He painted the joyous freedom of a nomad's life with the skill of a great artist, and all the swashing colors of a Tibetan sunset. His brush, it is true, was a leg of mutton, and his pigments mostly sour milk and lukewarm tea softened with rancid butter. But what of it? He was a master of the only materials he knew, and the clean winds of the world's high places swept along the airy vistas of his canvases. Rosita's alluring brown eyes and dank black hair, the set of her gunnysack garb, her quick understanding of his simple ambitions, and her inexpressible state of dirt had unlocked the elemental gates of paradise for this unsophisticated son of the Tibetan highlands. His life henceforth would run in deeper channels.

No doubt he some day would marry and beget sons and daughters, for such is the end of all great lovers. For something infinitely delicate and as universal as the colic's of childhood in Rosita's manner warned him that he could never be hers, and that his must be the way of pain. But from that hallowed hour till his last breath he never would forget this, divine, incomparable girl who had first shown him what heaven was. These hours by the embers of the dying campfire on the high plateau would be a sanctuary to which, in future years he might retire from the jangling discords of domestic infelicities. In the long years to come his body might be that of a faithful husband to one woman, but his secret soul most certainly would be that of a joyous, unblushing bigamist, subject occasionally to long spells of self-pity and sweet melancholy. None but he should ever learn the secret of that spiritual mating in the high wilderness and its immaculate ecstasies. His must be a life of renunciation. He sighed and manfully braced his thews for the next lap of his never-ending supper.

The others had long since dropped breathless out of the race, leaving their guest to beat the world's record or burst, as he should see fit. The white man's stomach is less elastic than his conscience. Ford slumbered unabashed. Joicey began to nod. Only Rosita remained attentive and sympathetic. And what girl in her fix would not? The pure, white flame of a first love is irresistible. She accepted the gift of this man's soul as a cat accepts fish, or an American Indian a scalp, because she could not help herself, and because her mother Eve took everything that was offered her.

At last he ran out of tea and rice. Having now reached the finicky stage of feasting, he cast a critical eye over the broken remnants of the sheep, and decided that mutton without rice or tea was unattractive. He licked his fingers, dried them on his hair, took a huge pinch of snuff, and sneezed Ford awake. Then he looked reverently over the embers toward the black bulk of the Holy Lama Joicey, squatting silent and Buddha-like on the other side. The sudden conflagration of a first love smothering beneath the soothing solemnity of a full stomach worked its perennial miracle. His deeper nature was about to erupt. He wished now to discuss the destiny and purpose of man, both here and hereafter.

"Master," he began diffidently, "you must be very Holy."

"I am," Joicey assented.

This foolhardy admission let in the flood. For hours the Holy Lama wrestled with the black devils of doubt which had made this young nomad's otherwise empty mind their favorite roosting place and filthy habitation. No sooner did he succeed in standing one legion of the bat-like creatures on their horned heads than another swarmed in, right side up, agog with eager and perplexing questions. The great Rinpoche himself might have sat at the feet of the Lama Joicey and in half an hour learned more Buddhism than he had absorbed in all his fifty years of laborious study and patient contemplation. What Joicey did not know he invented, and what he could not fabricate he borrowed shamelessly from every creed and philosophy in which he had ever dabbled. Schopenhauer's breezy pessimism but cleared the way for Plato's moony optimism. Kant fought it out with Mahomet, and the gentle Confucius wrangled bitterly with the Salvation Army. Step by step, the black hosts of doubt were driven from the young Buddhist's mind, but not before the Eastern stars wearied and grew wan was he purged of unbelief.

Doubtless a job of that kind takes longer on a Buddhist than a follower of any other creed. For his perpetual contemplation of eternity somewhat dulls his perception of mere time. However that may be, the issue in this case was a happy one. The young nomad emerged from the conflict purified and radiantly joyous. Never again would he question the wisdom of the Grand Lama, his spiritual master, or dispute the mystic dogmas of "the spotless jewel of the lotus flower." Cleansed in spirit if not in body, the young Tibetan at last rose to take his departure.

"And why are you, learned Lama, wandering this far place?" he asked Joicey.

"We are on our annual pilgrimage to Lassa," Joicey replied with ready untruthfulness.

"Then you shall pass my camp in the morning, and I shall see you again," he grunted joyously, his eyes resting on Rosita.

"I fear not," said Ford. "We take a shorter way." It was a bad blunder.

"There is no shorter way. There is no other way," the young man declared emphatically.

The situation might at any instant develop real danger. Of course, they could easily have not hesitated to take the lives of scores of innocent "savages" on even less provocation. More than one Tibetan has been murdered for as little, by men who call themselves courageous. Such a thought, however, did not occur to either Ford or Joicey. By temperament and training both men preferred brains to brute force.

If this troublesome questioner persisted, he must be silenced, or he might bring a pestiferous horde of horsemen about them before they reached the desert. On fast horses a troop of Tibetan cavalry, summoned from even thirty miles away, could easily intercept them long before they had traversed the last of the plateau. It might, of course, have been a week's journey to the nearest jong, but they had no detailed knowledge of their location, and obviously to question the young nomad would be fatal. They must, therefore, silence him by diplomacy. This they did by telling him one half-truth and two falsehoods.

"There is an easier way," Ford said quietly. "Only you don't know of it."

"What is this other way?" the nomad demanded suspiciously.

"I cannot tell you fully," Ford replied, "for it is a secret known only to the Holiest of the Lamas. But this much I can tell you: before we come to the first step of that other way, we must cross the desert which begins over yonder at the edge of this plateau."

"Now I know you are lying," the Tibetan remarked with childlike directness. He was not civilized enough to express himself equivocally.

"Why?" Ford demanded.

"Because not even a bird can cross that desert and live. It is a pen of fiery devils who consume everything, dead or living, even to the very rocks."

He spoke unaffectedly from the depths of a profound conviction. What he stated, was to him an obvious well-known fact.

"You say nothing can cross that desert and live," Joicey broke in quietly. "Look at me. Am I a dead man?"

"No," he answered slowly. His eyes expressed something of doubt, mingled with wonder and dread.

"Then come over here with me to the last embers of our fire and I will show you something," Joicey continued. "The stars grow dim in the coming day, but the light is not yet strong enough to show you all that which you must see."

Unwillingly, but fascinated and compelled by Joicey's manner, the young nomad followed him to the last embers of their fire.

"Why, shepherd, do I wear these gloves of sheepskin?" Joicey asked, kneeling by the embers and holding his hands out to the red glow.

"I cannot say, master, unless it be to keep your hands warm against the cold winds of this high place."

"Not so," Joicey answered. "My hands burn." He drew off his gloves, exhibiting his cracked palms and the seared withered flesh of his fingers. The young Tibetan recoiled in horror, for although the hands were much less terrible than when Ford and Rosita had first seen them, they still were not good to look upon. "See, they are white," he said. "The fiery breath of the devils in the desert burnt them almost to ashes," he continued. "For when I crossed the desert, I was a Lama, but not a Holy man. And so when the devils leaped upon me and I strangled them with my bare hands, their throats and poisonous breath burned my flesh, and I became Holy. Now I may cross the desert without fear, for I have slain devils. They shall not come near me. Tell no man of this, or that we cross the desert, lest some who are not Holy Lamas foolishly try to follow in my footsteps and perish."

"I will tell no man," the young man swore. "I go to care for my two sheep. Tomorrow I return to my brothers who are far away."

"It is a pen of fiery devils who consume everything living—even to the very rocks."

Plainly for the moment he was terrified half out of whatever wits he had. He desired nothing so much as to flee from the immediate vicinity of one who had actually seen and battled with the hideous devils of his nightmares and religious musings.

Rosita softly asked if she might accompany him a few steps of his way to bid him good luck. It was just the idle whim of a moment on her part, conceived and born in a second, as are most of the things that men and women spend fifty years of their lives in regretting after it is too late to think. The poor nomad forgot even his fiery demons in transports at the prospect of a tête-à-tête by waning starlight with the loved one. Conversing in low murmurs they strolled off in the direction of his camp. What they talked about Rosita never told.

When at last she returned alone, half an hour before sunrise, she heard her uncle snoring and beheld Joicey towering black as a thundercloud above the white ashes of their fire. At his feet lay the sorry remains of the feast and Rosita's bowl of rancid butter. It was almost impossible to be masterful or heroic amid such homely surroundings. Yet somehow he managed it and looked quite fierce.

"You've been gone an awful time," he snapped.

"Has it seemed long?" she asked sweetly.

"It isn't what it seemed, it's what it was," he retorted hotly. "You've been away two hours and a quarter."

"How strange a thing time is," she said reflectively, in the best manner of a Buddhist fakir. "To me it seems but five minutes since I left here."

His only reply was to give the unoffending bowl of rancid butter a savage kick that sent it spinning far and messily over the landscape. He stalked off toward the faithful ponies.

With a low laugh of utter bliss Rosita crept into her primitive tent for a short nap.

CHAPTER SIX
To the Desert's Rim

DESPITE their late revels they rose two hours after the sun and at once began preparations for the last and most dangerous lap of their long journey. From their camp to the edge of the desert was less than an easy day's march, so they had ample time to take every precaution for a safe passage. They were to change their disguises, march to the edge of the desert, and rest there till an hour before midnight before essaying their first penetration of the fiery wilderness.

The cleaning up process lasted over two hours. Boiling water, fine sand, wet ashes and one priceless cake of carbolic soap which circulated freely so long as it lasted, were the chief agencies in the miracle of transforming three Tibetans into their white equivalents. Rosita's hair proving the most obstinate stronghold of local color, the men accused her of selfishly taking twice her lawful third of the soap. At last, however, the entire party attained the blessing of cleanliness at the expense of a tingling skin, and once more they recognized one another.

They next burnt their Tibetan costumes and changed into clean, light garments of somewhat similar cut but more pleasing lines. Beneath these, each member of the party wore a close-fitting woolen shirt with numerous pockets containing the necessities of the white man who travels, revolvers, a small electric torch, maps, and so on, and in Joicey's case, a gold watch, a compass and a monocle.

"If we do have to return this way," Joicey said as he watched Rosita's travel-worn yak boots blistering in the embers, "we manufacture our costumes before we start back. It should not be impossible."

Rosita felt sure she could duplicate everything provided cloth and hides were available, and of this there seemed no reasonable doubt. Next they filled all their water skins and loaded them on the ponies. They had water sufficient for three days. If necessary it could be stretched to five, but no more. Rations in like proportion were next packed. Joicey had already cached the rest of the outfit beneath an inconspicuous cairn of stones and gravel. There remained but one thing to do before starting.

"Rosita," said Ford, "as you are the only woman in the crowd, we shall try it on you first. Come on, you're the goat."

"Too bad we didn't bring a dog," she retorted. "I balk. Captain Joicey got us into this, so he should be the first."

"Ford forgot to buy the bally stuff," Joicey objected, "so he ought to pay for his negligence by showing us that they didn't give me the wrong color."

He was about to doctor his lame case when Rosita seized one of his arms, Ford the other. Between them they brought him sprawling down like a steer for the branding.

"I say—" he expostulated.

"Hold quiet, can't you? Don't buck, or you'll spill the stuff. Rosita sit on his back."

She did so, and Ford with the aid of a large watercolor brush expertly dyed the victim's hair a beautiful deep blue.

"I hope it's a fast color," Ford said, letting him up. "Otherwise we shall be out of luck, for it's all we have."

"Let me see the bottle," Joicey requested. "All the genuine coal tar dyes have a special trade-mark."

Ford guilelessly surrendered the bottle. With his free hand and one leg Joicey deftly spilled him full length on the sand. "You re next," he said.

He took his time, lingering ticklishly on Ford's bald spot with the loving touch of an artist putting the finishing touches to his masterpiece.

"Now, Rosita, it's your turn." Ford advanced, grinning, to lay hands on his niece.

Joicey suddenly seemed puzzled. "Hold on a bit." He was trying to recall some essential detail. "Were there any women represented in that procession on the rooks?"

"There were not," Rosita declared emphatically. "I took special plans to look."

"The deuce of it is," Joicey continued, "I can't recollect whether the wise women also dyed their hair blue. In fact, I don't believe I ever heard anything about it, one way or the other."

"Your ancestor's narrative did not refer to it." Rosita was growing quite hopeful.

"I know that, of course. But I'm trying to remember what the man with the sapphire sphere said. He told me a great deal about the legends concerning the wise women."

"Just what did he tell you?" Rosita demanded suspiciously.

"Oh, all sorts of queer things," he fenced. "I shall give you the whole yarn tonight before we start across the desert. You must have it, of course, to prepare you for your part when we get across. But just now it would take too long."

"Still, telling it might refresh your memory. You had better begin."

"No, really, it wouldn't. I'm positive. That detail has gone completely. This is a case where reason and judgment are useless. We must take a chance and trust to luck. We shall have to toss up."

Searching about he found a large flat pebble, gray on one side. Slightly blue on the other. "The blue side is heads, the gray tails. If it falls heads, your hair shall be dyed blue; if tails, then you remain as beautiful as nature and carbolic soap have made you."

He flipped the pebble high in the air so that it described a wide curve and fell some twenty feet away. He beat Rosita to it by a matter of inches, but not before she had seen which side lay uppermost.

"Tails," he announced, swooping down on the pebble. "You escape, and I'm jolly glad of it. Gold is more becoming to you than blue. By Jove, though…" He sighed, "…I hope the god of chance hasn't played us a dirty trick. If he has, you shall have no head next week, gold or blue."

Now, Rosita could have sworn that the pebble had fallen heads, and that her hair by rights was doomed. She was not absolutely sure, of course, because she was still upright when Joicey's hand closed on it. But she had a strong suspicion.

"You know more than you let on," she said.

"What man doesn't? If I told you the tenth of what I know it would turn your hair bright green."

"Is this desert of yours so bad as all that?" she asked with mock seriousness.

"Not the desert, but some things on the farther side of it. I saw them take a man once—" He stopped short.

"Yes?"

"Nothing. We should have started half an hour ago. Come on."

Though she teased him all day as they marched easily along, she could not get out of him what they did to that man.

"Then I shall have to see for myself," she said gayly. "Just like Bluebeard's inquisitive wife."

"If you do, you'll be sorry," he replied. And he was right.

THE terrain now became rolling and more barren. Topping a long high swell, Joicey halted and pointed some miles away to a vast expanse of bluish silver glistening in the hot afternoon sun. This was their first glimpse of the desert which they must cross. Distant though it was, it filled them with an uneasy sense of present evil. The slanting rays of the declining sun seemed to awaken something infinitely old and wholly bad in that broad band of gleaming, bluish white, shimmering with a faint phosphorous in the sunlight.

This, then, lay between them and their goal. There was yet time to turn back. Joicey, divining their unspoken fear, pointed back over the plateau by which they had come. They shook their heads. Without a word, he led the descent down the other side of the dune, and until nightfall, they saw no more of the terror toward which they were marching.

A curious change came over Joicey's features as they neared the desert. The profile seemed actually to become more aquiline, like that of an old Roman, the lines of expression deepened, and the last trace of well-bred banality vanished. When at nightfall they halted and dismounted to rest for a few hours before taking the decisive step, he was a different being from the easy-going companion of their march across the Tibetan highland. He had lapsed into the man whom they had first seen lying unconscious on a hospital cot at Darjeeling.

"Shall we join your uncle and take a look at what lies before us?" Joicey asked Rosita.

She assented, and the three strolled up the gentle rise to gaze out over the desert. It was now dark. The stars had come out with a rush some five minutes previously, but as yet, the moon had not risen. Of the three, only Joicey was fully prepared for the sight which met their gaze as they topped a swell of sand which had hid the desert proper. As far as the eye could see, the floor of the desert below them glowed with a soft bluish light.

While they gazed a sudden gust of wind plowed a long furrow, perhaps half an inch deep, in the level sands about thirty-five feet from where they stood. Instantly the blue fire above the furrow deepened. It was nature's warning to them to turn back. Then as they watched, fascinated, the deeper blue paled, and nothing remained to mark the way the wind had taken. Only the blue phosphorescence lay still and unbroken from their feet to the horizon.

"Does it remind you of anything?" Ford asked his niece.

"Yes. It is like the blue light the sapphire sphere gave off, only much dimmer."

"It may be more than mere resemblance," Joicey remarked. "Well, we shall probably know before we're a month older. Now, do you want to take a nap before I tell you a few things that you must know before we get to the other side? You may have three hours; I can cut my explanations short if necessary."

"I couldn't sleep," Rosita said.

"What about you, Ford? No? Well, neither could I. In fact, I've been counting on our wakefulness. It's an effect of the desert air, I suppose. At any rate, I noticed it the first time I crossed. Suppose I tell you what you must know in the ancient Tibetan?"

"Fine!" they exclaimed. "And," Rosita added, "speak fast. We both are pretty sure now of the ancient language, but a final drill in following rapid speech will clinch our knowledge."

"All right," he agreed, speaking in the ancient tongue. "You have both done remarkably well at it, but then you had a lot to build on. Shall we sit here?"

And so, looking down on the evil phosphorescence that they were to enter within four or five hours, they sat listening to Joicey's account of how he acquired the sapphire sphere.

"I NEED not tell you," Joicey began in the ancient language, "how I first reached the desert, nor need I say more about my first crossing than that it was direct and without accident. I simply walked across it. The return was a different matter, owing to trouble with my compass. Before telling you how I got my sapphire sphere, I must briefly describe the lay of the land so that you can follow the essential steps of my adventure. On the other side of the desert is a considerable range of rock mountains cleft by a high, but easy pass. You shall see this for yourselves. Crossing over the pass, you come to the first outcroppings of the intense blue rock which is a distinctive feature of the country beyond.

"Tradition, I learned later, asserts that the same disaster which overwhelmed the Great Race and created this desert, changed also the red rocks of the surrounding country to a vivid blue. According to the legends, the colors once were much brighter, and the rocks themselves transparent—at least near the edges or in the thinner sections. From the top of the pass, you look down over the vast region inhabited by the small remnant of the ancient people. They are gradually becoming extinct, it appears, and only a very small part of their vast tableland is inhabited. The other wall of mountains bounding the tableland on the north—the one which in ancient times shut out the Chinese barbarians of the Stone Age—is not visible from the pass.

"So near as I could judge from what I picked up, the tableland must be at least six weeks broad, that is, the ordinary caravan would take that long to traverse it. It is plentifully provided with game, fish and wild fruits, so that an experienced traveler would have no difficulty in exploring it, even on foot. The length east and west is uncertain. On all sides the tableland is said to be shut in by high mountains beyond which stretch almost waterless deserts, thick in some regions with the fragmentary remains of forgotten peoples.

"Now I must mention one vital detail about the inhabitants themselves. For ages past this degraded remnant of the Great Race has maintained constant but very distant relations with the Tibetan nomads beyond the deserts to the west—not this desert, but those at the western edge of their tableland. This they seem to have done, establishing communications centuries ago, in order to glean if possible some tradition concerning the fate of the southern faction of their race which, if you remember, departed to the south in prehistoric times, two generations before the disaster. For obvious reasons they have learned nothing except one most curious fact which puzzles them greatly. And I may say that it puzzles me, too.

"The Tibetan language, they have discovered, has close affinities with their own, and evidently is descended through long ages from the same parent stock. Their blue-headed priests study the modern Tibetan diligently in the hope of finding in its obscure folklore, some clue to the fate of their southern faction. For that the Great Race still flourishes somewhere in the world they have not the slightest doubt. This faith in the continued earthly existence of a golden age which must have perished when the greater part of Europe lay under thousands of feet of ice, is to me inexpressibly pathetic, still it persists, like our own faith in a future happiness. I sometimes think that quick and merciful death for the whole remnant would be the most humane disillusionment.

"Now, one more important detail, and I shall proceed to my application of all these preliminaries. If Tibet to us is difficult of access, the ancient land of the Great Race is infinitely more so to the Tibetans. They are forbidden absolutely to set foot on the deserts surrounding the mountain barriers. If any are foolhardy enough to transgress, they either perish in the desert or are captured wherever they appear on the mountains and put to death in the City.

"Yet, in spite of all precautions, their forbidden land has been violated at least three times within this century by disguised Tibetan Lamas. The last violation occurred during my very brief visit. The priests had found the wretched man and stripped him of his disguise but two days' journey from the caves."

"Is he the man you were speaking of this morning?" Rosita asked.

"Yes. And as I said then, I shall never forget the way in which they put him to death. They had taken me to the 'place of execution' to witness what my own fate should be if they detected me in fraud. These priests, I may mention, are coldblooded, scheming, cruel, ignorant, credulous and superstitious, and constitute well over half the entire population. These are the blue haired beauties; so you and I, Ford, are now members of their engaging fraternity. 'Priests,' is perhaps an incorrect term for them;

'keepers of the traditions' would be more accurate, but it is too long.

"They have no religion whatever. In fact, one of their chief grounds for hating and despising the poor Tibetans is the faith of this people in something beyond the remnant's hard materialism—which is all that survives of the scientific traditions of the Great Race. Another, as I learned later is the 'family skeleton' of the remnant. The Tibetans, they say, are a degraded offshoot of their own people, and their religion, folklore and superstitions are all that remain of their former intelligence.

"ALL religious beliefs they scorn with the utmost contempt. I doubt, in fact, whether any of the priests has ever given five minutes' thought to anything unconnected with the past glories of their race, and the material ease which they suppose would follow from a knowledge of how to use the last flame of the ancient fire.

"All their existence is focused in this one thing: the consuming passion to rediscover the lost knowledge of their people. For this they scheme day and night. To this end they have sent envoy after envoy, spy after spy across the mountains and deserts in vain efforts to capture someone who might possibly be a descendant of the lost southern faction, and whose inherited instincts or manner of life might give them the clue to the fire, even if the captive himself were ignorant of the precise significance of his acts. They still cling obstinately to the tradition that only a woman can successfully manipulate the fire. This, of course, is a survival from the legend of the wise women.

"The first of these spies to penetrate the regions to the south of their own country undoubtedly was the man whom my ancestor met in Sikkim. Since then there have been sent out at least five hundred in fruitless attempts to repeat his success. All but one of these failed to return. They either have perished from natural causes or, as I think more likely, the majority have committed suicide on seeing from their first glance at modern civilization the utter hopelessness of their quest."

"I can guess who the one returned spy was," Ford interjected.

"So can I," said Rosita. "It was General Wedderburn's intelligent friend, Singh."

115

"Undoubtedly," Joicey agreed, "although when I first heard of him I doubted his existence. For the priests in the City with truly brilliant deceit had never mentioned him. Their skill in telling only half a fact is unique, and is the great forte of their lying. For there is no more efficient way of lying than telling a small fraction of the facts and letting the listener guess the rest. My first glimpse of the possible truth came seven years too late, as you know, when I heard all the details of little Evelyn Wedderburn's abduction.

"Now, I can show you in short order the high lights of my own escapade. I remarked that my first passage of this desert was without accident. It was not, however, uneventful. About thirty miles from the other edge, I stumbled upon the first evidence that I was not the only explorer who had attempted to cross. The winds had laid bare the bleached pelvic bone of a man. It was deeply pitted and worn, and evidently was of great age. A mile or so farther on I found two white yak vertebrae. These also were of extreme age. From there to the very edge of the desert, I came upon, at ever diminishing intervals, remains of men or animals. Note that I found nothing on this side of the desert.

"The caravans or solitary explorers had all started from the other side, and their bones remained to mark the extreme limits of their advances. Some had perished a few yards from their starting place at the farther rim. These, to judge by the very advanced stage of decay of their bones, must have been the earliest would-be explorers of more recent times. That the desert hid much more than was visible to a casual glance was evident from the sharp, wind-cut gullies.

"On the steep sides of these, to a depth of twenty feet, were the hard pockets left by the impress of human or animal bones. The bones themselves had long since rotted to dust under the action of whatever it may be that causes this whole desert to phosphoresce like decaying flesh.

"I had already begun the ascent of the pass on the other side when, chancing to look back at the desert, I noticed a mile from the edge several black lumps sweltering in the intense violet haze. Of course, I turned back to investigate. The lumps were the putrefying carcasses of eight yaks. Their saddles, of a curious design unlike any I had ever seen, also their packs, were still securely roped by leather lariats to the bloated bodies. The packs, however, of all but two of the animals, were empty. It was not difficult to guess the truth. The caravan had been overtaken by sudden disaster of some kind which I was unable to imagine (but of which I later learned more than I cared to know) shortly after venturing onto the desert.

"Although the animal had perished, the men somehow had escaped and had returned after the danger was over to rescue enough of their supplies to support themselves, either until they could make their way back to their starting point, or until a messenger could bring help. Although I searched carefully, I could find no human remains, and in fact, as I was presently to learn, there were none near the dead yaks.

"I at once began searching for traces of the survivors. My first discovery was that of a new grave in the gravel beyond the rim of the desert. Evidently, then, the caravan had not been Tibetan, or the survivors would have thrown their dead to the vultures. Opening the grave, I found the body of a man clothed approximately as I am now. Unwinding his headdress, I found as I expected that his hair was stained blue. Having removed his outer garment and his footwear, I closed the grave.

"There were in all eleven mounds; some members, if not all, of the expedition, had traversed on foot. I next sought the stores which these men must have rescued from the desert. Although they were not over fifty yards from the graves, it was more than three hours before I found the cache in the shelter of a large gray boulder. There is, I should say, an old moraine covered with such boulders about a mile from the ascent to the pass. This place evidently is well beyond reach of the decaying agencies of the desert, for the boulders are all firm rock, not rotted, as they otherwise would be.

"TURNING over the stones I found what I wanted and proceeded to stain my hair blue. The dye used by the priests is evidently a colloidal suspension of some pulverized mineral, for it is sticky like glue and after a time the coloring matter wears off gradually as a very fine powder. This, by the way, accounts for General Wedderburn's failure to observe that Singh's hair was blue.

It probably wasn't, as I knew very well. But isn't it remarkable what a little suggestion will do? The general half believed that he had never seen Singh without his turban, whereas he must have done so every day. The General however, was a prince of doubters compared to some others whom I have taken pleasure in bamboozling.

"Well, having dyed my hair, I next changed my clothes, putting on the headdress, outer garment, and footgear of the man whose grave I had opened. Except that I knew not one word of the dead man's language, I was ready to trust my wits.

"Luck favors the man who courts it. I made a thorough search of the vicinity in the hope of finding the survivor who had buried the last of his eleven fellow priests. Toward nightfall, I discovered him in a pitiable state of hunger and thirst, not a hundred yards from an abundance of water in skins and fresh food in hermetically sealed earthenware jars. He evidently was delirious, or he could not have failed to find the supplies.

"The first thing was to get him back to sanity. In the week of constant nursing that followed I worked my luck to its limit. Every sound that he made I carefully mimicked and remembered. By following his gestures, I followed every idea his clouded mind strove to express. In this way, I learned the names of the several foods, of the articles which he desired, and of the parts of the body and their functions, also some words expressive of various sicknesses. The words 'I,' 'me,' 'you,' or 'thou,' and certain of the commonest verbs such as 'bring,' 'give,' and so on, I guessed from his requests and manner of address. By the end of the week I had mastered over a hundred words of the ancient language—which not till later did I suspect was ancient Tibetan—and could frame simple sentences such as 'I bring water,' 'You want rice,' 'It is cold,' 'You sweat, it is hot,' 'It grows dark,' and the like.

"On the morning of the eighth day he sank into an easier sleep and I waited anxiously for him to awake. All that day I never stirred from his side. I was richly rewarded for my patience. Toward evening he began tossing uneasily, and presently he was in the throes of a raging delirium, his last for a many long day. He raved without ceasing far into the night. Of all that torrent I understood nothing except one word. Could I have been mistaken? No, the man certainly had uttered the common Tibetan word for 'yak.' It might of course have been a mere coincidence. The word itself was beyond doubt, but what did it mean? Was it a chance identity of sound in the two languages, signifying something quite other than a yak in the sick priest's tongue? I could only wait until the man recovered his mind, for that he must die that night or recover his senses before daybreak I felt certain.

"Dawn at last broke. Was it to be life or death? The man was frail and long past the prime of his manhood. I bathed his face in cold water, and waited. He opened his eyes. They were as yet without understanding.

" 'Do you want water to drink?' I asked him in his own language—the ancient Tibetan. His eyes turned in my direction and he saw me.

" 'Bring me water,' " he whispered.

"I held the skin to his lips and he drank a few drops. The cool drink seemed to give him new life. He sighed and whispered a sentence, every word of which was new to me. Then I played my desperate trump.

"The eight yaks died in the desert," I said in modern Tibetan.

"His eyes closed wearily, and I waited in an agony of suspense. Had he understood? Then to my inexpressible joy I caught the faint reply in Tibetan—not the Joicey—ancient language, but the modern in which I had spoken to him:

" 'Yaks cannot run like men.'

"All that day he mended rapidly. He seemed content to accept me as a fact for the time being; doubts as to my priestly character he could sift when stronger. During the week that followed, I more than doubled my knowledge of the ancient tongue. To avoid rousing his suspicions as long as possible I used both the modern and the ancient Tibetan in the routine of daily life without favoring either. But in extracting information regarding the objectives of his caravan and the customs of his people, I was forced to use the modem Tibetan exclusively, lacking words to express my ideas in the ancient language.

"To my chagrin he frequently replied at length in his own tongue. Of course, I never put a direct question. So long as it lasted, the method gave excellent results, and I learned much that later was of the highest importance. But any moment might bring the turn in my luck. One slip, and I should have to change my tactics immediately. I did not trust to chance. So when at last on the evening of the ninth day of his convalescence the priest got up to take a few steps for exercise, and I made the inevitable blunder, I was not unprepared.

" 'How glad your wife will be to see you again, alive and well,' I remarked. At the time, I did not know that the priests are forbidden to marry. It was a foolish slip; I should have guessed the true state of affairs. I saw my mistake instantly, but it was too late. He gave me a keen look.

" 'You are not of our race,' " he said.

"I plunged. 'You are right,' I said. 'I am not of your race.' "

" 'Then I must give you up to the killers,' he returned. 'I am sorry,' he continued; 'for without your care these many days this old body of mine should have perished like the others. Did you know that the penalty for entering our country is death?' "

" 'Not for me,' I replied. He had no means, so far as I could see, of enforcing his threat. Yet he spoke as it he could back up his words with actions if he chose, and in any case I was not yet sure enough of my ground to end our friendship by a trial of weapons.

" 'Why not for you? No man who is not of our race shall enter this land and live.'

" 'No man? Have you forgotten the race from which your people are descended? I am of the Great Race.' "

"He looked at me long and doubtfully. At first he seemed merely incredulous. Then gradually, as he searched my face for some mark of resemblance to the traditional likeness of his vanished ancestors, his own face grew dark and troubled.

" 'Give me a sign,' he whispered.

"Now, I had carefully secreted about my person the few paraphernalia of civilization which I considered necessities for finding my way back. These included a surveyor's compass, maps in an oilskin ease, a revolver, and two electric torches fully charged."

"Your monocle also, of course," Rosita murmured in English. There is no equivalent for "monocle" in ancient Tibetan or in modern, for that matter.

"Of course," he replied. "Couldn't have seen without it after I got back over the frontier. Well, all of these things were strapped on next to my skin; these comfortable woolen shirts are your uncle's idea. I now reached in and got one of the electric torches.

" 'Can you make light without fire?' I asked the poor old priest. He shook his head. I handed him the torch and showed him where to press the button. 'Press it, and make light,' I suggested. He did so, casting a brilliant spotlight on a boulder near where we stood. Evidently he was impressed. But he tried to minimize the feat. And indeed it was cheap enough trick, though the best in my bag.

" 'This is a little thing for one who is of the Great Race.' He again pressed the button, illuminating this time a stone about the size of my head. 'If you are of the Great Race,' he commanded, 'change that lump of rock into copper.' "

"Phew!" said Ford. "He had you there."

"Not by a mile," Joicey rejoined. He tenderly fished out his last cigarette, lit it, and inhaled a few luxurious puffs before continuing.

CHAPTER SEVEN
The Spirit of the Desert

HE RESUMED his narrative in the ancient Tibetan. "The too cautious priest had given me the chance for which I was playing. I wished to air my knowledge of the traditions, and here he was begging me to do it.

" 'Has your remnant of the Great Race sunk so low that it has forgotten the wise women and their dangerous office? Do not you know that only the wise women are trained to the hard task of taming the fire to be the slave and not the master of mankind? And where are the tools?'

"He admitted the force of my argument, but he was still sorely puzzled as to who I might be. That I really was what I claimed he seemed half inclined to believe. Then suddenly he put a question that all but floored me.

" 'Why,' he asked quietly, 'do you speak always the language of the degraded Tibetans, whom we hate and despise, when you talk of the greatness of our race? Our own tongue you use, like a menial, only for low things.'

121

"In a flash I guessed the truth that had been shaping itself at the back of my mind the past two weeks. This man's language was in some way related to modern Tibetan. The structures of the two languages were in many respects similar, say like ancient and modern Greek, or like Latin and Italian. Here was a clue, and trusting to luck, I now followed it boldly.

" 'Let me tell you,' I began slowly, to gain time, 'wherein your remnant of the Great Race has erred blindly for many ages. You hate the Tibetans, whereas they should hate you. For they are your own children.'

" 'That is true,' he said. 'But why should those degraded creatures presume to hate us?'

" 'Because your cruel race turned them out of your fruitful land to sink down to degradation on the cold, inhospitable uplands, where men toil all their days to earn their scanty food and covering.'

" 'That version of their history is the false one!' he exclaimed. 'They lie who say we turned away our own children. It was ages ago, but we who jealously hoard the last flame of all-creating fire know the truth. They left of their own willfulness. For in that long-forgotten time many, more than half our remnant, grew weary of watching with the faithful They said no man should ever cross the desert to bring back a child of the Great Race; they cried that none should ever traverse the flames to learn from those who ages before had gone south the secret of the fire.

" 'The true way to overtake our ancestors, they said, was to travel west, not south across the fiery desert. For the second time our race divided. This time less than half of the remnant stayed at its source, the rest flowed out toward the setting sun. Cold and hunger, wind and the sandy deserts dispersed them. They forgot even the little that we know of our great past, and became nomads. These are the degraded and faithless dregs of our race whom we despise, the squalid Tibetans.'

" 'Yet you speak their language,' I said coldly, 'when it pleases you.'

" 'That is only that we may learn from their base beliefs whether any of all the multitude which went west ever came upon the highway of the Great Race. We hope in their superstitions to find some clue to the present dwelling place of our common ancestors.'

" 'You have erred,' I repeated. 'It is true that the low Tibetans are children of your remnant and grandchildren with you of the Great Race. But they are children with you of the Great Race. But they are not all. They are the debased offspring of the stragglers and weaklings who dropped early out of the arduous, age-long march of the courageous host that traveled on unwearied, ever toward the setting sun and the new land of the Great Race. Their generations marched for centuries. And at the end of their march they came once more upon the fair dwelling place of those who are the masters, and not the slaves, of brute nature. They found again the southern faction of the Great Race, wiser, more powerful and infinitely happier than ever it was before the unleashed fire of the wise women created this desert.' "

"You told men a whopper while you were about it," Rosita remarked. "My, won't your wife have interesting experiences?"

"She won't if she is a wise woman," Joicey replied. "At least, not interesting in the way you mean. And I rather imagine she will belong to that great order of seekers after truth. Well, diplomacy worked, as it always does when administered in drastic doses. The poor old priest swallowed my yarn at one gulp. In such cases you should never stop at half-truths; remove them completely. Half a truth in international affairs—my little flurry was really such—is as troublesome as the snag of a decayed tooth. Pull it out."

"I foresee you will be prime minister before you retire," Ford chuckled. "Being British born puts the Presidency of the United States beyond your reach. Otherwise you should have our votes. Go on."

"FOR a moment I felt heartily ashamed of my success," Joicey resumed. "The poor old fellow broke into tears and asked me why we, the Great Race, knowing the plight of the remnant all these centuries, had made no move to help them. I felt as mean as Lazarus must have felt when poor old Dives asked him for a drop of water to cool his tongue, and Lazarus refused because he was quite comfortable where he was, in Abraham's bosom; while Dives through his own stupidity had fallen into a very hot place. There was nothing for it but to seek refuge in a fog of morals, which I did.

"The remnant had erred grievously, I said, in two respects. First, they had let over half their number depart without proper precautions on a dangerous enterprise. They should have seen to it that only a few of the strongest attempted the western route, sending out from time to time small but well-equipped expeditions. As it was, their callous indifference was the real father of the degraded Tibetans. For this reason we had decided to let them stew penitently in their own juice until they should succeed in getting a messenger of their own across the fiery desert to us.

"Even then, I said, we should take our time about forgiving them. For the Great Race had grown very humane in its new life, and mercifully permitted transgressors to purify themselves of error by suffering for their stupidities. Secondly, I told him, we believed that if any man had a great deal of anything he should be given more of the same thing; whereas if he had only a little it was but right to take away what he had. Now the remnant, I pointed out, had shown great obstinacy and not a little stupidity in seeking all these ages to force a passage across the fiery desert. They should have learned early that to beings of their degraded stage of intelligence it was impassable.

"Here I ventured a random shot. Only one man, I said, of all the thousands they had sent out had succeeded in traversing the desert and coming upon the remote outposts of our civilization. I meant, of course the man described in my ancestor's narrative, not knowing of Singh. He nodded, and I secretly congratulated myself on this lucky bull's-eye, little suspecting that I had missed the target by a mile. But of this presently.

"Well, I concluded my moral lecture by applying its precepts to his people. Since they had no common sense, as shown by their idiotic attempts to do the impossible, they should get none from us until some idle traveler, like myself, should pay them a visit from curiosity to see just how thickheaded they really were. Then if his remnant chanced to get anything from the traveler, our race was so wise, rich and comfortable that it would not miss the few crumbs of knowledge that they might pilfer. The men of the Great Race, I added casually, of course had full knowledge of how to cross the fiery desert without inconvenience to themselves. In fact, I had just strolled over it myself to see what kind of numbskulls lived on the other side.

"These fabrications convinced the old priest. For as I have said, the priests are cruel, crafty and cold-blooded. Only callous and heartless judgments, like the perfect beauty I had just pronounced on his wretched people, appeal to their cold understanding. He was now reduced to a state of the most abject humility. I felt like kicking myself, but took comfort in the reflection that the end justifies the means."

"You are painting yourself up blacker than the devil," Rosita laughed, "just to shock me. I shall believe in your portrait of yourself when I actually see you in politics. Now what was this precious 'end' of yours? If it was anything more than the perfectly justifiable one of saving your own life, I'm willing to admit that your political career has begun with a flying start."

"Ha," said Joicey, lapsing into English, "deuced unpleasant having to shock a charming young woman, but I can't help it. I can think of nothing to tell you, don't you know, but the bally truth. My end..." He resumed his story in the ancient Tibetan, "...was to gain possession of the sapphire which I guessed that old priest must have hidden somewhere in the vicinity. For, you remember, the priest of my ancestor's narrative carried with him a magnificent sapphire, saying it was his 'passport to the intelligence of the Great Race.' My venerable friend had not concealed his 'passport' about his person, for I had carefully searched all his clothing, as well as the stores, during his sickness. I now boldly asked the old fellow to show me his 'passport.'

"Trembling with anxiety to gain my favor he conducted me to a flat round stone, about a foot in diameter, lying near the edge of the desert. It was inconspicuous, being one of hundreds roughly like it. Without his kind assistance, I never should have found it. I lifted it for him, and he proceeded to scratch away the loose gravel underneath. Presently a cubicle box of lead, about eight inches each way, came to light. It was covered with inscriptions in several different kinds of characters, the writing being of the sorts with which you are familiar from your own passport. I asked him to read the characters, saying that I wished to see how faithfully his remnant of the race had preserved our secrets.

"HE BROKE down, crying that he could read only the one line in his own language, the ancient Tibetan. All the knowledge of the meaning of the rest had perished ages ago, and was blindly copied from one set of lead boxes to another, clear back to a forgotten original, by the priests who manufactured the boxes. There was a carefully preserved copy of the entire set of inscriptions, possibly the original itself, on the lead casing of the rocks at the entrance to the caves.

"This he assured me with humble pride, his sect was particularly jealous in guarding. Of course, I forgave him his ignorance, and told him the reading of the single line which he knew would be sufficient. It was the injunction to keep the jewel always in its lead box. By this means I learned a few characters of the written language. But they were not of much use as I did not stay long enough in his country to make any systematic study.

" 'Would you see the stone?' he asked.

"I signified that I would be so gracious, and he opened the box. That was my first sight of the sapphire sphere. I shall always take great credit to myself," he said with a smile, "that I did not there and then begin a dance of joy or let so much as a grunt of satisfaction escape my guard.

" 'It is well enough,' " I said carelessly.

" 'Is it of the true flame?' the old fellow asked anxiously.

" 'Without doubt, I assured him, although probably I knew less about it than he did.

"What use, Master, did the Great Race, our ancestors, make of such jewels as these?"

" 'Has your degraded remnant forgotten even that?' I asked in contemptuous astonishment.

He was humbly confused.

" 'Not wholly,' he stammered. 'Is it not true, as our traditions assert, that the Great Race made from copper a rarer metal that lived, and gave them light and heat without loss to itself?'

" 'Aye,' I assented wearily.

" 'And did not they make the copper, which is not abundant in this place, from gold?'

" 'Why ask me questions that a child might answer?'

" 'And is it not true,' he faltered, 'that they made the gold which they required from lead, which is very common in this land?'

" 'Have done,' I said. 'These things are the sport and idle pastime of our children. I see that your remnant has sunk as far below the ancient glory of the Great Race, even as we have risen above it. You forget,' I added severely, 'that the Great Race, even in the old time changed the rocks into copper.'

" 'Not so, Master!' he exclaimed, 'I know that well. But they learned that secret only in their later years. Did not I ask you a little while ago to change a lump of stone into copper?'

" 'Aye. I had forgotten.'

" 'And we remember through our traditions,' he continued proudly, 'that the living metal which the Great Race thus made from copper was the fountain of all their happiness. For, it is asserted, this living metal, and the heat and light which it gave without ceasing, moved mountains, changed the very air into food, and gave all men who could control its light an abundance of all good things without labor.'

" 'All that is in our records, and even the babes know it. But you have not yet shown me that your remnant remembers the use of jewels such as this one.'

"Have I not? They used the fire of these stones to change gold into copper, that they might then make the living metal which was the source of all their happiness. Am I not right? From lead they made gold, from gold by the fire of this stone they made copper and from the copper the living metal.'

" 'They were children in those days,' I said irritably. 'We are those children grown to manhood. All these things we do now in an easier way, making the copper directly from the common stones which are everywhere. Your degraded remnant has more to learn than we suspected. You are indeed fallen.'

" 'Master,' he whispered insinuatingly, 'teach me to use the fire of this jewel!'

" 'In good time,' I responded. 'Now I will take the lead box and the sphere it contains lest you, in your weak state, lose the stone and the fire it breeds.'

"He gave me a wondering look. 'But Master,' he said, 'we are not so slothful as you think us. We have not forgotten the walled-up chamber where the last flame of the all-creating fire still burns, nor have we lost our way to the rock root above it. This stone is not precious. In the place where it drank the fire others may still drink, for the fire never dies. Were this stone and all like it to be lost, the stone cutters of our people could yet make thousands in its image.'

" 'You have indeed been faithful enough in this little thing of all our wisdom that your degraded race still remembers,' I said graciously. 'But it is nothing. Be not swelled up over it.'

" 'No, Master, it is nothing,' he humbly agreed. 'Would you see this place where the rocks yet drink the flame?' he asked solicitously.

" 'When you are strong enough to walk I may go with you.'

" 'Then will you teach us to use the fire?'

" 'Who knows? If you are worthy and not sunk too low to understand its mysteries, I may take pity on you. For I am a reader of nature's mysteries," and one whose word the wise women follow.'

"I took charge of the box and its contents. The old fellow was quite exhausted from his short walk and all the excitement of meeting an instructor of wise women. In return for all his unconscious instruction of myself, I gave him a rattling good supper and tucked him comfortably up for the night. There was some difficulty in overcoming his scruples against letting a mighty man of the vigorously living Great Race wait upon a degraded wretch of the dying remnant, but I finally succeeded. To have let him get his own supper would have been killing the goose that laid the golden eggs. He still looked as if with proper care he might lay another in the morning, so I neglected nothing that could add to his comfort.

"IN THE morning he was a little weaker, although eager to talk. Like a good nurse, I confined his remarks to his personal wants. And so it went for several days. Sometimes he seemed to rally, and then I let him have his edifying talk out, but always the net progression was downhill. He lived longer than I expected—ten weeks and three days in all, counting the day I found him. In that time, by constant practice I completely mastered the ancient language and wormed out of him the route to the city by the caves, a great deal concerning the actual life of his people, and much of their legendary history."

"Did he tell you how the rest of the caravan had been destroyed?" Ford asked.

"He did," Joicey replied, and hastily changed the subject. "Now, in my zeal to deceive the priest I ended by deceiving myself," he continued. "It was the carefully formed habit, I suppose, of saying one thing and meaning another that led me to put a construction upon the most important thing the priest told me, which was quite other than the straight forward, literal meaning of his words. I was speaking the language of diplomacy; he was speaking the truth. Consequently, he had the advantage. If only I had known at the time of Singh, I should have not blundered as I did from an excess of imagination and too much caution. But until you, Ford, on the way to Lem Anderson's that morning gave me an outline of the General's story, I blissfully believed that the priest of my ancestor's narrative was the only one who had ever succeeded in crossing this desert.

"It was only when you told me in a few sentences of Singh, the man of unknown nationality, who had abducted the young daughter of a white man, that I began to see light. My only chance of success I saw, as you were so careful to rub into me, lay in joining you and your niece. In a flash I realized that I had been an ass of the first magnitude. If only I had taken literally what the priest had told me, I need not have got into hot water. I should have started back across the desert the moment I had buried him, instead of blundering on like a bear into a trap. The whole plan of attack would have been different from the beginning."

"Then we should never have met," Rosita said softly.

"For that very reason," he replied, "I rejoice that I made an ass of myself. For it might have been ten years before I found a girl with the right qualifications for the job ahead of us. In fact, I should have had to train her by painful years of drudgery, whereas you were the manufactured article almost ready for use."

"I wish you would wear your monocle sometimes," Rosita sighed. "It is so becoming, and you see some things much better with it than without."

But Joicey ignored the hint. He did not feel like spooning on the edge of the desert. She was at a disadvantage here, for he knew how the priest's caravan and its twelve men had perished, while she did not. He continued his story.

"So when the priest spoke of the dead hero of the desert, I thought he was referring to the man whom my uncle had encountered one hundred and fifty years ago in Sikkim. And when he went on to say that his own caravan had started south 'at the bidding of the voice of the wise woman who dwells with the flame,' I thought he was speaking in metaphors of some oracle or another of their superstitions. I became quite convinced of this when in answer to my question he told me that this 'wise woman' was a child of the Great Race whom the dead hero of the desert had brought back with him to instruct their people and that her speech was 'music'. The last word was the only one in the entire description that was not literally true, and this helped to deceive me. This 'music' I thought doubtless some form of incantation used by the priests manipulating the oracle, according to the usual frauds practiced in such things by primitive and even cultured peoples. The dead 'hero of the desert' might have brought back some fakir with him; it was not impossible although she would have had a rough trip of it.

"But it certainly was impossible that she could still be living after one hundred and fifty years, no matter how wise she was when captured in a state of nature. Hence she was at present a myth perpetuated by the priests, and the 'music' of her voice which had sent twelve men and eight yaks to a horrible death nothing more than the 'oracle' run by one priestly faction working upon the superstitions of another in order to get it out of the way. Such was my entirely rational theory of what the dying priest in all guileless simplicity told me.

"I laid so little importance on this part of his revelations that my question as to why the 'music' had ordered an expedition across the fiery desert was more for the sake of politeness than anything else. His answer was of a piece with the rest of his story: 'To bring back another wise woman of the Great Race, in order that she and I together may use the fire to the benefit of all your people. For one of us alone cannot safely guide the flame. Do you therefore bring me a sister, that together we may bless you. Should I alone guide the flame, it may escape my hands, and again overwhelm your people as once it did in the forgotten time.' Such was the oracle's reason for dispatching the unfortunate expedition."

"Now what in thunder do you make of this?" Ford asked.

"Nothing definite yet," Joicey replied, "except that it sounds like an exceedingly clever call for help. If so, Wedderburn's daughter is no fool. Well, we shall see next week."

"She must be beautiful too," Rosita added pensively.

"If she has fulfilled the promise of that miniature the General showed me, she's more than beautiful by now. She must be exquisitely lovely."

ROSITA changed the subject. "Did you learn anything else of importance?"

"Several things. But as it's nearly time to pack up and start, I can give you only one now. The wise women, according to the legends, were the very cream physically and mentally of the race. The traditions declared that they were very beautiful, and went into minute details regarding the shape of their head, and features, the color of their eyes—invariably of the brown tints, and the hair that ranged from, light yellow to red gold and was usually curled closely. They were permitted no conversation whatever with men, in order that their dangerous work might suffer from no distraction. The women who waited on them considered it a great honor, and there was much rivalry for the coveted offices.

"When the priest told me that no man may see her, meaning the present lonely 'wise woman,' I thought he was speaking in parables, and that clinched her nonexistence so far as I was concerned. For of course, 'no one may see' even if he is insane enough to wish it, a woman who has been dead over a century. You, Rosita, will be interested in the reason why women and not men were trained for the work of 'manipulating the flame'. The Great Race found them more adaptable, patient and painstaking; also the greater sensitiveness of their fingers made them safer than men in the extremely delicate operations of their profession.

"Armed with all the information he had given me, and happily ignorant of my own dangerous ignorance, I joyfully set out for the caves the moment I had buried the old man, taking with me my 'passport'. I need not bore you with a description of the route which you shall see for yourselves, I hope; nor need I dwell longer on my three months' life with the priests.

"On arriving I showed them the sphere, saying that their messengers had safely crossed the desert and were now enjoying themselves in taking in the modern wonders of the Great Race beyond. They had dispatched me at once to bear the good tidings, I said, and in proof of my identity had given me their 'Passport'. They were soon to return with many other 'readers of nature's mysteries' and wise women who would at once set about restoring the remnant to its former luxury; I myself was merely a messenger on a preliminary survey.

"At first I was received everywhere with feasting and flattery, then with suspicion because I kept deferring my exhibition of miracles with the sphere; then the cold shoulder was politely offered in certain high quarters and finally they put me to a crucial test.

"My efforts to get into the caves were thwarted at every turn. I never even learned the way to the entrance. The priests were too many, too watchful, and too shrewd for me. The test which undid me was quite simple. I see this now, although at the time I thought it was a ruse of priestcraft for getting rid of a troublesome guest. As a last device for breaking into the caves, I had asked the priests if I might be taken near enough to hear what the 'music' of the wise woman might have to say to me. They at once assented, but on one condition. If I could speak a single sentence in her tongue I should be permitted not only to hear her, but short of entering her sanctuary which was forbidden to all men, I might go anywhere I liked in the entire country.

"They would recognize the language, they asserted even if the meaning were not plain. This seemed such a contemptible piece of trickery on their parts that I almost forgot myself and was on the point of swearing at them in English. If only I had not been so everlastingly cautious, and had given free rein to my tongue as the spirit moved me to do, I might even now have been peddling sapphires the size of my head from one crowned nincompoop to another. But luck was against me and I held my English tongue.

"Replying in the ancient Tibetan I said that their request was an insult worthy only of savages; that we of the Great Race went where we willed and saw what we chose; that I was sick of their dumb stupidity and that now I was going home. Furthermore, I should tell the Great Race to let this degraded remnant continue to fester in ignorance.

"The game was up. That was clear. But could I get away? Luck favored me once more. Some of the older priests began to grovel. Would I not stay? No, I would not. Then wouldn't I soften my decision and send others of the Great Race to succor them? Possibly I might, if there were any as foolish as I, who might out of the pity of their hearts come and dwell a few days with these barbarians and teach them how to live. Even I myself might come again, bringing others. I should take with me the 'passport' of their messengers now with us, lest some ignorant priest in the mountains should ask for it on my return in proof of my identity. Moreover, although I might safely pass the desert empty-handed, the fire of the stone aided me in quelling the fires of the desert.

"They were satisfied but sorry. Now, on first arrival in order to impress the priests, I had boasted like a fool that a man of the Great Race can cross the desert in one march without water or provisions of any kind, sustaining himself solely by drawing strength from the fires that slay the uninitiated. I had badly needed some miracle to overawe them at the beginning and that insane lie was my idiotic attempt. I now paid for it.

"Twenty of the older priests insisted upon seeing me off. Perfectly powerless, I was forced to take the desperate chance which I did. We camped at nightfall at the foot of the pass on the other side from where it comes down to the desert. I waited till three hours before dawn before making my escape. Stealing a skin bag full of water and taking my sapphire in its lead box, I then crawled away and started up the pass on foot. My companions had good horses. Consequently, I went up at the double. Shortly after sunrise, I heard the horses' hoofs pounding up the pass behind me. I was now within half a mile of the top.

"The heat in that rocky place was like the blast from a furnace. I threw away the lead box, which thus far I had kept; thinking the script on it might be deciphered to give facts of scientific value. I staggered on up with only the water skin and my sapphire sphere. The priests were almost upon me; less than a minute would bring them into sight. Knowing well what I did, I stopped and drank all the water I could pour down. Then I hid the skin behind a rock, and reeled on. For capture with that water bag in my possession meant death in the most horrible manner yet devised by the devilishness of human beings; whereas if I were taken with nothing but the sapphire I might yet save my life by diplomacy.

"The race down the other side of the pass to the desert was a never-ending nightmare. Far out on the desert I saw a perfect inferno of blue light whirling and eddying in the sun. A storm raging over it toward me, I beat my pursuers to the desert by a few yards, and the storm met me at the edge. They reined back in terror, and I entered the storm with nothing in my hands but that infernal sapphire. I shall leave you imagine the rest. Come, shall we go?"

THE moon rose huge and blood red on the far horizon as their feet entered the still, blue phosphorescence of the desert, and overhead the myriads of stars in the vast sapphire of the night grew dim and infinitely distant. Compass in hand, Joicey strode some twenty feet ahead of the others, setting a little better than a four-mile-an-hour pace. Every now and then, he made a slight detour to avoid some patch of deeper blue light at his feet. These shadows in the blue fire marked the furrows and gullies cleft by the fierce opposing winds that sometimes warred over the desert for days, to die suddenly exhausted by their strife in some flaming dawn. Ford followed next, leading Joicey's pony and his own, and Rosita brought up the rear by leading her own pony. Clear, and sharply outlined in the still glow, their footprints shone with a deeper blue, and looking back in the moonlight they saw their trail, a thin sapphire line vanishing to the south in the paler fires.

Within forty minutes, the rim from which they had started no longer was visible. The last vestige of a living world had vanished from their sight, and all about them shimmered the unbroken expanse of a cold decay smoldering out in still blue fire. For as they marched, they noticed a refreshing coolness about their feet and ankles, as if they were walking in the dews of early morning through fresh, green grass. It was not an illusion, for on putting down a hand into the glowing mist at her feet, Rosita touched the sudden chill of something as cold as a corpse.

Never slackening their stiff pace, though the ponies began to hang back on their halters, they marched without a break from two hours before midnight to dawn. Through all these hours not a word passed. Just as the paler blue of the far horizon ahead of them seemed almost to burst into white flame shot with violet, Joicey raised his hand for a halt. Immediately Ford and Rosita with Joicey's help stripped the ponies, even to their light headstalls, washed their mouths out, and gave each a long drink of the precious water which they had so faithfully carried. Then they gave them their fill of crushed barley.

"That's all you fellows get to eat for the next twenty-four hours," Ford informed them, "so make the most of it. Now for the mere human beings."

The blinding sun leapt over the desert's rim, and instantly the blue fires crawled into writhing life. It seemed as if the whole floor of the desert for miles about them was a vast, intricate tangle of enormous sapphire blue serpents coiling and uncoiling sluggishly in the level rays of the sun. With incredible speed, the temperature of the air rose from the sharp chill of night to an almost intolerable pitch of withering heat. One of the ponies, with a tired, long-drawn sigh, sank down to rest among the blue serpents. He nodded, and his muzzle dropped lower and lower until his nostrils were immersed in the evil sapphire mist. Joicey stood watching the poor beast, and a look of pity came over his set stern face. It was his own pony, and his chum of many long days and nights.

"Poor beggar," he said, "he won't be there long."

The pony's head jerked up, and again sank from utter weariness. Then with an amazed snort he was on his feet, the whites of his eyes showing in his wild astonishment. Ford and Rosita, saying nothing, regarded him curiously.

"Better sleep on your feet, old man," Joicey remarked, going up to him. "Here, I'll put all three of you with your heads together so you can get a little shade." He put on the headstalls and tied the halters together. "Now if you chaps decide to make a bolt for it," he said, putting his arm through the ropes, "you'll have to take me too. Well, shall we try to doze for an hour or two before the day gets hot? Come over here in the shade of the ponies. Now you two sit down, shoulder to shoulder, and I'll squeeze in between you. Then we can support each others' backs and rest comfortably. I shouldn't lie down if I were you."

"I guess we have as much sense as a pack pony," Ford laughed, as they fitted themselves snugly together. "Ah, this mutual cooperation beats self-support every time. How much have we covered, Joicey?"

"A little over thirty miles, I should judge. We have done first rate. If we can keep up this, we shall beat the record. But it's almost a run; we did over five miles an hour in one stretch. Are you two able to go on after two hours' rest?"

"Why not take it easy, and march all night? In ten hours we could make forty miles without killing ourselves."

"The truth is," Joicey replied, "I want to push on as fast as possible while our luck is with us. That's why I crowded the pace, so long as neither of you complained. There is no wind yet, but you can't tell how long it will hold off."

"I see," said Ford. "Well, I'm game. I can go at a six-mile trot if I have to. But I was thinking of Rosita."

"Don't, then," Rosita murmured drowsily. "I want to snooze, and your loud thinking disturbs me. Don't worry, I can keep up the pace for a week if necessary. Go to sleep."

In spite of the terrific heat they dropped off. Their utter oblivion was a stupor rather than a sleep, but it filled them with new strength. Suddenly the men were wakened by a violent struggle. Rosita's head had dropped forward upon her knees, and the two men had slid closer together, their elbows pressing against the small of her back. She was now madly struggling to get to her feet. Springing up, they pulled her with them.

"Oh," she gasped. "I thought I was going mad."

The men looked silently down at the seething fires about their feet. In the fierce rays of the sun the blue mist had expanded until now it undulated in a blinding layer of slowly heaving violet light two feet deep.

"Let's go," said Joicey. "Help me with the packs."

In three minutes, they were wading through cold blue fire up to their knees, under a brazen sky that all but stunned them with its blinding glare and intolerable, massive heat.

"Well, we fooled it to the extent of two hours' rest, anyway," said Ford.

Joicey looked down at the seething fires. "Can you do four and a half miles an hour and keep it up?"

"Yes," they answered, lengthening their stride, "if the ponies can."

"If they can't, lug them till they drop. They'll give out before we do. Here, I can lead my own and guide too, as long as everything is all right." He took his pony's halter and marched ahead. Smiling aside her protests, Ford took charge of Rosita's pony and his own. She fixed her eyes on Joicey's back and kept, like a machine, just four feet behind him.

FOUR and a half hours of steady marching through that inferno of heat and light passed without a word. The human beings stood the killing pace without flinching. But the wretched ponies, lacking foreknowledge of their goal and undriven by mad ambition, hung back miserably and had to be half dragged.

"That's twenty miles less of it to do," Joicey called, signaling for a halt. "Don't sit down, it only makes it seem worse when you start again. Besides—" He glanced at the seething wilderness without finishing his sentence. "Just rinse your mouths out, then lean up against each other for a short spell. I'll give the ponies theirs."

Rosita objected to being "nursed." Ford helped Joicey with the ponies. "How long shall we have to keep this up?" he asked in a low voice. "Rosita, you know—"

"Don't worry about me," she said sharply. "I hear what you are saying. Now, as I told you, I can keep this up for a week if we must, provided I get two hours sleep out of the twenty-four. Don't you know me by now?"

"Yes, but we never tackled anything like this before," her uncle replied dubiously. "This is a different proposition from a regular caravan route across an ordinary sand desert."

"Provided the wind holds off," Joicey assured her, "you shall get four hours sleep beginning at midnight when this infernal stuff subsides again. But until then we simply shall have to keep up the pace. Now, I don't want to make a speech or anything of that sort. Nevertheless, I must say something. I am not doing this forcing willfully. This is one of the two or three occasions that come in every lifetime when human beings must show that they are made of better stuff than the beasts, by living on and fighting on sheer nerve for days after they should have died. If we are not to perish like beasts just because brute nature wills that we shall perish, we must draw on our reserves and spend them to the limit.

"When we stumble and fall from utter exhaustion we must somehow or another get to our feet again and keep on beyond the limit of endurance. Now those poor beggars," he pointed to the ponies, "don't know that they have a second wind. We do know. Through ignorance of what they have in them, they must leave their bones in this desert. We shall get out alive no matter what happens."

"We're with you, Captain," said Ford. "Go ahead with your compass."

Hour after hour, they slogged steadily ahead through the stunning heat and the slowly rising fires of the desert. The cold blue flames now washed well above their knees, and as the sun crawled down the steely vault to the horizon behind them, the poisonous fires seethed with a quicker, more evil vitality. The ponies began to stumble, Joicey's collapsed. The poor beast staggered on blindly a last few steps and sank to his knees, his head immersed in the fiery mist. He did not jerk it back. He was done.

They halted in silence and Joicey bent down to undo the pack. The sinister blue flames lapped about his face and broke over his head as he worked, but he paid no heed. Straightening up with the water bags, he slung them over his shoulders.

"Will you put him out of misery?"

Without reply, Ford reached into his robe and drew his revolver. They heard the shot before they had gone ten yards. Overtaking them, Ford tried to make Joicey share his burden, but Joicey refused. His face wore a look of triumph.

"Stand and rest for ten minutes," he said. "Rosita, be sensible and lean against your uncle. That's it. I learned something while I was getting those water bags, that has given me the strength of a dozen men. You noticed those infernal cold flames played about my face, and that I breathed them? Well, they were just like so much air to me. I feel no effects whatsoever; my brain is as clear as crystal. Bend down, Ford, and take one breath—careful, not too deep."

Ford jerked back his head almost before he had inhaled. "Am I drunk?" he muttered. His eyes gleamed with an unearthly light. "The stuff goes directly to the brain. It's a poisonous gas of some sort. One mouthful of it would drive me crazy."

"Or me," Rosita agreed. "That was what happened while I was asleep this morning. I said nothing at the time because I thought it was just my nerves beginning to go. I was five years old again. I saw my father and mother, and yet something all the time kept whispering, 'They died in the plague fifteen years ago.' It was hellish; I thought I was going mad. We must not rest in this. Keep on; I can last forty-eight hours if necessary. By then we should be surely out of it."

"If the wind doesn't rise," Joicey replied. "Our real danger will begin about an hour from now when the sun sets and the cool air rushes down the mountains ahead of us. I want you both to do one thing, make up your minds now to obey me without question in everything. Exert your wills now and compel your sane selves to keep some sort of a grip on your actions no matter what comes. At the worst, even if the wind does rise, we should not be more than thirty hours longer in getting out of this. With a clear brain I shall be able to find my way somehow. And if the worst does happen, both of you will be helpless for perhaps days as I was. Now make a supreme effort to get a hold on yourselves so that you shall subconsciously remember my will."

"My determination is fixed," said Rosita. "Even if, as that time this morning, I lose all sense of my surroundings I will yet go on like a machine. And I will hear and understand when you speak, even if I am powerless to answer."

"You can count on me, too," said Ford. "But what if you give in?"

"I shall not. If I were still susceptible to the poison, it would have taken effect while I breathed my fill of it just now. It must generate its own antitoxin in the system that resists its first attack. I am now immune, just as a man who has had a bad case of smallpox has nothing to dread from further exposure to the disease. Those twelve priests died before the poison worked itself out of their systems. Besides, they were old and feeble; both of you are strong and vigorous. And I, being stronger both physically and mentally than they, lived through the madness and became immune, although I probably breathed thousands of times as much poison as they. But I had absorbed so much of it, without water even to wash out my mouth and nostrils of the poisoned dust, that for six years I wandered through Central Asia in a daze trying to find my way back to India.

"In all that time I had nothing but my blind instinct of self-preservation to protect me from myself. Everything but the will to live and keep from being robbed of my sapphire vanished in whirling black clouds that rolled up everywhere and marched before me. I have no clear knowledge of how I ever did find my way back through Tibet into India. The six years is all a stumbling blur of endless marching and strange faces asking stranger questions. But I won through to the goal I had set myself when the priests drove me into the storm on this desert. And so shall you reach yours in spite of the worst, should it overtake us, for your wills are unalterably fixed to obey mine. It will not be I who shall save you, but your own will power, the spirit of the desert, which keeps alive human beings long after they should have perished."

"HOW long were you in the desert?" Ford asked. "The second time, I mean."

"I don't know. I seem to remember a succession of eight pitch-black and blinding blue hells in the storm. Then I felt nothing until in a sudden flash of sanity I knew that the wind had dropped and the storm was over. I was still in the desert. How, when and where I emerged from it is a blank. Now you are rested. See if we can't do ten miles before sunset. That should bring the mountains in sight."

They made their objective. As the sun rushed flaming down into the fiery sea behind them, they saw far ahead, and beyond the desert, the rosy-tinted snow peaks of their goal.

The sun was down. In five minutes, darkness would drop upon them. Already they noticed the fall in the temperature, as if a furnace door at their backs had suddenly been closed. Joicey moistened the back of his hand and held it toward the northeast. The motion of the air, imperceptible to the unsensitized skin, betrayed itself in the cooling moisture.

"The wind is coming," he announced. "Remember your resolutions. Rosita, carry two of the water bags; Ford, you carry four. I'll take the rest. Now, shoot the ponies."

They obeyed without a word.

"Now tear off all you can, without ripping the pockets of your woolen shirts. I've just had an idea. The cloth of the tunics would be better, but we can't risk arriving in rags that will be seen."

They handed him the material. He quickly folded it into bandages, and soaked these in water. They guessed his purpose, and helped him to tie the bandages firmly on so that their mouths and nostrils were covered by the wet flannel. As they did so, a refreshing breeze played about their faces. But it also rolled the heaving blue phosphorescence into long billows that raced over the fiery swell toward them from the far shore of the desert. The wind freshened from the distant mountains, and the billows all about them curled noiselessly over in league-long breakers of blue flame.

"One of you take hold of my right arm, the other the left," Joicey ordered. "Do not let go whatever happens. If you need water I'll see to it."

A long tongue of gleaming blue spray licked hungrily up his side and broke in a shower of violent sparks over the compass in his hands.

"Look at the needle," he said.

Fascinated, they gazed at the compass needle. Neither made any sound, for adequate thought failed them. The needle was spinning round and round, now in one direction, now in the opposite, resting only for fractions of a second at the random points where it changed direction.

"It's useless," said Joicey. "I shall steer by the mountains when the moon rises tonight, and the sun tomorrow."

That was their last sane memory in the desert. All the rest became a blind confusion of battles against black whirlwinds and blue flames, of clinging to something that kept moving and would not let them die in peace, and of the hideous nightmares of madness broken only at intervals of ages by cool dreams of sweet water.

CHAPTER EIGHT
"The Way Was Long"

"ROSITA! Can you hear me?" Surely, she thought, it was Joicey speaking to her in English. But now, it must be the ghostly beginning of another of those terrible dreams. She could see nothing. Either she was dead or she had gone mad.

"Remember your resolution in the desert," the tense voice continued. "Use everything that is in you. Don't try to understand anything yet; obey. The blindness will leave you soon when all the poison works itself out. We have rested here twenty-three days and nights. The priests are impatient. They are getting suspicious. I can keep them from you no longer. We must go on. Your uncle understands what he is to do. You are to ride. Hang onto your horse somehow. The priests insist on a sign from you before we start. You must do one thing now. Our lives depend on it. You must do this: Say a few words to me in English."

She struggled to lift her reason above the black cloud that stifled it like heavy smoke, but the poisoned madness of the desert still racing through her blood rocked her brain. Yet she must conquer her desire to die. And she could do it, she knew, although she had no conscious knowledge of the means. She vowed that she would obey Joicey's command, and before she knew that she had uttered a single word, she had spoken.

"Shut up, will you?" she heard a querulous voice complaining. "Can't you let me sleep in peace? Go away."

"You're a brick!" she heard Joicey exclaim under his breath. "We're safe now for a few days—"

She heard no more of what he said. A jubilant clamor of many tongues drowned his voice in a tumult of ancient Tibetan, of which she caught only the reiterated refrain.

"She is a wise woman! She speaks the tongue of her sister!"

Abruptly the shouting ceased. There was a bustle of preparation all about her—runnings to and fro, the stamping of horses and sharp orders given in the ancient language.

"Now is the time to endure beyond the limit." It was Joicey's voice again, whispering to her in English. "Get up and mount your horse." He helped her to rise. Somehow, she obeyed him although she could see nothing. "Now grasp the thongs in both hands and lean far back in the saddle. It has a high back and will support you. I'll see that your horse keeps the road."

Then, raising his voice, he addressed the priests in ancient Tibetan. "The wise woman has not yet ended her long meditation," he announced with grave respect. "She wishes still to ponder on the journey to the caves. There are many dark and difficult things which she must tell her sister in order that they together may master the secret of the flame and control it to your health and happiness. Therefore, she commands that none of you speak to her unbidden. This command you will obey on the long journey over the pass and by the blue precipices."

"We shall obey! She is a wise woman."

"My brother, the reader of mysteries," Joicey continued, "also wishes to ride in silence. He would observe closely the signs of the flame which devastated your land in the forgotten time. For, as I have told you, in the desert and in the story of your destruction he has discerned many hints of new secrets of the perpetual fire. These he would now ponder more deeply as we traverse the regions which the flame touched. Therefore, that he may not be disturbed by your idle words, he would ride behind you with the wise woman. Proceed slowly so that he and I may observe the rocks, and thereby learn much for your health and prosperity."

"He is a creator of wisdom and knowledge," the spokesman of the priests answered. "Such were the men of our sect before the flame destroyed us. His word is our law. But will not you, Master, honor us with your company while your brother and sister meditate? You have told us much, these last three and twenty days while they pondered in silence, and still we thirst for your wisdom. We are humble; ride with us, Master."

"No. Your lack of understanding disgusts me now as it did when I visited you before. In the years between my visits you have sunk yet lower, such is the swiftness of your decay. Ride on with your degraded fellows. Keep your brothers well ahead of us so that we may not be disturbed by their idle chatter."

Rosita heard the priests' cavalcade file off. Presently a hand was laid on hers, and Joicey spoke in a low voice.

"Stick it out for five or six days. You are rapidly getting better of the poison and should be able to see in less than a week. We shall reach the caves in about five days. Prepare for a supreme effort when we get there. Your uncle is nearly better. Is the dizziness going?"

"Yes," she answered faintly. "Don't talk to me. If I need anything, I'll tell you. See that I don't fall off my horse."

"I'll look after you. Lean far back in the saddle. That's it. Now we're off."

HE SPOKE to the horses and they followed the priests at an even walk. Rosita held her balance comfortably. Hour after hour passed in an uneasy dream. The air, at first dead and stifling, steadily freshened and became cooler. She passed into a dreamless sleep. When she awoke, a keen wind seemed to quicken her whole body into new, young life. It was like an ice pack to a fever patient.

"That wind is blowing off glaciers and snowfields," she thought.

"I don't like the way her blindness hangs on," her uncle said.

"If it hadn't been for the wet bandages," said Joicey, "she would have been dead long ago. They were as blue as indigo when I wrung them out and rewetted them. I'm sorry now that I removed them at all during the storm, for that probably is how she came to get such a dose of the stuff. Yours were much thicker, and I didn't have to wet them nearly so often."

"It should be possible," Ford hazarded, "for a man in a gas mask to cross with perfect safety."

144

"Perhaps, but I shouldn't like to try it in a five-day blow. Do you feel a queer sensation when the full glare of these infernal blue rocks strikes the back of your head?"

"Yes," said Ford. "I have kept quiet about it because I thought it must be an after-effect of the desert poison. There was no sense in bothering you with my troubles; poor Rosita is enough worry for both of us."

"Well, since we both feel the same thing, it must be something more than imagination. How does it affect you?"

"I begin to see things that aren't there. It is like a fitful recurrence of the desert madness. There is nothing steady about it; the spells come and go like a sort of erratic drunkenness."

"Exactly," Joicey agreed. "Do you know, I'm beginning to wonder whether those blue-headed priests are such idiots after all. The stuff they use for dyeing their hair is exactly the color of these rocks."

"What of it?"

"Well, yours and mine is the right color, but that's all. I suspect the priests use a powder ground down from these rocks as the base of their dye. You remember that when I was here before I used the dye which I found among the stores of the priests' caravan, also that I discovered how the dye rubs off in a fine blue powder and must be renewed from time to time. Now, during both my former journeys past these blue cliffs, and all the time I lived with the priests and wandered about in the vicinity of similar blue rocks, I felt no ill effects whatever."

"I see," said Ford. "The dye those fellows use is no mere beautifier. But how does it act? What does it do to their skulls to keep them from going insane—for that's where I shall soon be if there are many more of these blue cliffs that we must pass."

"We shall swerve away from this wall after a while," Joicey replied. "How the dye works, I can only make a vague guess. These rocks contain some mineral perhaps that gives them their intense blue color. Notice that the rocks are largely masses of whole unbroken crystals. You know of course how diamond crystals and some other kinds of precious stones give off light for a considerable time if they are put in a dark room after exposure to the full sunlight?" Ford nodded. "Well," Joicey continued, "I imagine there is something of the sort going on in those large blue crystals. The light which the diamond gives back in the dark is of a different quality from that which it absorbs.

"My guess is that the mineral which is responsible for the blue color of these rocks has a somewhat similar power of changing the nature of the light rays which the crystals absorb. It is these changed light rays impinging on our skulls that cause all the trouble. Possibly the changed light is analogous to that from, say, a naked mercury vapor arc, which gives off ultra-violet rays that may even cause blindness. These rays, of course, must be something quite distinct, but similar. They may act something like an X-ray, jarring and disintegrating the delicate nerve cells of the brain."

"All that may be so," Ford admitted, "but why should the blue dye neutralize these harmful rays—if they exist?"

"There is the puzzle of the whole thing," Joicey replied. "And I can only make another wild guess. If the dye really is made from the powdered crystals as I suspect, then it would very probably have the power of stopping or disintegrating the harmful rays emitted by the unbroken crystals. It is similar to grinding down a piece of transparent blue glass, I imagine. Look through the glass as it is first, and you see everything blue, because the glass transmits only blue light, stopping all the other colors. But try to look through the same glass after it has been ground down to a blue powder, and of course you see nothing at all. The powder is opaque, which is only another way of saying that it stops all color, transmitting none."

"THAT reminds me," Ford laughed, "of the awful times I had trying to learn crystallography in college. I decided it was less work to get out and find some real sapphires than it was to read in books about what they do, or don't do—I've forgotten which, to the plane of polarization. Also, there's a sight more money in it."

"Ah," said Joicey, "you're practical. I'm not. You may believe it or not, but it would give me infinitely greater satisfaction to know why Singh neglected to keep the dye on his hair when he was in Sikkim, while the man in my ancestor's narrative kept his religiously dyed blue all the time, than to get another five million out of Anderson."

Ford eyed him shrewdly. "I'm glad you said 'another' five million. Otherwise, I should have had to disbelieve you. Why, if I had twenty-five million dollars in the bank I might begin, like you, to take an interest in what kind of cabbages grow on the other side of the moon. But your question about Singh and the other fellow is easy—to a practical man. It's simply this. In Singh's day—twelve or thirteen years ago—a man with blue hair would get his picture into the newspapers from Calcutta to Moscow inside of a month. Did Singh want publicity? He did not.

"As for the other fellow, a hundred and fifty years ago, nobody ten miles from him would ever hear of his existence. The ignorant natives in his immediate neighborhood would set him down as a holier sort of holy fakir than usual, and bring him all the fattest bananas. Then again, he may have thought that all rocks might be injurious to a certain extent, so he found it easier and more prudent to keep on dyeing his hair instead of breaking off the habit of a lifetime and running possible risks. But when Singh saw that the English, the rulers of the country, as well as the natives, had civilized hair, he followed suit to avoid making a monkey of himself. Anyway, that's what I should do."

"Like most explanations," Joicey said, laughing, "it's ridiculously simple when you know it."

"Well," said Ford, "whatever the truth of the whole question, I wish we had some of the priests' stuff for this poor girl's hair. Unless we can do something for her soon, she may die."

"She won't turn to dust," Joicey asserted with calm assurance. "She has too much sand."

That quiet expression of belief in her grit was the tonic she needed. She longed to thank him for it, but her struggle not to collapse before her energies might be called upon in a crisis, absorbed all her will power. And so it went. She sat her horse or dismounted at night like a machine, only to climb machinelike into a saddle with the first glimmer of dawn. They had found some food for her—what it was she neither knew nor cared—that she could swallow, and this gave her strength. At last, one noon the hideous march ended. She heard Joicey instructing her in a tense whisper.

"Rosita! Wake up. We have reached the City; we are outside the chamber of the oracle. The priests demand that you pass a crucial test before they will go on with this. Our lives are in your hands. You must get control of your mind and use it. If you understand what I am saying, answer, 'Yes, perfectly.'"

"Yes, perfectly," she answered.

"We knew you wouldn't fail us. This is the situation. You must understand this. The other wise woman of the priests, who undoubtedly is Evelyn Wedderburn, is a sort of oracle or something of that nature. Don't try to puzzle out why she is; your uncle and I do not yet see through it. The priests say that she delivers long chants in a 'sweet music.' These chants are always the same.

"The priests do not understand a single word of them. She has told them the general nature of these chants—they have to do with manipulating the flame, she says—without divulging their precise meaning. The priests have memorized the sounds and reduced them to a sort of writing, although they cannot reproduce the sounds vocally, they say, nor understand what they signify. Don't puzzle over this now. Concentrate everything that is in you on the next, which is to be a crucial test.

"You are to hear the 'oracle' chanting. The priests are to break in on the oracle, silencing the chant. You are then to go on with the chant in the same words and tones that the oracle, or 'wise woman,' would have used if she herself had finished the chant. The priests declare that if you are a 'wise woman' it is impossible that you should be ignorant of how to continue the chant of your 'sister.' These 'chants' are all, she has told them, part of the common wisdom of all the wise women of the Great Race. The priests say they will recognize at once whether your performance is correct. If it is not, we are to be taken up at once to the 'place of execution' and be cast forthwith into the 'ever-living flame.' But if you do successfully continue the chant, they will accept you unreservedly as a true wise woman of the Great Race, and your uncle and me as 'readers of nature's mysteries,' as we have claimed for you and ourselves.

"Rosita, you must continue that chant. We guess that their 'oracle' Evelyn Wedderburn sings or recites in English. If you can't go on rationally with her interrupted chant, say something at any rate in English. Use your wits. Then face down the priests if they tell you that you have failed by insisting that they are so degraded that they cannot recognize a song of the wise women even when they have heard it sung for years. Demand that you be left alone for a week, with only one woman and ourselves to wait on you. This will give you time to rest. Now, you are going to win. Whatever happens, remember that your uncle and I are near, and that we shall all stick together. Here come the women to take you to the oracle."

"Shoot me at once if I fail," she said. "Promise."

"I promise," Joicey replied. "You won't." Afterwards, in recalling what followed, Rosita said that she remembered only telling the women attendants to lead her carefully to the oracle as her eyes were not yet accustomed to the dimmer light. Although still blind from the desert poison, she guessed from the "feel" and coolness of her surroundings that she was being led along a narrow passageway into a spacious stone vault. She was conscious of the priests in the vault, their tense expectancy betraying itself in whispers and subdued rustlings. There was a deathly hush of a few seconds, and the "oracle" began to chant. At the first clear words, uttered in a woman's voice of caressing sweetness and purity, Rosita all but fainted from relief and joy. For the "oracle," the "wise woman" was reciting with all the artless rhythm of a child nothing more abstruse than Sir Walter Scott's *Lay of the Last Minstrel*:

> "*The way was long, the wind was cold,*
> *The minstrel was infirm and old*'"

...rippled the lilting voice of the oracle, and instantly, not waiting for the bidding of the priests, Rosita took up the legend:

> "*The harp, his sole remaining joy*
> *Was carried by an orphan boy.*'"

She got no farther. A deafening shout from the priests reverberated against the rock roof, drowning the long, shuddering cry of the oracle in a paean of victory.

"Mother!" the voice had cried.

"Silence!" Rosita commanded the priests in their own tongue, and again. "Silence!" She had summoned all her strength for a supreme effort and must spend it immediately before it ebbed. The shouting ceased. When its last echo had died away, and only the sobs of the oracle lingered on the still air of the vault, Rosita again addressed the priests, speaking rapidly in ancient Tibetan.

"My sister has a command which you must obey. First, I would speak a few words with her. She must learn the fruits of my long meditation." She resumed clearly and slowly in English.

"Evelyn. I am your sister. Your mother is not here. Your father waits for you in India. Two men and I have come to take you to him. We are in great danger. They may hurt us. Ask me nothing now, and do not fret if I go and stay away for one week or even for two. I shall come back. The men and I will take you to your father. You must do everything that I tell you to do, both now and later. Tell these priests or men now, in their own language, that I must think long and study hard before you and I tame the fire. Say that I must speak much with the two readers of secrets before it will be safe for me to work with you. Tell them to send only one woman to wait on me. If you do not understand anything I have said, ask now, quickly. If you do understand, give the orders at once."

Rosita heard the oracle without an instant's hesitation, and without a quaver of the voice, lay her commands upon the priests. Then, while the tumult of joy still raged, she asked the women attendants to lead her back to the "readers of secrets." After that, she recalled nothing clearly, although she had a dim remembrance of the elation on her uncle's face and Joicey's, and a painful consciousness of the exasperating ceremonial slowness of the woman who prepared her for bed.

"WHILE the men explored the city of flat-roofed stone houses nestling in the crescent of a sheer red cliff that rose twelve hundred feet or more above the plateau, five days of utter restfulness passed quickly for Rosita, restoring her to health and sanity. The blindness was the last effect of the desert poison to disappear completely. On the third day, she recognized Joicey, and her uncle, who from time to time paid her brief visits, and on the fifth, the last symptom vanished in a rapid succession of short spells of total blackness.

The men told her only the most encouraging news. Although the priests, under the guise of guides anxious only that their distinguished guests should miss nothing of interest in their extensive city, kept a close watch on their movements, prohibiting them from visiting either the "wise woman" Evelyn or the vicinity of the caves, yet they seemed friendly enough and apparently accepted the travelers at their own valuation.

The only fly in Rosita's ointment was the woman attendant. She was efficient in her ministrations and doglike in her devotion, almost worshiping Rosita, yet she was an intolerable nuisance. Even the most trivial service was hedged about by an elaborate maze of exasperating ritual. A simple request for a drink of water started the conscientious pest off on an endless chain of sanitary precautions sufficient to immunize an entire nation against all the plagues of Asia.

Rosita was not allowed even to wash her own face. The attendant did it for her in fifty different lotions, lingering over each sticky mess until Rosita longed to rise and shake some speed into her. Such were the penalties of being a wise woman. It would not be the fault of the attendant if this golden haired "child" of the Great Race succumbed to measles or chicken pox.

As she recovered, Rosita took note of her surroundings. Her chamber was a large, cool vault, lighted and aired by four vents in the ceiling, each about six feet square and open to the wonderful sapphire blue sky. There were no windows, and only a single door. The bed was a pile about a foot high of soft furs, with sheets of some purple fabric of a texture like that of the finest silk. Blankets were not needed.

The table was of wood, black with age. The dishes, beautifully designed works of art, were of some strange metal resembling gold but with a noticeable greenish tinge. When tapped, they rang like Bohemian glassware. These naturally excited Rosita's curiosity, for they were like none that she had seen elsewhere, either in museums and shops or in pictures. She wondered if possibly the peculiar, rich-looking metal were a by-product of the ancient process of which the priest had told Joicey, whereby the men of the Great Race changed lead to gold, the gold to copper, and finally copper into the "living metal" which was the source of all their material happiness.

She secretly planned to take back with her at least one of these marvelous dishes as a souvenir.

The walls, floor, and ceiling of her chamber presented even more difficult riddles. Every foot of the surface was lined with a dull gray metal; and of this lining, all but the metal on the floor, every inch was deeply engraved with innumerable minute characters. These characters were closely similar in appearance to the undeciphered inscriptions on the small lead box in which Singh had carried his sapphire disk or "passport." No two of the inscriptions on the walls appeared to be alike; the whole presented an amazing treasury of forgotten knowledge. On scratching this metal lining with her thumbnail while the attendant was absorbed in "purifying" a drinking cup, Rosita verified her guess that it was lead, gray, and deeply oxidized from long exposure to the air.

"I would offer anyone a sapphire as big as my head for a pocket camera, at this moment," Joicey remarked when the attendant finally had performed all the ceremonies of closing the door, leaving Ford and himself alone with Rosita. "That writing may, of course, only be ritual or some rubbish of some sort," he continued, "and not worth deciphering. Still, the men who knew enough to cut these multitudes of tiny characters into lead with such perfect precision, probably were not such fools as to preserve only a lasting record of the etiquette of shutting a door. Those inscriptions mean something." He peered at a square of the microscopic characters on the wall as if trying to memorize them by sight.

"Well Rosita," said Ford, "it's the sixth day, about seven in the morning, I judge, since you've been cooped up here. How would a little sightseeing tour strike you? Feeling all right for a walk?"

"Fine!" she exclaimed. "I never felt better or more clear-headed in my life. What's the program?"

"We thought you might like to pay Evelyn Wedderburn a visit. The poor girl must think we've deserted her."

"That's splendid. But will they let you two see the 'wise woman'? I thought men were forbidden anywhere near their quarters in the caves."

"They are. We shall stay here and entertain the priests with diplomatic accounts of our greatness. But we have arranged everything for you to go whenever you feel like it. Joicey, you invented our yarn. Tell her."

"The priests are eager enough for you and your 'sister' to begin operations at once," Joicey explained. "In fact, they are just a little too eager. As your uncle remarked, they want to spill the beans before they're properly cooked. They want to shut you two wise women up together in the caves, like a pair of owls in a sack, and keep you there until you produce results. When you have 'tamed the fire' to their uses, the priests will let you out again, not before. Now that of course wouldn't do at all. It's difficult enough to get one young woman out of those beastly caves, let alone two. And, for all I know, if you two highly unscientific young women did get to fooling with 'the flame'—whatever that may be—you might finish by sending us all back to India in an airline. For that there is something real and dangerous behind all this nonsense of the traditions, I am fully convinced. So you must be free to enter and leave the caves as you please until we get everything for which we came.

"NOW, the scheme is this. Your uncle and I laid all the results of our conferences with you before the priests. We told them," he continued with a smile, "of your obstinate refusal to attempt anything until you had thoroughly mastered all the instructions contained in the encyclopedic inscriptions on the walls and ceiling of this room."

"Joicey didn't think of that himself," Ford interrupted. "Those fool priests themselves put it into his head. They almost begged him to make monkeys of them, or like chumps they confided to him where they got these inscriptions. They originally adorned a wall of the very chamber of the 'perpetual flame' where our friend Evelyn is supposed to be working day and night in an effort to 'tame the fire.' The remnants of their race who were not wiped out in the great disaster of their traditions removed all these precious records from the cave that was still intact before they sealed up the entrance. They couldn't read a single line of it, for all the 'readers of mysteries'—men like Joicey and myself—had perished in the disaster, and the survivors were only law-abiding, unscientific citizens. Yet they hoped that in time either they could unriddle all this themselves, or that someone with more brains than they had would come along and do it for them.

"The descendants of the remnant, our blue-headed friends the priests, are still hoping. They thought Evelyn would do it, but somebody with a head on her shoulders put Evelyn up to saying that she had left her happy home in the Land of the Great Race before her nurse had taught her the ancient written alphabet. Joicey, of course, told them that you enjoyed this kind of thing better than a novel, that it was the very stuff of your mind, and that you could read and understand every word of it with your eyes shut."

"Your uncle is right," Joicey agreed. "They asked me to spoof them, and I did. When I told them of your determination to master this prehistoric encyclopedia, they groaned, suspecting that it will be a long job. But we pacified them by explaining how you had already discovered from these records that the ancient way of 'taming the fire' differs greatly from that which the Great Race now uses, and (here's the joker) how their 'chamber of the undying fire' is constructed so that only the ancient way can be used in it with any safety.

"They were much impressed by your important discovery that any attempt to use the modern, infinitely more efficient method on their antiquated remains must inevitably precipitate a second disaster that would make the one which created the desert look like a cool spring breeze. They agreed readily that you are very reason-able in your demands that you be allowed to study their flame chamber at will and compare what you observe there with the instructions preserved here. So you personally may go to and from the caves as you see fit.

"They even saw clearly, as your uncle has hinted, that it might be necessary to teach your half-educated 'sister' to read these inscriptions and study them with you. For, of course, your 'sister' was stolen by that reprobate 'hero of the desert' before she was old enough to read the most ancient and noblest of all languages, which our wise women still carefully preserve, but more as an accomplishment than as a thing of any intrinsic value. For the priests clearly understand from your preliminary researches that any premature attempt to control the flame can end only in terrible disaster; and before the dazzling splendor of your surpassing wisdom they are blinder than bats and meeker than Moses."

"Well," Rosita laughed, "as I remarked once before, the woman who is guileless enough to marry you will lead an exciting life. Thanks, though, for all your trouble. Everything now should be easy. Shall I bring Evelyn back with me to study the inscription this afternoon?"

"We think it better not," Ford replied. "She's important, but she's only half of what we came for, and until we get all the sapphires we can pack, she will only be in the way. It would be a pleasure, of course, to have her with us; but I never did believe in mixing pleasure with business. She's safe enough where she is until we figure out some way of getting the sapphires and making our escape. At present, we have no earthly idea how we are to do either. Now, are you ready to go?"

Rosita nodded, and Ford continued. "All right. We have kept one little detail till last. Two or three of the more conservative priests talked the others over to what they call a measure of safety. They believe in us, but think it more in keeping with their cast-iron traditions that we wait here for you, and that you be blindfolded on your way to and from the caves. It is little more than a matter of form they assure us. As soon as you and Evelyn decide to begin operations on the fire, this last precaution will be abandoned, and you will be shown the way, unblindfolded, to the entrance. Now, just for a little counter precaution of our own. If you are not back by nightfall, Joicey and I are coming to fetch you.

"We have our revolvers. So don't you worry. We'll be right after you if the priests are up to any monkey business. Try to get back about fifteen minutes before sunset if you can. We shan't be anxious, though, till one minute after sundown. Here's your faithful nuisance to blindfold you. Keep your nerve and use your eyes when you get into the caves. We shall be waiting for you just outside this door when you come back."

"I'll steal you each a sapphire," Rosita whispered as the woman humbly advanced with the bandage. Having blindfolded Rosita—and she did a very thorough job—the attendant led her to the door and the men followed her outside. Two waiting priests advanced respectfully. With a diffidence not unmingled with awe, each took one of Rosita's hands. Apologizing for the liberty, they led her away. The men saw her disappear with the priests at the end of the long street of stone houses.

DIRECTLY in front of them towered a sheer cliff of reddish rock at least five thousand feet high in the main mass, and dropping abruptly to a sort of crescent shaped bay of only twelve hundred feet a little to their left. In this bay, the main part of the town was situated. Somewhere within the interior of the vast cliff, which stretched in an apparently unbroken wall as far as the eye could see, must be the caves, for behind the street where the men now were standing the city extended mile after mile out on the open plain with no other mountains visible beyond it.

The streets were laid out on the rectangular pattern, clean and well spaced, but otherwise uninteresting with their interminable vistas of one-storied, flat-roofed stone dwellings. Nevertheless, the huge crescent-shaped bay of sheer rock twelve hundred feet high which bounded it on the south gave it a sort of dignity; and the rugged beauty of the steep break which made this bay in the precipitous ridge of naked rock nearly a mile high and possibly a hundred miles long, gave the city an air of mysterious grandeur such as no other capital city of the world can claim.

Neither of the men felt any anxiety for Rosita's safety. They were soon joined by several blue-haired priests. These gentlemen, all friendliness and deep respect, hungered and thirsted for information regarding the Great Race in its modern splendor, and the two 'readers of nature's mysteries' were not backward in supplying them with graphic details, for the most part of their own invention from what scientific knowledge they possessed.

Joicey, happening to mention something about wireless, struck an unexpectedly convincing note. Either the priests were his superiors at romancing, or their traditions really did assert that their people had once, in their glorious past, conversed at will across space with only the simplest portable instruments to aid them. Ford's casual mention of aeroplanes fell rather flat. The priests easily outdid him with their legends of the Great Race having mastered mechanical flight only to discard it for something "much better"—a sort of levitation, it seemed—which the southern faction of the race used on their journey to the "new land."

In fact, they said, if only a few of the "readers of mysteries" had been left alive by the great disaster, the remnant of the race might easily have used this means to overtake the others; but like everything else that was of any practical use, the knowledge of how to do it perished with their scientific sect. The one survivor in a hundred thousand seems to have been a rather unintelligent person, which perhaps accounts for the stupidity of their remote descendants, the priests. Ford delicately intimated this to them, and candidly admitted the utter childishness of flying machines, saying that he had mentioned them merely because he thought they might be within range of the degraded priests' understanding. Between fact and fancy, the little knot of truth-tellers managed to kill the long day quite pleasantly.

At last, just as the sun touched the sharp summit of the high cliffs, Rosita reappeared with her two guides. She was blindfolded. One of the priests ran for the attendant to remove the bandage; Rosita's skillful fingers must do nothing but the most delicate work of manipulating the flame. The devoted woman came on the run, just as Rosita joined the men.

The bandages off, she turned to her uncle a face radiant with success. Then, seeing the expectancy of the priests she spoke a few words in their own tongue, assuring them that within a year their people should be restored to all its former greatness, and even more. For she now felt confident, after having seen their chamber of the flame, which really was quite good of its inferior kind, that her sister and she could easily control the fire to human use. But, before attempting this, many more visits to the chamber of the flame and much further study of the inscriptions were imperative necessities.

Only after such protracted study might they begin work without danger of precipitating an overwhelming disaster on the entire world. And now, she concluded, would the priests kindly retire and leave her to sift all that she had discovered through the fine minds of these two readers of nature's mysteries? In other words, although she did not say it openly, of course, would they be so good as to go and bury themselves and leave her in peace?

The jubilant but awestruck priests melted away like snowflakes on a river at her polite, caressing request. The moment they were alone, Rosita turned to Joicey, her face beaming.

"Evelyn is a beauty, a darling and a wonder," she said. "Wait till you hear her story. She told me everything. You two come in with me and I'll get rid at that everlasting woman."

The attendant humbly emerging from Rosita's room just then; Rosita dispatched her to supervise the preparation of an extremely complicated dinner for three. "That should keep her fussing till the cows come home and hang their hats in the hallway," Rosita remarked as the faithful creature bustled off to execute her mistress' commands.

THEY were just about to enter Rosita's chamber when the distant shouting of an angry mob arrested them. The shouting rapidly grew louder and clearer; evidently the mob was heading in their direction, although as yet it had not entered their street. The men felt under their tunics for their revolvers and stood ready, their hands and forearms concealed within the folds of their garments.

"You had better shoot me," Rosita said, "if they are coming for us. Evelyn told me what they do to spies."

"If we can't make a run for it, I will," Ford agreed. "Then Joicey and I will give these fellows a taste of hot lead before we cash in our chips."

Suddenly the yelling mob burst round a corner and streamed down the street directly toward them. The men never moved, determined not to draw their revolvers until sure of the mob's intentions. The leaders, blue-headed priests, were now almost level with them. Spying the wise woman and her companions watching them they stopped. Then one of the priests darted up to them.

"What is the matter?" Joicey asked evenly. Both his gloved hands were concealed in the folds of his robe, and each grasped the handle of an automatic.

"A filthy Tibetan!" the priest exclaimed, and Joicey's heart stopped, but bounded on again when the priest spat and pointed to the center of the mob. "The watchers of the mountains caught him seven days ago. He had crossed the desert. Show the degraded beast to the wise woman," he shouted to the mob.

The mob parted, disclosing a huddled wretch of a Tibetan cowering in his filthy rags between two guards. He had been shamefully mistreated and was now dazed and but half-conscious. His hair was matted over his head and face with the dried blood from great gashes in his scalp, and here and there, his rags were soaked with crimson. They dragged the poor wretch up to confront Rosita.

Her first full look nearly paralyzed her. "Good heavens! It is our nomad," she gasped in English.

Ford and Joicey too had instantly recognized their companion of a night on the Tibetan highlands. Their hands froze. Then Joicey spoke in English. "He can't possibly recognize us," he said. "We are white people now. When he saw us we were Tibetans."

"What are you saying?" the spokesman of the blue-haired priests demanded suspiciously.

"We are saying that this spy looks more like a degraded beast than a man," Joicey replied in the priest's language. "Is it possible that anything in human shape can sink to such depths of filth and bestiality? What are you going to do with him?"

"Do with him? Give him to the never-dying flame! That is the end of all spies."

"Very proper," Joicey replied.

"Shoot the priests," Rosita whispered in English. "Then run."

But Joicey never moved his hands within his garments to slip off the awkward gloves, and Ford's ready fingers made no stir beneath his robe.

"Is this man a Tibetan?" Joicey asked the priest.

"Look at him!"

"I see him," Joicey answered coldly. "Is he a Tibetan?"

"Yes! You have but to see him and his filth to know his degraded race."

"Has he a swinging needle such as travelers of the degraded peoples use to find their way through deserts and through the darkness of starless nights in the mountains? Has he such a thing, without which the low races are lost like cattle in the desert wilderness? Did you find one on him when he was taken?"

"No. He had nothing but a water skin and some filthy remnants of a sheep."

"Then how, if as you assert he is a Tibetan, did he find his way across the fiery desert? Only the true children of the Great Race have that secret knowledge. Only they can feel with their bodies which is north and which south; only they by the pull on their minds can tell the east from the west, and they alone can find their way even as the birds through the mountain passes, without erring and without a needle of the degraded peoples. This man is not a Tibetan."

"Then what is he?"

"How should I know? That is for you to learn, by questioning him and asking him his business. What drew him straight across the fiery desert to the mountains and the pass into your land?"

"He did not come by the pass," the priest exclaimed. "The watchers at the mountains found him in the high rocks two days' journey east of the pass."

"Then that settles it," Joicey said. "He is not a Tibetan, or he could not, without a needle, have found that shorter though more arduous way to your City. Take care, I say, that you do not deliver up a true son of the Great Race to the flame. Sift this dangerous matter well."

"If you make a mistake in your haste," Rosita added in a voice that was cold steel, "my sister and I shall visit you with our displeasure. Cleanse him and feed him for two days. Clothe him in raiment like your own, and you shall see what he is. Then I will help you to a judgment, the day after tomorrow."

"Is it a command?"

"It is. Now go. Take this man and treat him tenderly. Ask him nothing that I do not hear, and nothing that these men, my brothers, the readers of mysteries, do not hear and sift through their wisdom. He may be a son of the Great Race. If you disobey me in the least thing," she suddenly flamed, "my sister and I shall destroy you and all your people in the flashing of an eye."

"And all our wisdom shall aid these wise women," Ford added, "to blast your place with fire from the earth which it defiles. Destroy this man's filthy rags before night, lest they pollute your city with disease."

"Go! Obey!" Joicey shouted.

Cowed by her threat and the aspect of her companions, the mob dispersed in slinking fear. The priests led away their stunned prisoner who had understood nothing in his dazed terror. When they had disappeared round a corner, Ford withdrew his hands from his robe and wiped the sweat from his face.

"Whatever made the fool come here?" he asked in bewilderment.

"The power of love," Joicey replied with a short laugh.

Rosita ignored his explanation. "How can he possibly have crossed that terrible desert?"

"Luck. Just as I did the first time. He hit a thirty-six of forty-eight hours with no wind and simply plugged ahead. Probably he rode his horse until it pegged out. He may have struck a shorter way across; he didn't come by the pass. He must have entered the desert about three weeks after us. We got the storm; he, like the lucky fool he is, missed it. That's all."

"But the compass?" she objected.

"He may have had one for all I know. If so, it is probably tucked into some hole in his rags. That was a truly brilliant idea of your uncle's commanding them to destroy his rags before night."

"You certainly put up a good bluff," Ford remarked appreciatively; "when we get back to civilization I hope you'll play me a game of poker with sapphires for chips. We might even invent a new variety of the game, 'sapphire ante.' I hope the priests don't search the poor devil."

"If they do, he's gone."

"Not while I have any brains left," Rosita snapped. "And not while you, Captain Joicey, have a bluff left in you. If I got him into this mess, I'm sorry. I'll eat all the humble pie you order me, if only you'll help me to save him from that horrible death, and I'll never again, so long as I live make a fool of any man. There, is that enough? You'll help me, won't you?"

"Of course, I will," he said rather uneasily. "You know I was only joking when I said that just now. I ate the poor chap's mutton, didn't I? Well, then, I must use everything I've got to help him out of this hole. My own idiotic yarn about strangling the devils in the desert with my bare hands probably was at the bottom of his imbecility. For I made him a 'holy man' that night, so of course he could cross unharmed, whereas the devils had given me a hot time of it merely because I was anything but holy when I tackled them."

Thus did he make amends for his spiteful remark about the power of love.

"I knew you would all the time," she said gratefully as they passed indoors.

CHAPTER NINE
The Forbidden Caves

"WELL," Rosita began when they were comfortably seated in her lead-lined chamber, "I promised each of you a sapphire. Here they are, just alike, so you won't quarrel over the spoils." From the folds of her garment she produced two three-inch cubes of the flaming gem and presented them to the men.

"Gad," Ford exclaimed, "these are finer quality than Joicey's sphere. This thing is priceless—look at its intense violet fire."

"This certainly beats the sphere," Jokey agreed. "One of these is worth a dozen of the others." He turned his cube over and over, examining it with open-mouthed admiration. "It has a fresher, more 'alive' brilliance than the sphere had, even at its best."

"It should," Rosita laughed. "Evelyn just made them for me less than two hours ago."

"What!" Ford exclaimed. And Joicey almost shouted, "Has she found out the secret?"

"Oh, even the most ignorant of the priests can do that trick," Rosita said with a superior air, "although not nearly so quickly as she. You see, they only get the leavings of the 'flame' after it has passed through a quarter of a mile of solid crystal. But you shall see for yourselves tomorrow—if you have the nerve."

"How?" Ford demanded. "Tell us that and don't worry about our nerve."

"It's quite a story. Before I tell it, let me give you the end first, my big piece of news. I can get you into the caves."

They gaped at her in astonishment. "Rosita," said Joicey, "you're a wonder. You may flirt with all the nomads in Tibet if you like."

"One is enough." She turned to her uncle. "And some day, not tomorrow, because Evelyn can't make arrangements yet about lead boxes for them, you can go to the caves with a sack, or a barrel—if they have them here—and shovel up all the sapphires we can pack away. If we can get horses to carry them, I'm going to take back enough to line the basin of a small fountain which I intend to have in my city residence."

"Don't," Ford begged. "You are killing me by inches. Oh, Lord, why didn't we bring a steam shovel?"

"All right," said Rosita. "They really are as common here as you like to make them. That old priest of Captain Joicey's was a truthful man. Now, first about those sapphires in your hands. You had better be careful how you carry them. They must not be handled while the sun is shining on them. To do so for long will certainly cause terrible burns and mortify the flesh."

"So I have suspected," Joicey quietly remarked, looking at his gloved hands.

"When these sapphires are incased in lead," Rosita continued, "their destructive rays are stopped and the lead cases may be safely handled. The same effects are produced by long handling of the bare stones away from sunlight, but the burns are very much slower in appearing. Evelyn had no boxes for these, so you had better be careful.

"Next, another warning. You must keep out of shadows while the sun is shining. Every foot of the sun and rocks is impregnated with some mineral that gives off a heavy, deadly gas. This gas has somewhat the same effects as the fumes of the desert, producing temporary blindness and insanity if inhaled. It is not exactly the same thing, for full sunlight either destroys the poison or rarefies it so that it flows onto the cooler spots. It is dangerous even to sit close to the ground with your back to the sun, for the poisonous gas piling up in your shadow may reach your mouth and nostrils."

"Ah," said Ford, "friend Singh wasn't such a chump as the General thought him, after all."

"Singh was one of the keenest men that ever lived," Rosita warmly agreed, "even if he should have been caught and sent to the penitentiary for kidnapping Evelyn. But I shall have a lot to say about him presently. Singh, by the way, wasn't his right name, of course, but it will do, as we have known it so long.

"Another precaution: you must not go under overhanging rocks or enter a cave anywhere in this country unless the whole rock or cave, including the ground under it or the floor of the cave, is lined with lead. Otherwise you will get the full strength of the poison. It never disperses from unsunned places. The lead apparently prevents the gas from generating in the rocks or soil and escaping into the air. This taboo is so important that the mothers here train their children as soon as they can crawl to avoid all overhanging things, holes, cupboards, tables, and so on. Then the avoidance is fixed as a life-habit as soon as the children can run about and understand what they are doing."

"Our quarters too," Ford interposed, "and presumably also every room in this city, is lined with lead. These people are no fools."

"Not fools, perhaps, but ignorant, degraded, and superstitious. They do everything by rote and rule, blindly following traditions they ceased ages ago to understand. Captain Joicey, your estimate was right. Singh was one man in hundreds of millions, the one intelligent mind this race has produced in perhaps thousands of centuries. Of course the man of your ancestor's narrative was miles above the average, but he wasn't in Singh's class, I should judge. Singh was a freak."

"A 'sport,' or possibly a 'reversion to type,' the biologists would call him," Joicey remarked. "Our own people have examples of the same thing occasionally—Newton, Darwin, Pasteur, Einstein, Madame Curie—and then the whole race strides ahead a hundred or a thousand years. But go on."

"Singh was one of them. But, poor fellow, the ignorance and superstition of his people were too much for him, and he died in trying to lie them into greatness. I shall give you, as clearly as I can the outline of what Evelyn and her personal attendant, Ana, told me. Evelyn, of course, has grasped the situation only gradually as she developed from childhood to womanhood, but now that she is a woman she understands Singh's great motives and bears him no malice.

"SINGH, as I have said, was a man of extraordinary genius. His mind developed fully when he was little more than a boy. Being the son of a priest—although the priests are not permitted to marry, they frequently have 'morganatic' families—Singh was doomed to the priesthood and drilled mercilessly in the traditions. Among other tasks in his long preparation was the memorizing by sight of a great number of the inscriptions on the walls and ceiling of this room. Traditions, which he later verified from the inscriptions themselves, asserted that all these inscriptions had once been tablets on a wall of the one undestroyed cave of the 'perpetual fire' where certain wise women formerly worked. None of the priests understood a single character, nor did he while he was memorizing their appearance. Between all of them, the upper priests at any time were able to reproduce exactly all the characters inscribed on the walls and ceilings of this room. This was a precaution against the accidental destruction of the inscriptions.

"Not satisfied with this unintelligent drudgery, Singh's keen mind, when he was barely twelve years old, seized on the whole mass of inscriptions with the resolve to decipher them or perish. I don't believe you realize just how stupendous an undertaking this really was.

"In the first place, the inscriptions are in seven languages, all dead for tens of thousands of years, with only the ancient Tibetan as a very slim clue to one of the easier of the seven dead languages. In the second place, no two of the inscriptions duplicate each other; the information in each is different from that in all the others. Last, these are not mere lists of kings, battles, and accounts of foolish expeditions that any good decipherer might attack and blunder through with luck and patience.

165

"They were something far more difficult: whole books on forgotten sciences—physical, mathematical, chemical—in the highest state of their development, and that state, I should remind you, was far in advance of the scientific knowledge which we have today. He had to guess at the meetings of processes that were dead arts before his own language was born. And on top of this, these inscriptions contain but a very small fragment of the science of which they are a part; the rest perished in the caves that were destroyed.

"These contain the more difficult and advanced parts; the elementary 'books' were obliterated in the disaster which destroyed the ancient race and created the desert.

"Now you may agree with me that a man who could make real headway against such a problem was a genius of the highest type. I know," she said with an apologetic laugh, "it isn't considered nice and young lady-like for a girl to worship brains in a man rather than beef, but I was born that way and can't help it."

"You'll do," said Ford. "I shan't kick so long as you follow your own taste and don't marry one of those young fellows who pose for the white collar advertisements, go ahead."

"Five years of incessant labor gave Singh his first clue, and in one year more he had mastered their entire meaning, although of course many of the instructions contained in these 'books' were, to say the least, obscure to him. It was both a triumph and a defeat, for he learned of the incompleteness of these records and of his own inability to perform the actual experiments and processes which they called for. Before he could take another step forward, he must get into the caves.

"He told the priests nothing of his discoveries, determined to work out the salvation of his people without their ignorant, meddling interference. The outwitting of their cowardice and superstition was a much harder task for him than the reading of the inscriptions, and without his sweetheart Ana's help, he could not have taken the first step. Ana was then his own age, eighteen, attractive, much above the general intelligence of her race, and devoted to Singh.

"He tried to teach her to read the inscriptions, but failed completely. Ana had ability but not a spark of genius. She had—

and still has—a passionate admiration for her sweetheart's genius, his ambitions, and his hopes. Better, she had a practical mind admirably adapted to scheming and plotting. Singh confided to her that he must gain entrance to the caves before he could advance a step farther toward his goal, and she pledged her life that he should gain his end.

"THE difficulties were tremendous. Ages ago, shortly after the disaster of the tradition, the entrance to the caves had been completely sealed up by a mass of masonry at least two hundred feet thick. Evidently, the survivors in their terror of the single remaining 'flame' that still lived in the undestroyed chamber, did this as a safeguard against a possible recurrence of the disaster which had overwhelmed them. For it became the iron law of the land, and thus firmly imbedded in the present traditions, that not a stone of the sealed barrier should be moved until some 'wise woman' or 'child of the Great Race' might be brought back to teach this remnant of the race the lost secrets of controlling the flame to the use of man. The penalty for a violation of this traditional law was death in the 'all-consuming fire.'

"But how could they inflict the penalty?" Ford interrupted. "The remaining 'flame' was safely blocked up in the caves."

"As Captain Joicey evidently knows, they inflict the death penalty, not in the caves, but on the top of the cliff, where the rays from the 'flame' pierce sheer through the solid rock crystal of the cave's roof. You will understand better when you see things for yourself tomorrow."

"All right, go ahead."

"It was Ana's scheming mind that solved the puzzle, and she did it in a straightforward, common sense way, just as an intelligent woman unties a troublesome knot by using a pair of scissors. She did the obvious thing. If only a 'wise woman' or 'child of the Great Race' could gain entrance to the chamber of the undying fire, then they must capture one or the other, or at least secure a substitute that could be palmed off on the ignorant and superstitious priests as the genuine article. The entrance to the caves could then be un-sealed by law; they could thereupon introduce their captive or accomplice, and Ana could accompany her as personal ministrant in accordance with the traditions. The rest would be comparatively easy. With a clever confederate in the caves, Singh himself could possibly gain entrance or, failing that, Ana could report minutely what she found; perhaps make drawings.

"The difficulty was where to get their 'wise woman'. Singh himself believed that the Great Race—the southern faction— either had long since become extinct or had gradually degenerated, losing its control over nature and its scientific knowledge step by step in the course of ages. Otherwise, he argued, in all the ages that had elapsed since they had departed for the south, they surely would have established communications with their ancestral home, for sentimental reasons if for no other. Still, he thought, there might be yet found far to the south degraded peoples, remote descendants of the Great Race, with at least some of the characteristics which tradition ascribed to the 'wise women' the brown eyes, golden hair, and so on.

"He decided, therefore, to follow in the footsteps of all his predecessors who had sought to overtake the Great Race, and take the desert route south. Now, not one of these foolhardy explorers had returned—so your ancestor's man, Captain Joicey, did not get back, as you guessed. Singh set himself to discover why, and soon found a possible reason in their ignorance of the laws governing storms on the desert. These he next investigated, and found that almost invariably wind storms on the desert followed in cycles of two days' storm, one day calm, three days' storm, two days' calm, one day storm, five days' calm, when the whole series would repeat in the same order. There were regular, accountable changes with the seasons, Ana found later.

"The plot was now matured except one detail. What sort of woman was Singh to capture and bring back? She must be golden-haired, brown-eyed, and have as nearly as possible the correctly shaped head and peculiar physical beauty demanded by the traditions. A grown woman, unless she acquiesced in the plot and came of her own free will, could not be considered for an instant. She either would kill herself or Singh rather than be coerced to brave the perils of the journey, or she would go mad and die from terror on the way. And further, if she came unwillingly, she probably would be useless for their purpose when she arrived. They searched the traditions.

"Taking a long chance, he decided to interpret 'child of the Great Race' literally, and trust to their wits to convince the ignorant priests that a mere child, provided only she was of the Great Race, would have sufficient knowledge and keen enough instincts to attack the problem of safely manipulating the flame with a reasonable chance of success. This, of course, was a desperate expedient, and they again scrutinized the traditions for some detail that would make their claims for the 'child' more plausible.

"To their great joy they found what they were seeking. The wise women, according to the traditions, although not permitted to bear children themselves, were given a selected few of the very cream of the race, four-year-old girls, to train from the beginning in the delicate manipulations which they later must perform when they grew up and became wise women.

"The training consisted of games to develop skill with the fingers, and the memorizing by rote of songs or chants describing the movements and operations in controlling the flame. This training lasted five years, until the girls were nine, when the rudiments of the process had become fixed life-habits of speech and manual dexterity. After that the 'readers of nature's mysteries' trained the girls for five years longer, when the training again changed, alternating for a period of five years between the wise women for the actual operations, and the readers for the underlying science. Singh and Ana cared only for the first five years of all this, when the girls were between the ages of four and nine.

"The way was clear. Any intelligent little girl with the proper physical characteristics would serve their purpose. Her childish patter and naive songs in her own language would be sufficient 'chants of the wise women's teaching' for the ignorant and credulous priests. By kind treatment, Ana would win the child's affections and confidence and ultimately, perhaps, develop her into a successful accessory to Singh's ambitions. The plot was now complete. The next thing was to put it into action."

AFTER a hurried inspection to see whether her devoted attendant was still safely busied, Rosita continued her story of Singh.

"Singh departed on his search. Ana bid him farewell at the edge of the desert, which he entered on the first day of a five-day calm. With the permission of the priests, she took up her abode in a tent among the boulders at the foot of the pass to wait and watch for her lover's return. Her father, and later the priests, visited her once in every four months, bringing her food and other necessities. In the eyes of the priests, she became a sort of holy woman devoted to her age-long quest for the Great Race. Her word became law to them, and she lived in comfort confidently awaiting Singh's return.

"She waited and watched the desert for nineteen years. Then one morning, just as the last blue sheets of flame after a terrible windstorm whirled across the desert, she saw a figure reeling toward her out of the blinding fires. It was Singh. In his arms, he carried a large bundle.

"They reached the edge of the desert at the same instant. She got him to her tent. There he placed his bundle on the ground and motioned her to undo it. It was wrapped up in his tunic, and she noticed as she unrolled it that the cloth was wet in one spot. Unwrapping this she came upon the face of a golden-haired little girl, the mouth and nostrils thickly swathed in wet cloths torn from Singh's garments. The cloths on the outside were stained deep blue by the fine dust or gases which they had absorbed; those next to the child's face were practically fresh and uncolored."

"Singh also had an idea at the right time," Ford remarked to Joicey. "You're not the only pebble on the desert. Go on, Rosita."

"She removed the wet cloths. Singh knelt down and put his cheek to Evelyn's lips. Having assured himself that she still breathed, he staggered up, fell into Ana's arms, and died.

"For days, of course, Evelyn was near death, but Ana saved her. When at last her mind returned, she cried inconsolably. Ana could not comfort her, for Evelyn understood nothing of her language but the single word 'water.' Broken-hearted over the death of Singh, and stricken to the soul by the misery which their ambitions had inflicted on a helpless child, Ana vowed that henceforth she would devote her life and all her talents for scheming to the

170

righting of a wrong for which she, no less than Singh, was responsible. She has kept her vow.

"It would not be difficult, she guessed, to convince the superstitious priests that the dead Singh's golden-haired and brown-eyed find was indeed a child of the Great Race and an instructed pupil of its present wise women. The final conviction Evelyn herself unwittingly supplied.

"By a stroke of good fortune the priests had visited Ana just two days before Singh's return and death. She therefore would have almost four months alone with little Evelyn before the next visit.

"Evelyn at first cried herself to sleep. But soon, nature reasserting itself with the return of perfect health, she became less miserable, and instead of crying, sang. She used to sing over all her nursery songs, one after the other, 'to keep from forgetting what father and mother looked like,' she told me. Then, because she was lonely with nobody to speak to her in English, she began reciting to herself all the poetry her father and mother had taught her—and it was a lot.

"By signs and small gifts of trifles Ana encouraged her to keep this up almost incessantly, for she noticed the musical rhythm of the verses even if she could not, of course, get their drift. At the same time, she drilled and drilled Evelyn by sheer rote in a few sentences of the ancient Tibetan. Evelyn herself readily picked up the names of the foods, and so on; but of this formula, which she learned like a parrot, she understood nothing until years later when she had learned the language thoroughly from Ana.

"Days before the priests paid their next visit, Ana had Evelyn splendidly prepared. But she left nothing to chance and spent the remaining time before the visit in constant rehearsals with Evelyn of the fraud she was about to perpetrate. When at last she saw the priests coming, she concealed Evelyn behind a big boulder and by signs and kind words bade her not to be afraid. She then at once conducted the priests to the shelter of another boulder well within hearing distance of the one where Evelyn was.

"The rest almost happened itself. Ana urged Evelyn to sing and to recite her English verses, and then made her repeat like a parrot the formula in ancient Tibetan in which she had drilled the child to the point of rebellion. Evelyn reeled it off like a veteran.

"The substance of this formula which she had learned by rote was this: 'I am a child of the Great Race, taught these chants (meaning the nursery songs and her poems) of instruction by the wise women, my elder sisters. Your brother, the priest who died to bring me to you, and my elder sisters the wise women command you through my words to unseal the chamber where the flame still lives, and to let me live and grow up in the chamber of the caves where your wise women dwelt. Then as I grow, ever seeing the flame and living in its chamber, I shall understand the chants which my elder sisters have taught me, and I shall give back to you all the secrets of the flame. Let no man come near me now, or ever. Let this woman Ana be my servant, for so your dead brother commanded me to ask; and let the wisest of your young women be my handmaidens, that I may be tenderly nourished.'

"ANA'S strategy has been a complete success. I need describe only one phase of their life in the caves; the rest you will doubtless hear some day from Evelyn herself. It was Ana who invented the 'oracle.' She induced the priests to cut a window in the rock between one of the outer caves and a large, lead-lined rock chamber, or sort of vestibule, accessible only from the outside— that is from the city, but not from the caves. All they had to do was to drill from the outside a hole almost anywhere in the face of the cliff, for the entire mountain is honeycombed.

"The oracle, then about twelve years old, began her weekly practice of keeping the priests informed of her rapid progress in 'mastering the secrets of the flame.' As she grew older and gained a better knowledge of the ancient language, her reports of course became more elaborate. She always, from the very first, included a liberal slice of English poetry. This, by the way, has helped her to retain her native language.

"Nor was all this sham. Between them, Ana and Evelyn really observed a great deal. They can do numerous extraordinary things with the 'fire'; but naturally, they are afraid to experiment too far. The priests know nothing whatever of the genuine progress that Evelyn and Ana have made; all they get from the 'oracle' is a nonsensical tickling of their avaricious imaginations. You shall see some of the real wonders yourselves tomorrow.

"Now Ana never does anything for the pure fun of it. The oracle was the first step in a truly brilliant scheme. As soon as they were comfortably installed in the caves, Ana, still faithful to Singh's ambitions, determined to carry on his work. But she herself could understand nothing vital of the numerous strange things around her. If the flame was to be tamed and used as in the days of the traditions, it must be by a race of an intelligence far higher than hers. Evelyn had told her what she remembered of her childhood in England and India, describing among other things the railway trains and engines, the electric trains, steamers, telephones, electric lights, gas lights, watches, clocks, printed books and newspapers, the sending of telegrams and cablegrams, automobiles-'motors' she calls them—and flying machines.

"The last were a great novelty when she saw them, so they made a deep impression on her childish imagination. She had seen only two, but they are as vivid today, after twelve years, as when she saw them at some fair or another. Ana decided that a race civilized to that extent should be able to unravel the mysteries which surrounded her in the caves, and again her will triumphed. Having finally satisfied herself that Evelyn was telling the truth about the life of her people, and not merely romancing in the way common to children, she devised her plan for bringing men of Evelyn's race to study the caves. The first step in the plan, as I said, was the oracle. That was about eight years ago.

"The rest is pretty easy to guess. It was Ana who instructed Evelyn to say that she must have a 'sister,' or helper, of the Great Race before she could safely manipulate the flame. Through Evelyn, she commanded that an expedition of twelve men be sent across the desert to fetch the 'sister.' She calculated that at least one or two would get across alive, that these would be captured and, when they would understand their captors' language, be questioned as to their country. The captors would then, out of curiosity or greed, invade this country, oust the priests by means of their superior skill and intelligence, and so gain entrance to the caves. Although, only thirteen at the time of the expedition, Evelyn saw in this her one hope of rescue. For if the men were captured, and an expedition of Englishmen or other Europeans was the result, she was almost certain of being found.

"You already know the fate of this expedition. It is the one of which you, Captain Joicey, discovered the remains and the last survivor. They perished before they had well started. But the priests never learned of this disaster. For they no longer visited the other side of the pass near the desert, now that there was no 'holy woman' to be fed.

"THEN, soon after, came your visit, Captain Joicey. Ana and Evelyn heard of your coming the day you arrived in this city. From the description which the priests gave of you to the oracle, poor, hopeful thirteen-year-old Evelyn guessed at once that you must be an Englishman.

"You yourself have told us of the suspicions of the priests, and of their final test to decide whether you were of the Great Race as you claimed. The wretched Evelyn herself was the author of that test. She imagined, naturally enough, that you were some man sent by her father—who had been unable to come himself, why she couldn't think—and that you had found her only after long years of searching. Ana and she planned and plotted to get word to you. Then came the priests' consultation with the oracle. What should be their course of action? How could they decide that this man was really of the Great Race? Ana and Evelyn held a council of war in whispers behind the oracle window while the priests waited for their answer. What could every man of Evelyn's race do?

"Ana suggested, rather fatuously, that he telephone. This put the idea of the actual test in Evelyn's head. What simpler and at the same time more convincing test could she tell the priests to set you than the speaking of a few words in her own tongue and yours, English? All the priests had to do, then, to convince themselves that you were the genuine article, was to ask you to say something in the oracle's language."

"Jove, what a blind fool I was not to see through it," Joicey groaned.

"No, you weren't. You had never heard of Evelyn's abduction, so how on earth could you have guessed that English was required of you? Well, of course, you were sent back. Evelyn, heartbroken and despairing, decided that you could not be English, and that you had never heard of her. But Ana disagreed. She said you had failed deliberately because the priests were too many for you, and that you had gone back to your own country for help and would return as soon as possible."

"That hits it exactly," said Joicey, "except the part about my stupidity being deliberate. I have never yet made a fool of myself on purpose. It has always been involuntary."

"What about your monocle?" she laughed.

"Oh, that's different. Can't see a fellow countryman or an American without it, you know. But go on. I have a feeling that infernal woman of yours is about to break in on us with her rotten dinner."

Rosita continued. "In order that there should be no unnecessary accidents when you did return, Ana, through the oracle, commanded that the priests set a constant watch, day and night, over the desert for a mile on both sides of the pass."

"That accounts for the enthusiastic welcome they gave me when I marched in with you two," Joicey remarked, somewhat crestfallen. "Good old Ana. I thought it was just the after-effect of my parting lecture to those beastly priests. If they hadn't been there waiting for us with water and food we shouldn't have been here now. We owe Ana our lives. You both were pretty far gone, and I had just enough energy left to hide the water bags and be diplomatic to the priests."

"So I've suspected," said Ford. "I'll get it out of you yet how long you dragged us through that hellish storm."

"Both of you walked all the way," Joicey lied unblushingly. "I hear that confounded woman of yours rattling her pots and pans. Rosita, it's all up."

"Just one more thing. She always takes half an hour to get in. Evelyn remembers that Singh, so long as she was conscious in the desert, never took a single drop of water after his yak died. He gave her all she wanted to drink, and kept her mouth and nostrils covered with wet cloths."

"Then he's not the man I thought he was," Joicey admitted. "I beg the poor chap's pardon. Did you tell Evelyn of her mother's death, and who we are?"

"Yes, just before I left her. The fact that her father is still alive and longing for her softened it a little."

"Does she recall how Singh eluded the search parties?" Ford asked.

"Not distinctly. Twice they passed under a tree in which Singh was hiding with her, and once by the edge of a brook her father almost stepped on her hand. Singh evidently was as cunning as an animal. Once out of the town he made straight for the jungle and the hills, following no road or trail. After crossing the mountains he stole the yak from some Tibetans. He must have followed an entirely different route from ours, for Evelyn remembers nothing of the rock tunnel with the colossal sculptures, nor anything of the great waterfall."

"It is possible, then," said Ford, "that he needed no compass?"

"Probably an absolute fact," Joicey replied. "You remember his sense of locality that puzzled the General. Many of these priests have the same queer gift. I wasn't bluffing when I said that this afternoon. They can tell the points of the compass by instinct. It seems to be the one trace of an intelligence higher than our own which has survived their pitiful degradation. Here's that dashed woman."

JUST before daybreak the next morning a priestly ambassador from Rosita waited on Ford and Joicey.

"The attendant of your sister, the wise woman, asks me that you be led to your sister."

Exchanging glances of triumph the two men rose hastily from their unfinished breakfast of goat meat, sour milk, barley cakes, and green fruits, and followed the messenger to Rosita's apartment. They found her ready to start on their perilous expedition to the forbidden caves.

"My woman is on an errand," she explained hurriedly, "and will be back in a moment. When she comes, tell her at once to fetch an escort of priests, the more the better, to take you to the chamber of the oracle."

"I can find my way there without a guide," Joicey interposed.

"Of course, but the priests are essential to Ana's plan. Say that you two readers of mysteries have very important instructions

176

concerning the perpetual fire which you must explain to my sister and me together. We are to be listening at the small opening through which the oracle delivers her messages."

"And are we to squeeze in through it?" Ford asked.

"Ana isn't such a fool as that, even if the opening were big enough, which it isn't. Wait and see; there's no time to explain now. You two will have to use your heads. Captain Joicey, you visited the place of execution when you were here before? Well, keep your eyes on it all the time you are in the chamber of the oracle; it can be seen by looking down the passageway leading into the chamber. If anything unusual happens, you two must rush out with the priests and mingle with the crowds. Keep a sharp lookout for me. When you see me, shout in ancient Tibetan, 'It reddens!' and follow me. If on the other hand you see nothing unusual at the place of execution, stay in the oracle chamber. You will be unable to enter the caves. Here they come."

In obedience to Rosita's command, the two priests accompanying her attendant blindfolded the "wise woman" and led her away to consult with her "sister" in the caves. Joicey then ordered the obsequious woman to fetch "twelve times twelve" of the upper priests to conduct them to the chamber of the oracle. He briefly and impassionedly explained the grounds for this extraordinary request, saying that the priests might as well begin now to learn the secrets of the flame, and concluding with the solemn assurance that this great day was to mark the beginning of a new and glorious era of prosperous sloth for the entire remnant of the Great Race.

The priests came on the run. Everything went exactly as prearranged by Rosita. Arrived at the lead-lined chamber of the oracle, Ford asked to be taken before the opening in the wall that he might instruct the wise woman, while Joicey, declaring that he must meditate in silence a few moments, turned his back on the chamber and gazed through its entrance. The long, straight rock passageway, also completely lined with lead, by which they had entered, commanded an unobstructed view of the center of the crescent-shaped "bay" in the red cliffs, rising sheer up twelve hundred feet above the wide expanse of flat-roofed dwellings.

Directly in the line of vision and on the crest of these red cliffs was a depression in the long level skyline, so slight as to be unnoticeable from below unless looked for carefully. An observer knowing where to look and what to see would just discern, rising vertically up against the intense blue sky above the cliffs, an extremely faint shaft of purplish light. Joicey, fixing his eyes on this barely visible discoloration of the skylight, waited tensely, for the faint purple shaft marked the place of execution.

He had not long to wait. Evelyn's musical voice floated through the narrow "window" of the oracle.

"My brothers, have you brought the readers of mysteries to instruct my sister and me, as we commanded?"

"We are here," Ford replied in ancient Tibetan, and the united murmur of a hundred and forty-four priestly voices confirmed his assertion.

"May we with safety unite the fifth and seventh rays of the flame?" Evelyn asked, still speaking the ancient language for the benefit of the twelve dozen priests.

Without an instant's hesitation Ford took his cue, delivering himself solemnly in the ancient language of the first nonsense that entered his head.

"You may," he said profoundly, "if you exercise great care. It is a thing of extreme danger, but necessary to the taming of the fire for this degraded people's happiness and good health. Mingle together no more than a fifty-seventh part of the fifth ray and a seventy-fifth part of the seventh, and all will be well."

The murmuring priests were so deeply impressed by this profound philosopher's parade of wisdom that they missed their oracle's immediate reply. To Ford, listening with all his ears, it sounded suspiciously like a delighted but subdued chuckle.

"You are wise," the oracle replied in mellow tones. "My sister and I go to perform your wonders that this people may be great as of old."

Four minutes later the old-womanish buzzing from the round gross of priests was instantly hushed by a wild yell from Joicey.

"The flame!" he shouted, pointing to a broad pillar of hard, blinding white light that shot vertically up from the high place of execution to pierce the very root of the heavens.

IN THEIR wild stampede down the narrow corridor, the panic-stricken priests trampled each other like maddened cattle. Joicey had leapt back into the chamber of the oracle to let them boil out, and now he and Ford hurried over the prostrate bodies of the less agile priests to mingle with the shouting multitude. The terrified inhabitants of the city were pouring into the streets from their flat-topped houses and streaming along the broad avenues which ran from the red cliffs out through the city toward the open country miles beyond. There was something pitiable about their unreasoning terror; it was like the flight of a populace from a sudden volcanic eruption.

But the two men had no time for pity. Their own lives and those of the two women, they knew, were in the hands of these ignorant mobs; and a single mishap meant a horrible death not only for themselves but for Rosita and Evelyn as well. A shrieking, gesticulating woman attracted their attention. It was Rosita, Cassandra-like, prophesying disaster.

"It reddens!" Joicey yelled at the top of his lungs.

Paralyzed into immobility for an instant, those who heard the shout, infinitely terrifying to them because they understood nothing but would believe anything of what it portended, froze in their tracks and stared up at that hard pillar of dazzling white fire. For perhaps ten seconds they stood thus, petrified. Nothing happened. Then in a flash the blinding white changed to the color of newly shed blood. With a groan of utter, abysmal fear the spectators broke and ran pell-mell for the open country.

Ford and Joicey found themselves pursuing a fleeing figure that raced toward a dim cavern, one of several apparently just like it, at the base of the red cliffs. Rosita disappearing into the misty depths of this cavern, the two men panted after her, to stumble presently over the body of a guard slain by his own imagination. The other had escaped. Catching up with Rosita just as she reached a massive double door of lead, they helped her to swing open the doors and, once inside, to make fast the stout bars of the same metal which locked the leaden doors on the inside. Exit was easy; entrance without the consent of the wise women, impossible. They were within the forbidden caves.

Panting from their exertions they leaned against the doors and regarded their surroundings. They found themselves in a funnel-shaped amphitheater of lead-lined rock, about six hundred feet in diameter at the bottom and open to the sky, which showed as a bright blue circular window over a thousand feet above the floor. The floor of this funnel was also completely covered by lead plates, so closely fitted that the joints between the plates appeared as thin straight lines engraved on the level surface.

On the farther side of this amphitheater, a system of spacious corridors pierced through the cliff in all directions to the interior, and in the center of the floor was a deep well some fifty feet across. The shaft of this well, the corridors and, in fact, every inch of rock which they observed in the vast system of caves and open runnels, they learned later had been lined with lead in prehistoric ages.

Approaching the well, they peered over the sheer edge. Far below they made out a tiny spot of dull crimson, apparently no bigger than a pinpoint, so great was its depth below the floor.

"That's red-hot lava," said Ford. "This whole place must have been hollowed out of the crater of an extinct volcano."

"No," said Rosita. "Ana told me yesterday the traditions assert that all these caws, funnels, corridors and wells—Ana and Evelyn in their explorations have found over eight thousand wells just like this one scattered all through the caves—were burned out of solid rock of the cliff's by the Great Race. The only natural thing about any of all this is the vast mass of native rock cliffs or mountains which was here when the Great Race first came to this region. All the rest is their work. According to the traditions, the wells were sunk in order to expose the subterranean fires because in some of their 'taming of nature,' the Great Race used enormous quantities of terrific heat for long periods."

"The lead lining of this well can't go down to the lava," Joicey observed, "or it would evaporate long before reaching it."

"Yes, the well is lined all the way down. You are looking through a mere hole in the rock roof high above a lake of red-hot lava miles below us. At least that is Ana's account of it. Shall we go on? Evelyn's quarters—her living place—are less than five minutes' walk down that third corridor to the left."

THEY hastened down the dark tunnel in silence, overawed by the colossal wonder of these vast workshops and laboratories of a long-forgotten race. A small but rapidly growing oblong of light directly ahead told them that soon they should enter a second amphitheater open to the sky, and presently they emerged. Rosita, of course, had seen it before, but its unexpected charm drew a low exclamation of delighted astonishment from the two men.

This second open funnel was at least five times as broad as the other, being about a thousand yards or over half a mile across, and was a perfect little paradise of winding paths through brilliant flower beds and little clumps of young trees and blossoming shrubs. At this early hour of the day the shaft of sunlight from above shattered itself on the high western wall of the amphitheater, casting a soft reflected radiance like a summer dawn over the lovely garden, and arousing the late sleeping birds to their first sweet morning songs in the dewy leaves.

Under a rose bower not far from where they stood entranced, they noticed a low couch with bright coverings. Nearby a bench and table of some dark wood bore the remnants of an early breakfast—broken bread, fruits and two drinking cups of the peculiar greenish gold metal which they had seen in Rosita's chamber.

"That is where Evelyn sleeps," Rosita said, pointing to the couch; "and that is her summer breakfast room. The oracle's window is just over there, behind those hanging vines with the bright purple flowers."

"Where is Evelyn now?" Joicey asked.

"She and Ana are attending to the fireworks." Rosita laughed. "They will have to keep it up as long as you two stay. Otherwise the fright of those stupid priests may turn to awkward curiosity."

"Gosh," said Ford, admiring the delicately rich beauty of the scene before him, "I envy her. What do you say if we just camp here the rest of our lives and let the priests hammer their fists black and blue on that lead door?"

"I'm with you," said Joicey, ambling toward the table. "I wonder what the oracle had for breakfast this morning?" he rudely speculated.

"Ah, bread, fruits, and water. Excellent for the complexion, I'm told. Rosita, introduce us to the guardian angel of this earthly paradise."

"Ana?" Rosita asked innocently. "Er—ah—yes, of course."

"I shall be delighted. Down this way. That's the entrance to the cave of the flame over there. You couldn't live here very long, I'm afraid, without developing a man-sized thirst," Rosita continued as she led them toward the entrance. "Every drop of water that comes into this place is carried in by women attendants. The priests might object to their going back and forth to minister to a mere man."

"Where are these blessed women now?"

Joicey asked in sudden consternation. "They'll pitch us down one of these beastly red-hot wells if they catch us here."

"Ana packed them all off the first thing this morning to fetch in fresh supplies of dirt for the plants. She had observed that the soil in some of these beds is all but exhausted after its eleven years of constant cultivation. All this, of course, was carried in soon after she and Evelyn imprisoned themselves."

Joicey sighed his relief. "Good old Ana. I shall embrace her."

Rosita laughed. She had seen Ana; Joicey hadn't. "That's a promise," she said. "And we'll make you keep it, too. Well, here's the center of the mystery. Take your fill of it, for we can stay only a few minutes. Evelyn and Ana are nervous about fooling too long with the fire."

CHAPTER TEN
Joicey Keeps a Promise

THEY had entered a vast chamber filled with a soft radiance like bright moonlight. The floor of the chamber was hollowed out like a vast bowl, the sides sloping down very gradually from the surrounding walls. Glancing up, they saw a sublime vault of sheer, transparent crystal arching over the entire cavern.

"Ah," said Joicey, "this must be directly under the place of execution. The priests told me about that crystal roof. According to them, it was once dense red rock, like the rest, sealed over with lead, but the constant impact of the flame beating in a narrow beam for ages against its center and then 'mushrooming' out over the entire vault, dissolved the lead and slowly changed the rock of the roof to transparent crystal. But where is the flame? According to what they guessed, it should be a narrow pencil of rays striking the crystal at its center. I see nothing but this diffused moonlight."

Rosita found it. "Do you see that spot of red on the crystal of the roof, a little to the right of the center?" She indicated a blood-red patch on the vault almost directly over the center of the enormous bowl. "Well, that must be where the red ray you saw from outside enters the crystal."

"I see," said Ford. "In passing through possibly four hundred feet of crystal the ray gets spread out, just as it would by a very thick diverging lens. But where are the operators?"

"Look down now, just beneath the red spot. See them?"

Through the soft haze they dimly made out two small figures, like neat little dolls, standing by what looked like a low, flat pedestal. Toward these they now hastened down the gently curving surface of the vast bowl.

"They seemed absorbed in their work," Rosita remarked, "and no wonder. Ana accidentally discovered the trick of changing the colorless 'flame' into a ghastly red about nine years ago when she first began fooling with things, and she hasn't tried it since. It was at night, and only two of the women attendants, who happened to be out and returning late, saw the momentary blood-red flash of the pillar outside. Ana talked them into believing that it was their imagination, and bound them to secrecy by threatening to have them declared mad if they repeated what they had told her.

"The flash lasted only a second, Ana immediately putting things back as she had found them. It scared her half to death. Since then Evelyn and she have found out a great deal about the machine that generates the flame. Ana remembered how she got the red, so she and Evelyn turned it on this morning. The machine really requires two operators for convenient handling."

They were now within easy vision of the operators. The two women were standing over a low solid block of the peculiar green-ish gold metal from which projected two thin rods, each about six inches in height. From these two rods the two operators never lifted their eyes.

"Mind where you are going!" Rosita called out sharply. "That block is on a platform over one of the wells."

They halted just in time. From the sides of the well, sixteen narrow footwalks, at regular intervals, sprung across the abyss with its crimson dot far below, to meet directly above the center of the well in a circular platform about fifteen feet across. The narrow lead-covered footwalks were evidently girders of metal or possibly stone, supporting the central platform with its block directly above the lava beds miles beneath. The block, over which the two women were intently bending, was in the exact center of the platform. From the center of its top surface a thin pencil of vivid red rays shot vertically up to the crystal vault above. In the lead paving around the block a number of square holes had been drilled clear through the stone or metal of the platform, so that an observer standing near the block could look straight down the well and observe the crimson lava spot without changing his position. There was ample room for safely walking round the block from one of its short projecting rods to the other. A slip, of course, meant a plunge down the well into the boiling lava. From the rim of the wall to the central platform was a somewhat dizzy walk of about seventeen feet along an eighteen-inch girder.

"As I told you," Rosita said as she took the lead to the central platform, "they have counted over eight thousand of these wells dotted about in the different chambers of the caves. On the floor of this bowl alone there are over five hundred dotted about. This one is unique. It is the only one that is even partially covered. Possibly the machines above the others were burned off in the great disaster and fell into the lava." She had reached the platform and now glanced back to see what progress her companions were making. "Captain Joicey!" she exclaimed, stamping her foot, "do walk in the middle of the path."

Joicey complying with her request, Rosita proceeded to the block.

"We are here," she announced, approaching Evelyn.

"I heard you coming," she replied, "but we dare not stop with this." She had answered in ancient Tibetan, it being easier for her to think automatically in her adopted tongue than in English. As she spoke she put out a graceful hand, and with the greatest delicacy of touch gave her rod an almost imperceptible turn to the left. "There is something wrong," she continued. "Is the air hotter or colder in here than it was yesterday?"

"Hotter—very much," Rosita answered.

Without looking up, Evelyn addressed her companion. "Ana, try turning your rod so that the second mark on it comes opposite the fifth deep line on the scale."

Ana's wrinkled hand endeavored to make the adjustment. With a premonition of impending danger the men held their breath. Whether Ana blundered, or whether Evelyn's guess had been incorrect, they never knew. A thin, blinding rod of intense blue light leapt from the bottom of the block sheer down to the crimson spot in the well, and instantly the entire substance of the block itself became as transparent as glass. To their amazed eyes was disclosed a sight which perhaps no human beings had ever seen.

The block stood revealed as a bewildering tangle of some unbelievably intricate apparatus of green crystal embedded in solid metal, now miraculously rendered transparent by unskillful manipulation of the controlling device. Yet, for all they knew, this sudden transparency of the block might be nothing else than the correct preliminary to its proper functioning, accidentally rediscovered after the lapse of ages. The men could only gaze at it in fascination, seeking in that brief revelation of a forgotten science to master some slight detail of its baffling complexity.

Ana's hand dropped to her side. She stood rigid with fear at what she had unwittingly done. Without haste, and without the least sign of nervousness, Evelyn walked round to Ana's end of the block. Her steady, beautifully shaped hand approached the rod.

"I do not know what I am doing," she said in English. "The air is getting warmer. I must try something."

She gave the rod a turn to the left so slight that it barely moved. The intense blue downward ray was extinguished and immediately the vast chamber seethed with a dull red light thrown luridly up from more than five hundred lava wells in the floor of the bowl; the floor trembled as at the jarring approach of an earthquake, and from beneath it a deep angry rumbling muttered through the distant caves and corridors. The block had lost its transparence and now glowed with the sullen hue of red-hot iron.

The entire substance of the block itself became as transparent as glass—showing intricate works.

Joicey stepped quietly to Evelyn's side. "Let me try," he said. "I can do no more than wreck it. Shut your eyes, everybody. It's a tossup whether you open them here or in heaven."

Before they realized this rash intention, he had grasped both rods in his clumsy, heavily gloved hands and given them a vicious, wrenching twist. The jarring under their feet ceased abruptly, but the vast chamber still seethed with crimson light. Then he turned one rod slowly round, twisting the other simultaneously, but faster.

"If I don't hit the right combination before each rod makes a complete turn," he said with a grim smile, "we shall never see a blue-headed priest again. Ah, that must be it."

As he spoke the air of the cavern gradually lost its blood-red hue, and again a soft light brooded peacefully over the vast bowl. The red spot on the crystal roof too had disappeared, and in its place was now a bright path of faintly purple light. Once more the chamber of the undying flame was in its normal state, or so it seemed to a superficial inspection. They could not guess, of course, whether their tampering with the block had produced any deeper change not visible to a casual glance.

"Oh," Rosita gasped, "let us go at once. We have time to escape before the people return to the city. Ana knows where we can get horses not far from the entrance to this awful place."

"But I haven't got what I came for," Joicey quietly protested.

"Evelyn will give you all the sapphires you can carry. Won't you, dear?"

"More," Evelyn said in a rich, low voice.

She was hungrily devouring Joicey's face with her luminous, wonderful blue eyes, for it was the first English face that she had seen in twelve eternities. Joicey thus far had given her only a casual swift glance—he had been absorbed in the metal block and the operations of the two women. He now returned her frank, unfaltering admiration. Truly, she was as beautiful as her childhood miniature had promised she would be, with a sweet gravity about her eyes and mouth. Her coloring resembled Rosita's, but her seriousness, with a touch of the child which she could never outlive, was her own.

"Thank you, Evelyn," Joicey said in English. "That is very kind of you, dear. But I did not come all this long way to get a load of blue stones." He tried deliberately to use only such phrases as an eight-year old girl would understand fully and immediately.

"Did you come for me?" Evelyn asked simply, with the honest directness of a child.

"Yes, my dear. Your father sent me with this man and this young woman. But I came for something else too."

"What, if not sapphires?" Rosita asked.

"Fun," he replied, addressing Evelyn, adding immediately for Rosita's benefit, "information. You forget that I'm worth five million pounds sterling. That's as much money as I can expect to use decently."

"Information?" Ford repeated in astonishment. "What about?"

"These caves, for one thing. This block, since I've seen it, for another. Have you ever seen anything like the apparatus embedded in it?"

"Yes," Ford and Rosita answered together. Rosita continued. "It was like one of those things the sculptural figures in the rock tunnel were carrying. I would guess it is a small-sized machine of the same kind as that which the eight colossi at the end of the procession were carrying between them."

"Not quite," said Ford. "I'm sure this is only about one quarter of the whole thing those eight giants had. What about it, Joicey?"

"I agree with you," he said. "This is only a part of one of their main machines; probably just one unit of some fourfold contrivance. Possibly all four parts must operate in unison in order to do their trick, whatever it is, completely and with safety. I'm going to find out how this thing works and what it does."

Ford laughed. "If that's what you came for, you can carry a sack of sapphires for me."

"Delighted, old chap, if you two agree to stay here till I have time to take this thing to pieces." Turning to Ana, he questioned her in the ancient Tibetan. "Did your sweetheart tell you anything of what he read in those inscriptions when he was a young man?"

"Much that I could not understand," Ana replied. "That is why I brought you here—to tame the fire in this block and to make my people great, as my sweetheart dreamed."

A BROKEN heart makes some women beautiful, others hideous. Poor Ana was one of the latter. Her wizened face was that of an aged and sad-eyed, dejected monkey. Joicey regarded her as if she were Aphrodite just risen in fresh beauty from the waves. "You remember at least something?" he persisted. "Tell me ever so little and I will make the dreams of your dead lover come true. For among my people are many wise men who gave their whole lives to reading the mysteries of nature. I am not one of these; I am but an ignorant traveler. Yet, if I show these others even the shadow of a truth, they will come after me to make your people great. Tell me, what did the Great Race do with the fires they tamed?"

"They turned the rocks to metals, iron, silver, lead; they made lead into gold, and the gold into a harder metal, more beautiful than gold; they took the barren metals and compelled them to bear offspring of heat, fire, light and the lightning itself, and from this offspring they made living metals such as are not found in the rocks of the earth. They drew forth food from the air, heat and light from the winds and from the dead sands of the desert, and they made cool gardens of the fiery wildernesses. Winter or summer was theirs at will, and the winds blew or were still at their bidding. Snow fell when they bade it, and the rains came when they were called. They were masters of life and death; they died when they were weary, and none died before his time. Nature in all things was their slave, for they were the masters of all her secrets. In these ways they were great, and in many others of which my lover told me, but which I did not understand. For I am not wise as he was."

"Be faithful to me as you were to him," Joicey said, "and the wise men of my race will restore all these things and more to your people. For we, too, travel the same way that your race took ages ago, only we have just set our feet toward the rising sun. Tell me, are there any more of these blocks or other relics of the Great Race in these caves?"

"No. This is all that remains unruined. In many of the caves are twisted masses of metals and strange crystal fused together by the flame which destroyed all, but these are of little meaning."

"I would see those too, but not today, for it grows late. Tomorrow there is much to do. Not until the day after may I visit you again." He turned to the wondering, wide-eyed Evelyn. "We shall take you away from here to your father soon. Don't cry, or be sorry that we do not go now. Can you still tell the time by a watch, my dear? Or have you forgotten?"

"Show me your watch," she begged with all the eagerness of a child.

He extracted it from an inner pocket of the shirt under his robe and handed it to her. She took it with glee, caressing it.

"What time is it now?" he asked.

She puzzled over the dial a few moments. "A quarter past three," she said.

"Good!" he exclaimed. "Now show me how much the big hand moves in five hours."

Her forefinger slowly made five complete circuits of the dial.

"Right. Now, if you do something for me, I shall give you the watch as a present. You may keep it all your life. It will make you think of the first people like your own that you saw since you were a little girl."

"What must I do?" she asked eagerly.

Evidently, she had not outgrown her childhood's ambition to own a gold watch. She was a strange mixture, this beautiful girl of twenty-one. In everything pertaining to her English life she was eight years old; in all else she was a woman with a knowledge of the craftiness and deceit of the oriental mind such as no English woman, and but very few men possess. And behind it all there was a "something" in her eyes that was older than the human race and as ancient as the everlasting hills. Her prolonged, almost solitary brooding over the mysteries all about her had brought her close to the heart of eternity, and the solitudes of those twelve vital years from eight to twenty-one had developed in her a thirst for the deeps of knowledge such as only the profoundest lovers of nature ever experience. Although one-half of her mind longed just now to master the secrets of the ancient fire with the wise men whom Joicey had promised to bring to these caves, the other half was wholly enraptured at the prospect of possessing a gold watch.

"What must I do?" she repeated, her pleased face one rosy blush of joyous anticipation.

"This." He instructed her in the ancient language lest the English words prove too difficult for her unaccustomed ears. "This. When your sister, the wise woman, brings you word that we are about to go up to the place of execution, look at this thing. When the big hand has gone round five times, that is," he added in English, "after five hours—go to the chamber of the oracle. If your sister the wise woman is not there, outside, to say that all is well, hasten back here as fast as you can. Then," he now included Ana in his instructions, "you two women must do again, without delay, what you did today. Send up the blood-red light, for only thus may we escape with our lives. Then leave this place at once, go to the lead doors that bar the entrance to these caves, open them, and wait outside for us until we come. If on the way you can get two sacks of sapphires, do so. We shall not fail you. Now I see," he said, glancing up toward the crystal vault, "that the spot of light above us is faintly purple. Is this block now as it usually is?"

"It is," they answered.

"Then hasten now, wise woman," he said to Evelyn, "to the place of the oracle. Tell the priests who will question you there before long that all danger is now past; that you and your sister, obeying the two readers of secrets, easily controlled the fire. Do you understand? We must go before the guards return and prevent our escape. Do you, Ana, let us out."

She looked at him with all the pent-up hope of a frustrated lifetime in her eyes. "You will bring the wise men of your people to read these mysteries?"

"I will. Though sometimes I lie, I never break a promise."

"Ahem!" said Rosita

"By Jove!" Joicey exclaimed. "I almost forgot."

To Ana's intense disgust and astonishment, Joicey caught her in his arms and kissed her fervently on both wrinkled cheeks. Ford and Rosita applauded vigorously. Ana wiped her face. It seems that the degraded remnant of the Great Race had lost the greatest of all arts along with the rest which their ancestors cherished, so the bewildered Ana took the kisses as some new and particularly revolting mark of disrespect.

But Joicey was not without reward for his virtue. Evelyn, moved by some childhood memory of farewell kisses from her father's guests, walked artlessly up to him and offered her cheek. With a sidelong leer of triumph at Rosita, Joicey hastily brushed his lips with the back of his glove. Then he took advantage of his opportunities like a man. Following Evelyn over the eighteen-inch girder to the brink of the well, he executed a wild sort of triumphal war dance, a foolhardy thing to do in midair over a bed of boiling lava, but very soothing to the emotions.

Rosita, following with her nose in the air, let him go as near the edge as he liked.

ALL went even better than they had planned. Before nightfall the women attendants had been summoned back to the caves by the reassuring commands of the oracle, transmitted broadcast by the more daring and curious of the priests, saying that in the passing of the danger the Golden age had dawned again on all their land. Before midnight even the more timid of the refugees had returned to their dwellings in the city. Many, indeed, had come back much earlier when from afar they saw the terrifying pillar of blood-red light suddenly vanish in the afternoon sunshine. Far into the night the city rang with songs of praise for the wise women and rejoicings that the readers of mystery had turned imminent disaster into brilliant victory.

Toward the end of the celebration an insane, ugly note muttered threateningly under the thanksgivings of the more ignorant. It was the degraded Tibetan, they said, who by his filthy presence had caused the new wise woman to falter in her task. Thinking of him as she had seen him the evening before, and disturbed by the memory of his utter bestiality, her hand had erred at a critical moment, endangering the lives of all their people. Like all mad rumors sown in the fertile soil of a mob's collective ignorance, it multiplied upon itself at compound interest. Joicey turned to Ford, where they stood with Rosita outside her quarters.

"We have those infernal priests to thank for that. They are determined to give him up to the flame tomorrow, and this is their way of manufacturing public opinion to back up their devilishness." His jaw set. "Well, we shall see. Let us turn in now and be fresh to trick their stupidity in the morning."

They sought their beds, and like soldiers before a decisive battle, slept dreamlessly till dawn. They were awakened before sunrise by messengers from the priests requesting their attendance at the trial of the "filthy Tibetan." They had already taken him to the place of execution where they now waited the arrival of the wise woman and her companions to "aid them to a just judgment."

Without an instant's delay, the three rose and followed the messenger, Rosita saying that she must stop a moment at the chamber of the oracle to give her sister important instructions regarding the manipulation of the flame during her absence at the trial. The guides readily acquiesced; in any case they must pass that way.

Arrived at the passageway leading to the chamber of the oracle, Rosita bade the party not to wait for her, and hurried in to deliver her message to Evelyn. Within two minutes she rejoined them.

"Was Evelyn there?" Joicey asked in English.

"Of course. It is exactly three o'clock by her watch. You forgot to wind it when you gave it to her, but she remembered the trick when she found it had run down. If she has not heard from us in the meantime she will leave the window of the oracle chamber when her watch says ten minutes of eight, go to Ana, and at eight o'clock sharp send up a red light or flame like yesterday's."

"Fall back a second," Joicey instructed Ford, "and look at your watch. Note the time exactly."

Having complied, Ford reported that it was three minutes past seven. "The fireworks should begin not later than twelve sharp, or possibly two minutes to twelve. I'll keep an eye on the time and let you know by signals. One finger up means one hour gone; bent finger, half an hour; touching left eye, fifteen minutes; right eye, five; lips, two. Add all the signals to get the time."

"Right," said Joicey, as they turned into a narrow lead-lined passageway in the face of the red cliffs. "We are about to climb over twelve hundred feet of pitch-dark circular stairway up through the cliff. Rosita, demand longer and longer rests every fifty steps. Go as slowly as you can without arousing suspicion. Don't crawl at first; pretend to be exhausted as we get up. We must take three hours if possible."

The long toilsome climb began. "Do not tire the wise woman," Joicey ordered. "Her finely made body is not like your degraded carcasses. What to you is a task of no weight is to her a heavy labor. A little work makes her hands tremble for many days, so that she cannot with safety control the flame."

The ignorant escort was sufficiently impressed. Between the priests' solicitude for the continued steadiness of Rosita's fingers and her own honest concern for her tired legs, they managed to kill three hours and thirty-five minutes in the dark ascent. Five minutes more were wasted in opening the massive lead trapdoor at the top, opening out on the place of execution. Ford, boasting that in his own country he was a strong man, refused the assistance of the escort in what was, after all, no difficult feat. But he made it appear so, with his panting and groaning.

Incidentally, he took careful note that the trapdoor could be fastened by two stout bolts, evidently of lead by their feel, so that entry to the stairway from the place of execution could be easily blocked by anyone on the stairs. There was at first some difficulty in shooting the bolts. Evidently they had not been used for some time. Having satisfied himself that he could readily work the bolts, Ford finally succeeded in his trial of strength shouldering up the heavy door. The party emerged into the place of execution and the escort carefully let down the trapdoor.

There now remained but one hour and forty minutes in which to succeed or fail in saving their nomad from a fiendish death.

THEY found themselves in a vast cup-shaped hollow on top of the cliffs, a long, slight dip in the rim of the cup at their backs marking the depression on the skyline of the cliffs which they had seen from the chamber of the oracle. The floor of the hollow was a level Circular expanse of pure crystal; the gently sloping sides were lead-lined rock. Directly above the crystal floor and sheer up to the limit of vision, the atmosphere exhibited a distant brilliance, like the beam of a searchlight passing vertically up through the clear sunlit air. At the edge of the crystal about eighty yards from where the newcomers stood, a group of perhaps forty of the blue-headed priests stood with their backs to the trapdoor, intently regarding the brighter radiation of their "perpetual fire," Joicey took the situation in hand.

"Degraded beasts!" he shouted in modern Tibetan, "is this how you welcome us? Where is the prisoner whom you falsely accuse of being a filthy Tibetan? Bring him before us that we may Judge between him and you."

They humbly obeyed. As they approached leading the nomad, Joicey clasped his hands behind his back, frowned on the subdued priests and stamped with well-simulated impatience. All this time he was keenly scrutinizing the face of the nomad. The wretched man had been thoroughly washed and given a clean robe or toga such as the priests themselves wore. Joicey fixed him with his eyes.

"Is there still on your body, lost son of the Great Race, any shred of the filthy rags in which these men found you?"

Before the nomad could answer, the spokesman of the priests replied humbly, "No, master. In obedience to your brother's orders we destroyed all his rags before nightfall, and according to the command of your sister, cleansed his body."

"Silence! Did I speak to you?" Then he roared at the trembling man in English, "That disposes of this poor devil's compass, you blue-headed idiot. Ford, keep these men away from the trapdoor. Stay near it yourself, and if they approach, curse these degraded dregs of the Great Race away from your august presence. Rosita, invent an excuse for leaving when I give you the clue." Joicey's face while he bellowed these English sentences at the shaking priest was black with passion.

"I do not understand the modern language of the Great Race," he stammered in his own tongue, looking appealingly from Ford to Rosita. "Only this wise woman and your brother who reads mysteries speak the great tongue."

"Liar! Does not your sister, the wise woman, deliver her oracles to you in our language?" Joicey shouted at him in modern Tibetan.

"She does," the thoroughly cowed priest replied.

"Then you degraded fools," Joicey said with withering contempt, "have treasured her chants and utterances without understanding a single word. Speak the tongue of the Tibetans in our presence, all of you! Your vile ignorance would soil even your own debased language."

By this simple and time-honored legal device of browbeating, Joicey contrived to make them conduct the entire trial in the one language which the prisoner could understand. If the man had any brain at all he should now be a material help in outwitting the abashed priests and saving his own life. Joicey felt confident that the fight was already won.

"My sister," he said, addressing Rosita, "it is not necessary that you stay longer here among these low priests. Our brother will open the door for you. Descend to your sister."

"We have much to do for the welfare of your unworthy people," Rosita said, addressing the priests. "I shall descend. Your petty affairs are a weariness to my spirit and a burden on my flesh."

"As fast as you can!" Joicey ordered her in English. "Tell Evelyn we shall not need the red flame. It's too risky. You have an hour and ten minutes before she leaves the oracle window. We follow in fifteen minutes. Hurry!"

Ford lifted the trapdoor for her and she vanished down the spiral stairway. He was about to close the trap after her when, noticing that Joicey had again engaged the attention of the priests, he left it open and unobtrusively took his place by Joicey's side.

All was going with perfect smoothness. Joicey, master of the priests and of the situation, was holding forth in lucid Tibetan on the infallible earmark of a true son of the Great Race, the ability to find his way anywhere without the use of a "needle" such as the barbarians to the north used, and without even glancing at the sun or stars. Many of the priests looked self-conscious and pleased; they too possessed this aristocratic gift. Joicey's keen eye detected their conceit.

"And so," he said, concluding his well-reasoned harangue, "it scarcely is necessary to question this man at length. Those of you who are more fortunate than others in retaining through life this gift of the Great Race which every one of you has in childhood, can understand how impossible it would be for anyone not born with this wonderful power to feign possession of it. The simple fact that this man found his way through the fiery desert by means of this high gift alone is sufficient proof that he is a son of the

Great Race." He turned to the marveling nomad. "Is it not so, my brother?"

The nomad gaped at him like a suffocating fish. Either he was as stupid as a fencepost or, like George Washington, he could not tell a lie. Joicey's heart stopped. Ford experienced a sudden nausea.

"I do not understand what you have been talking about," the truthful blockhead replied honestly.

"You damned fool," Joicey ripped at him in English. "I'll save you yet from frying yourself like a worm on a hot stove." Then turning to the priests he suavely remarked in ancient Tibetan, "I fear your harsh mistreatment of our poor brother has destroyed his mind. He has no memory of his most precious gift. Shall we accept him as one of us—which he undoubtedly is—or would you prefer to continue these questions when he has recovered his mind, say a month hence?"

The priests were only too willing to leave the decision entirely with their learned brother. The conciliatory tone of this wise reader of mysteries, not to say his subtle flattery of themselves, had completely enslaved their obsequious minds to his slightest whim.

"Very well, brothers," Joicey decided. "He is one of us. Your judgment does credit to the intelligence of our race. For the present, let him share my brother's room and mine. His mind needs a physician, and we are skilled in such things."

They agreed readily enough. Had not he with impartial justice called them "brothers"? They all but fawned on him as they made way for him to lead them down to the city. With a curt order to the nomad to follow closely on his footsteps, Joicey turned his back on him. In turning he unclasped his hands from behind his back, letting his arms swing comfortably at his sides. He had taken but two steps toward the trapdoor when a yell of terror from the nomad froze every drop of blood in his body.

"The Holy Lama's hands! His gloves!" the wretch shrieked, pointing at Joicey's gloved hands. To his muddled mind it was quite clear that the devils in the desert had at last got the better of the Holy Lama, had murdered him in some horribly complicated way, cut off his hands, stuck them, gloves and all, onto one of their own nefarious crew of demons and finally had dispatched the grafted devil to strangle him, the Holy Lama's proselyte, with the very hands which had put the finishing touches to his conversion. It certainly was just the sort of well-rounded revenge that any ingenious devil would take.

"Run for it!" Ford shouted. He made a dive for the trapdoor. Glancing back he saw that Joicey was already intercepted. He stopped as if shot.

"IT'S NO USE, Ford," Joicey said quietly. "We're done for. They would get you before you were down a hundred steps. We could shoot only twelve of them, and there are over forty. Keep them here as long as possible. When we don't appear, the girls will know. It's their one chance. They can hold out in the caves for a week, and then—" He did not finish. It occurred to neither of them to shoot the nomad. They were not in the habit of escaping from their difficulties at the expense of others.

"Rosita has a revolver," Ford remarked. "Listen to that fool reading his own death warrant—and ours, too."

"Shall we start the shooting?" Ford suggested. "I'm not going to cash in without giving these fellows a run for their money. They're twenty to one against us."

"No. Give the girls time. We might shoot and bolt for the stairway, but the priests would be right on top of us. We couldn't lift and shut that heavy door before they smothered us. And we could not shoot on that spiral, even if it were lighted. The priests would only drive us into the open. Then the game would be up for good. Well, I hear our intelligent friend filling them up with our adventures. What a fool I was to show him my hands that night over the fire. He will come to that sacred memory in a moment."

Into the amazed ears of the priests, the terrified nomad was pouring a detailed and circumstantial account of his endless supper with the Holy Lama, his companion Tibetan and the charming girl for love of whom he had followed them across the desert. With the invariable luck of an imbecile his only mishap in the desert was the death of his horse from thirst when but ten hours' journey from the hither side.

He confessed to having experienced thirst himself during the subsequent ten hours' tramp. Otherwise, he had suffered no inconvenience. He had made the journey "in a straight line" by means of a "needle" which he had acquired some years before on a holiday excursion to the "northern land"—evidently China. Between his fuzzy way of snarling up his story and the priests' eager questions, it was well over an hour before his revealing cross-examination ended.

"And you say the gloves with which this holy man of the filthy Tibetans covered his burned hands were of sheepskin?"

"Of sheepskin, with the wool outside. I thought he wore them because the winds where I live are sharp and cold. But it was not so. By the embers of their campfire he showed me that of which I have told you. These are not men; but devils who have slain the Holy Lama in the desert. The woman with the yellow hair also is a devil."

The unreligious "priests" greeted this theory with a sarcastic sneer. They knew nothing of devils, but with the deceit of human beings, they were tolerably familiar. They turned and scrutinized Ford and Joicey. The two men stood close together, indifferently regarding the intense broad shaft of purplish white light streaming up from the crystal floor.

"Let's shoot," Ford suggested. "The girls have had over an hour. They should have guessed by now."

"Hold your fire," Joicey counseled. "Rosita may have gone to her room to wait for us. Give her time to get to the caves. I think she would have sense enough to wait for us at the oracle chamber, but we can take no chances. It's my fault for not telling her."

The spokesman of the priests approached Joicey. The coolness of the two "readers of mysteries" during the long examination, and their apparent indifference as to its outcome, had somewhat disconcerted the priests. They were not yet ready to accuse the two men openly of fraud.

"Will you remove your gloves and show us your hands?" the spokesman asked diffidently. Without a word Joicey complied.

"What caused those burns?" a priest asked.

"My passport to your country which I once carried in my bare hands for many days. I had lost the lead box in which I should have kept the jewel."

"Have you still with you the jewel which you showed us in our camp by the desert?"

"It is here." Joicey reached into his robe for the General's lead box with its sham sapphire. A priest took it without comment.

"Is it not true," the spokesman resumed, "that you told certain of my brothers when you visited us before that you, being of the Great Race, could walk unharmed through the storms and fires of the desert?"

"It is. Am not I here? Your brothers saw me enter the storm. Not many days ago they again saw me walking through the blue flames untouched."

"Then how is it that the cold light of the jewel, which we know to be the same as the cold fire of the desert, burned the flesh of your hands?"

"Your childish questions weary me. When you have learned our wisdom you will know all these things. Have done."

THE man respectfully inclined his head. "I shall ask you but one more question, Master. Was the jewel in this box," he took the box from his fellow priest and held it up before Joicey's eyes, "made by your brothers of the Great Race?"

Joicey had no clue to the man's intention. He mentally tossed up a penny and with his mind's eye watched it fall. Heads was to be "yes," tails "no." The coin of his imagining fell heads.

"Yes," he replied evenly, "the jewel in that box was made by a man of our race. But we set little store by such trifles. I brought it merely to convince your childish minds." All of which was, of course, literally true. But it was a diplomatic truth; that is, as a keen statesman characterizes such things, "a truth told with the intention to deceive." He could not decide from the priest's face whether his intention had carried or miscarried.

The priest made no reply. He motioned to one of his fellows, who joined him. "Have you, brother," he asked the newcomer, "a piece of rock from which you fashion the jewel passports?"

Searching the voluminous pockets of his robe the man presently found among the simple implements of his trade some odds and ends of common gray sandstone, one of which he handed to the spokesman. Taking it, the priest invited Joicey to accompany him to the edge of "the flame." Joicey nodded. Before following he spoke to Ford in English.

"Stay here. If I see danger, I shall stick in my eyeglass. If after that a priest tries to touch me, shoot him before he does. Don't shoot until his hand is within an inch of me."

Reaching the edge of the crystal, the priest placed Joicey's imitation sapphire and the lamp of sandstone side by side on the lead floor, about a foot from the shaft of rays issuing from the crystal. "Bring the Tibetan," he shouted.

Four priests seized the trembling nomad and dragged him to the edge of the rays.

"Put his right hand in the flame," the head priest ordered.

Despite the frantic struggles of the shrieking wretch two of the fiends got him face down and powerless on the lead floor while the other two, straightening his right arm, swung it around so that his right hand entered the rays. There was a hiss as of steam on red-hot iron and the withered hand curled up and back, white and useless. They released him. He fled in a daze, too terrified for outcry, to Ford.

"That," said the head priest, "is what this fire does to flesh that cannot withstand its flame. If your blue stone is not a true jewel you shall show us that you are indeed of the Great Race by walking through this fire to the far side of this crystal floor. And if you do not reach the farther side unharmed, your brother, the 'reader of mysteries,' and your two sisters, the 'wise women,' shall follow in your footsteps. But have no fear," he concluded with an evil snarl, "this flame is of the same nature as the fires of the desert which you walked through unharmed. It is merely stronger. The filthy Tibetan we shall keep to show as a foretaste to the others who would deceive us."

Saying nothing, Joicey thrust his ungloved left hand into his robe. The priest continued.

"See the making of a true jewel." Touching the lump of sandstone with his foot, he deftly kicked it onto the crystal floor just over the edge, so that it came to rest in the extreme outer band of the rays.

For perhaps five minutes nothing happened. Then before his very eyes Joicey saw the dull sandstone gradually become transparent. As the seconds passed the clear lump assumed a rapidly deepening bluish tinge. Before six minutes had elapsed the cold rays of the perpetual fire had transmuted the worthless lump of common sandstone into a priceless sapphire.

"Have you nothing new to show me?" Joicey asked with acid contempt.

"Who knows? Your own jewel may show you that of which you have never dreamed."

"You fool. I could slay you with one look from my left eye." Contemptuously turning his back on the priest he drew forth his monocle and screwed it firmly into his left eye. He stood motionless, staring into the faint purplish white fire before him.

Presently his own imitation sapphire slid onto the crystal at his feet and came to rest in the rays. For six or seven seconds there was no change. Then in the space of two seconds he saw the glass crumble to white powder and vanish. Wheeling instantly round he looked the priests squarely in the eyes. The man's hand was already outstretched to thrust him into the fire.

"Touch me and you are dead," he said quietly.

In the same instant the priest saw the monocle. "His eye is crystal!" he yelled. "He will slay me!" His hand dropped to his side and he stood paralyzed by his own credulous terror.

"Degraded fools!" Joicey shouted. "See what your ignorant disbelief has done. Would you be slain by a fiercer flame than this cold fire which we, who are of the Great Race, walk through unharmed? If not, let us with our brother whose hand you have destroyed quit this sty of ignorance forever, untouched by your vile hands. Lay so much as a finger on anyone of us, or on our sisters, the Wise women, and you are dead. Do you believe? Let this man touch me now!" The man was beyond motion, even of a finger, and the others were too astonished to move. "Likewise," Joicey continued rapidly, "if you follow us now you shall die instantly. We—"

Astonishment froze the words on his tongue. The livid face of the priest before him had gone a ghastly blood red. Glancing behind him he saw the cause. Up through the crystal floor streamed a pillar of vivid scarlet light.

Before six minutes had elapsed, the cold rays of the perpetual fire had transmuted the worthless lump of sandstone into a precious sapphire.

"Don't run," he shouted in English to Ford. "Take the nomad with you and wait for me at the trapdoor. These idiots are paralyzed with fright."

He strode up between the terror-stricken priests to the trapdoor. Reaching it, he gave the nomad a kick which started him well on his way down the spiral stairs, helped Ford to raise the trap and lower it gradually as they descended the first five steps. Then, ducking their heads, they let it drop with a bang and shot the bolts.

"Down like the devil!" Ford shouted. "I felt the beginning of an earthquake."

CHAPTER ELEVEN
Each to His Own

TIME after time in their headlong flight down the spiral stairway, the three men were rudely buffeted from wall to wall, but they never hesitated in their descent. Violent earthquakes wrenched the solid cliff, crumbling to fragments the stone steps beneath their feet; yet they kept on, sliding and rolling down over the rubble. Through it all their luck stayed with them, for the falling chips from above missed their heads.

Suddenly, with the abruptness of a thunder-clap, the terrific uproar ceased, and a blast of sultry heat smote their faces, and they knew that they had all but reached the bottom of the rock stairway. Was the exit blocked? Did that hot wind blow from the rising waves of a flood of incandescent lava? Involuntarily they halted. Over the ruined stairway below them they heard the dull tinkle of falling rubble under light footsteps leaping up to meet them. A revolver shot rang out, and when its clattering echo subsided a voice cried in English:

"Is that you?"

"We're coming," they shouted.

"Quick! I've got horses."

Dashing down through the blinding heat and gaining the open, they found Rosita and Evelyn already mounted. There were in all twelve badly frightened horses, saddled and bridled, in four strings of three each. At a sign from Rosita, Joicey sprang onto Evelyn's trembling horse. Sitting behind him, she put her arms round his chest, and Joicey, digging his heels into his horse, galloped his string of three after Rosita's. Ford followed just as a terrific earthquake all but stampeded his horses, managing the two remaining strings; for the nomad, suffering intense pain from his withered hand; could do little more than keep his seat.

Amid the crash of falling buildings, the terrified horses galloped down the deserted streets, mad to gain the open beyond the city. It was impossible to look back; every nerve and instinct strained only to reach the comparative safety of the open country miles from the crumbling red cliffs. Not until they had overtaken and passed the fleeing multitudes, leaving the last straggling houses of the city a mile in their rear, did they rein up the staggering horses to recover their wind.

Turning in their saddles, they looked back. Great flakes of red rock were crumbling from the cliffs and roaring down in avalanches of broken stone upon the roofs of the city. Jagged fissures at the base of the cliffs revealed the dull, cherry red of the rapidly melting rock in the deep recesses of the cliffs. Under their feet the rising and falling rumble of subterranean detonations shook the quivering ground like a jelly. Their wills urged them to flee, but the heaving sides of their spent horses counseled the prudence of five minutes' halt.

"Where's Ana?" Joicey asked.

"Dead," Rosita sighed. "I wanted to go back and get some sapphires but she wouldn't tell me where they were, and went herself. The lava in the well by the entrance to the caves boiled up and covered the floor of the first amphitheater just as she started back dragging two sacks of sapphires from a tunnel on the farther side. She left the sacks and disappeared into the tunnel by which she had come. As Evelyn and I started to run a torrent of boiling lava gushed from the tunnel."

"She didn't deserve that," was all the comment of the men. Evelyn's face was wet with tears, but she made no sound.

"Did any of your priests escape?" Rosita asked.

"No," Joicey replied. "They stayed in the place of execution to pay for this chap's right hand."

Rosita glanced at the nomad's dead hand. She said nothing.

"What has happened?" Ford asked. On a few rapid sentences, she told how, after waiting in the chamber of the oracle thirty minutes for the men, she had guessed their extreme danger, and ordered the priests to admit her to the caves, saying that her sister urgently needed her assistance. Ana, Evelyn, and she had then tried desperately for half an hour to send up the red ray, but the block apparatus, evidently damaged radically by Joicey's rough handling the day before, was beyond their control.

The instant Evelyn touched one of the rods the block burst into brilliant transparency and again the hard blue ray shot down the well to the lava below. Struggling with the machine, they noticed the air in the vaulted chamber was rapidly rising in temperature, and on glancing down the well, saw that the lava was now a vivid scarlet and apparently rising fast.

Rosita, leaving Ana and Evelyn to wrestle with the machine till the last moment of safety, rushed out to give the alarm. Within twenty minutes, the entire population of the city was streaming toward the open country. Before telling the priests all, however, Rosita had ordered them to bring her instantly twelve fresh horses, saddled and ready for the road, saying only that the animals would be desperately needed by herself, her sister and the two readers of mysteries if they were to avert the threatened catastrophe. Having secured the horses, she commanded the priests to evacuate the city at once. She then drove all the horses into the small courtyard of a dwelling near the entrance to the spiral stairway.

DASHING back to get Ana and Evelyn, she had met them in the entrance to the caves. Evelyn and Ana had struggled with the machine until a sudden jarring under their feet warned them that the rising lava had surged up and struck the rock roof of its bed. One glance down through the holes in the platform of the block sufficed to show them that they must run for their lives. The scarlet spot far beneath was visibly growing larger. The lava had entered the well and was shooting up toward them in a fountain of molten rock. Not knowing the imminence of the fiery flood, Rosita had asked where the sapphires were kept, and Ana's tragic death had followed.

The girls then fled to the horses. Rosita left Evelyn with them, and started up the spiral stairway to see whether Joicey and her uncle were still alive, and if necessary, to aid them in escaping from the priests. At their answering shout, she had turned instantly and scrambled down again over the shattered stone. With Evelyn's help she somehow had managed to drag the stupefied horses from the courtyard and prevent them from stampeding before the arrival, a few seconds later, of the men.

"Evelyn rode a great deal when she was a little girl," Rosita concluded; "but it will be some days before she learns the knack again."

Poor Evelyn, weeping silently, said nothing. Rosita leaned over in her saddle and whispered to Joicey. "Let her be," she said. "The poor kid is heart-broken over Ana's death."

Joicey nodded. "Change mounts," he said. "When the lava boiling up through those wells fills the caves, there will be the devil to pay. How many wells did Ana say she had counted?"

"Over eight thousand five hundred, in the undestroyed chamber alone. She thought from appearances that there must be thousands more all through the ruined parts of the caves."

"Well, I hope so. Those blessed blowholes are the safety valves between us and a sudden ascent to heaven. But for them that whole cliff would have burst the roof of the sky hours ago," he remarked as he dug his heels into his fresh horse.

Hour after hour they galloped over the level plateau, leaving the lumbering two-wheeled carts of refugees from the farmhouses far behind, and urging their exhausted horses to the limit of their second wind. Whenever one of the animals which they were riding showed signs of collapse, they all changed mounts and rested the beasts for a few minutes. Then they were off again, relentless as ever.

By sunset, the towering red cliffs from which they were fleeing showed only as a low faint streak on the far horizon with a dim fan-shaped halo of whitish purple light radiating from one point on its crest, faint and evil against the calm, deep sapphire of the evening. This halo puzzled them, for certainly the block must have been destroyed hours ago.

"There is something happening to the rocks in the interior of those cliffs that we know nothing about," said Joicey, looking back. "Mere heat never sent up colored rays like those. We started the thing going with our ignorant fooling. Now nature will do the rest and finish the job once for all."

For four hours longer they reeled on over the plain. Then halting they flung themselves from their saddles, hobbled the horses and unsaddled them. Sinking to the ground where they stood, they slept the sleep of exhaustion.

In the hour before dawn they leapt dazed to their feet, awakened by the screams of the horses. All around them the vast plateau lay stark and blue in the glare of an unearthly light. Involuntarily they glanced behind them in the direction of the cliffs. From end to end the horizon was a sheet of seething blue flames licking hungrily up the sky halfway to the zenith.

"On your faces! Stop your ears!" Joicey shouted, flinging himself full length on the ground.

They were barely in time. The appalling concussion of the eruption which had shattered to dust the entire mountain range behind them, broke the legs of two of the horses and rolled the others over and over on the grass like balls of thistle down. Wave after wave of the terrific detonation volleyed over them, and the blue glare on the ground deepened, shade-by-shade to a dull red, then vanished suddenly in absolute black with the passing of the last explosion.

Like their own shadows in a fever dream, they staggered to their feet and reeled off to find the horses. The grass at their feet became faintly visible, and looking back Joicey and Ford saw the source of this new and ghastlier light. For one horrorstricken second their hearts stopped. From end to end of the horizon a vast, flickering wall of blue phosphorescence, like a tidal wave of burning sulfur, hung above the plateau.

Words were unnecessary. That wall of seething blue flame was of the identical hue and peculiar brilliance of the cold, poisoned flames of the desert. All the oceans of hell were rushing over the plateau to drown them in cold billows of hideous madness.

Four shots in quick succession brought the men to their senses. Rosita had shot the two horses with broken legs and had put two others, terribly lacerated, out of their pain. Somehow or another they got the remaining animals unhobbled and to their feet, and found their saddles. Instinct alone urged the cruelly hurt brutes to stumble on with their riders, for they were stone deaf and insensible to blows. Their flight now necessarily dragged more and more, a complete change of mounts being no longer possible. The stunned horses moved like machines, poor beasts.

Dawn broke, and once more the refugees glanced back. The tidal wave of fire was less than fifteen miles behind them. As the level rays of the sun struck the base of the mile-high wall of blue fire, the foot of the advancing wave seethed with a blinding light and slowly, majestically the crest toppled over toward them on the plateau in a silent breaker of sapphire flame. Within half an hour that wave must wash over them.

Gazing sadly at it, Joicey spoke. "I tried to bring those wretched people something of their great past, and now the last of them lies dead beneath that wave. It is always so. Shall we go on, or end it here? The horses are done."

"Lead them," Ford answered. "Eternity is long enough without our help. Ten minutes or a hundred yards may save us yet."

"Nothing can save us when that poison cloud overtakes us."

"It may not. There should be a strong wind before long, rushing in toward the hot lava beds. The lava must have flowed out for miles over the plain by this time. Besides," he added quietly, "I have a conscientious objection to suicide. That merely is my own view, of course. I do not presume to pass judgment on any of you who may think otherwise. Evelyn, take hold of my hand. You're tired."

By mutual consent they ran on, tugging their horses, and Joicey half dragged the nomad who was in a daze and helpless. In about ten minutes they met the first puff of the morning breeze.

"Saved," said Ford, quickening his run. "Don't look back till it's a gale."

The long-delayed hurricane rose with incredible speed as the cold air of the plateau rushed in at last to the far-distant lava beds. Looking back, they saw the tide of blue fire less than three miles behind them seized by the wind, and tattered into high-flung streamers of dazzling violet flame as the hurricane rolled the inferno of madness back over the plateau.

They were saved.

ONE morning some twenty months later, a messenger from the wireless room of the fastest trans-Pacific mailboat between Hong Kong and San Francisco handed the taller of two bronzed men who stood gazing down at the sapphire waters a sealed marconigram evidently just received.

"What new bee has found its way to the General's bonnet?" Joicey laughed, slitting the envelope.

"He wants you to try frozen orange juice on Evelyn. Poor girl, I'm genuinely sorry for her, though it is rather a joke; after eighteen months of roughing it in Chinese deserts and mountains without a murmur, it is a come-down to be bowled over by seasickness."

"Ha!" Joicey snorted when he had read the General's message. "Listen to this:

San Francisco. June 20.
Stay in your cabin until I board steamer. Anderson is here.
Wedderburn.

"What do you suppose he wants?" he asked.

"More sapphires at his own price, of course. Well, he won't get mine."

"Won't you sell?" Ford asked.

"Not for twenty million. That cube is to become the Chief cornerstone of the new age. It shall be kept in a lead casket engraved with this legend: 'This sapphire is one of the two last identical jewels made by exposing a cube of common sandstone to certain rays discovered, used, and forgotten by a dead race. The first person or persons duplicating the rays which this stone emits after exposure to sunlight shall receive a reward of four million pounds sterling. This reward is to be held in trust, and the income pending its final disposal administered for the good of humanity and science, by the Ana Foundation for the Destruction of Ignorance. The expert staff of the Foundation shall be the last judges of all claims for the prize.' "

Rosita had joined them. "You may as well make Evelyn a present of the four million now as later," she said darkly. "And what are you going to do with the other million pounds? You got five out of Anderson."

"Ah," he replied, readjusting his monocle to get a better view of her, "that remains to be seen."

"I think I shall go and see how Evelyn is," Ford remarked.

"She just had her lunch," Rosita warned him. "Take a stewardess with you." She turned to Joicey. "You haven't answered my question. The income from twenty million dollars should be enough to run your precious Ana Foundation. What about the rest of your loot?"

"Well," he said, putting his monocle in his vest pocket, "I shall probably enjoy life on the balance."

"How? Exploring? Racking your brain on those machines in the Himalayan tunnel? Washing the Tibetans?"

He glanced cautiously around the deck. Nobody was in sight. "I'll tell you," he whispered, bending down so that nothing might escape her. "But don't let it go any farther."

Before she realized fully what he had done, he had put his arm around her and kissed her.

"Well," she said, "if you think that sort of thing is worth five million dollars, your money won't last very long."

Her apparent indifference nettled him. Also it made him feel cheap and rather foolish. "Don't you care?" he said.

"Not half as much as you care for Evelyn."

"Oh, damn!" he exploded. "Can't you see that all these months I haven't once thought of her in that way?"

"Then how have you been thinking of her?"

"As an eight-year old child. She is charming and beautiful—as beautiful as you are—and the man who is lucky enough to get her someday will be in heaven all his life. But she still has to learn all that white people think and feel between the ages of eight and twenty-three. No doubt a year in London will do it, for she has a brilliant mind. But it positively gives me the creeps sometimes to hear her in one breath pattering like a little girl, with all the innocence of just eight years, and in the next picking her fellow man to pieces with the cold-blooded craft and subtlety of an aged oriental devil. Ana taught her thoroughly, I'll say that for her. Frankly, I don't envy Wedderburn his job in civilizing one half of her."

"Dear me," said Rosita, quite maddeningly. "Anything else?"

"Yes. She has an appalling sort of scientific mysticism that sometimes makes my spine stick up like a hedgehog's. Her eerie remarks about the impressions left on the grass by last night's shadows in the moonlight—she will actually show you the beastly things in broad daylight—or her ghastly insistence that it is much pleasanter and easier to walk north instead of east or west, give me the cold shivers. No doubt this is all a result of her long imprisonment with Ana in the caves, and will pass when she makes scores of friends her own age. But until it does, and she forgets all the traditions that Ana taught her, I shall like her best when she is just eight years old. And I can't marry a mere child, you know."

"All that is too logical to be convincing," Rosita remarked.

"Do you want me to be illogical?" he blustered.

"Of course. Love and logic are cat and dog. Wasn't there some illogical reason behind all your attentions to Evelyn the past year and a half?"

"If there was," he said craftily, "then I must be in love with her."

"Not at all," Rosita retorted sharply.

"You are illogical," he said, and she stamped her foot. "Therefore," he continued with geometrical precision, "by your own test you are madly in love with me. I knew it, I knew it!"

HE STARTED capering on the deck. She was so vexed with herself and so angry at him that she laughed. "Do have the common decency," she said, "to let me save my self-respect."

"Very well," he generously assented, coming to rest at her side. "I shall. My interest in Evelyn began, I hope you noticed, when you took to nursing our Tibetan friend's stump. That was all right. It was only proper that you should do everything possible to make the chap less wretched. But when you deliberately tried to make him believe that you were his lost love of that mutton orgy, and not a yellow-haired devil of the fiery desert, it was a bit thick. Suppose you had convinced him that you and his Tibetan sweetheart were one and the same girl. What then?"

"Well, what?"

"You would have washed him and married him."

"I would not. Absurd. The priests had washed him."

"Then why did you do everything in your power to win him back to you?"

She threw back her head and laughed. "You never will understand women as long as you live. Never mind, I like you for it. You've told me what I wanted to know."

"What?" he demanded.

"Why, that you love me, silly."

"I told you that twenty minutes ago."

"Oh, no, you didn't. Here comes my uncle. Let us keep it to ourselves a bit. It is too sweet to share, just yet."

"Well," said Ford, "she's coming to, just as we reach the Golden Gate." Evelyn had in fact just suggested that she might be able to take a short turn about the deck, but this made the smothered laugh with which Joicey greeted his remark no less puzzling to Ford.

"What have you two been up to?" he asked.

"Oh, nothing," Rosita answered. "We were just talking about our nomad. Poor fellow, he wasn't much good as a guide, was he?"

"As stupid as a dried prune. Fit only to be a lama."

"Well, that's what he is by now, and a very highly respected one too, no doubt. Can't you just see the Tibetans gaping at him when he brags how he led four evil spirits of the 'Forbidden Desert' through the forgotten mountains and lost them on the Chinese desert?"

"We do owe him a vote of thanks, though," Joicey remarked, "for blundering onto that caravan route while he was looking for grilled mutton chops in a dry river bed. In some ways that chap was a genius."

"I'll bet he never takes a wife," said Ford.

"So will I," Rosita laughed. " 'E learned about wimmen from me, 'e did.' Well, here we are, home at last. Dear, but it looks good. I'll bring up Evelyn."

213

Fifteen minutes later as the steamer crept into dock, Evelyn leaning over the rail gave a glad cry and instinctively stretched out her arms. Something about the white-haired man standing at the pier's end swept thirteen years from her mind, brought back her childhood in one overwhelming rush. He recognized her and waved. She sank sobbing into Rosita's arms. When at last the gangway was lowered, Rosita stole quietly away and left them to find each other.

Joicey in the meantime had completely forgotten the General's message. "I say," he exclaimed to Ford, "look at that fat little chap dancing all over the Captain. Excited, what?" He screwed in his monocle to get a better view of the interesting phenomenon. "By Jove, it's Anderson. I wonder what the Captain has been doing to him?"

Anderson spied them. "There he ith, Captain!" he shrieked. "Arretht him! He'th on your boat."

Joicey strolled up to the Captain. "Going to put me in irons, sir?"

The Captain grinned. "If you insist. I hope you won't, though, because it wouldn't be legal now that we are no longer on the high seas. This gentleman neglected to get a warrant and bring an officer."

"Ah," said Joicey looking through about three feet of invisible Anderson to the floor of the Customs Office behind him, "absent-minded beggar, I see."

Anderson fizzed with fury. The grounds of his complaint against Joicey appeared to be that he had purchased a worthless ball of gray sandstone four and a half inches in diameter for the exorbitant price of five million pounds sterling. He wanted his money back.

"But I say, old fellow," Joicey expostulated, "I didn't sell you your bally sandstone ball." He reached into his pocket and produced photographic copies of certain certificates, experts' reports, and receipts and quitclaims which Anderson had signed. He dangled them just a little too temptingly near Anderson's right hand. In five seconds they lay on the deck, worthless scraps of torn paper.

Joicey smiled. "Sorry, the originals aren't handy," he said. "They're in the vaults of that bank in Darjeeling where you and I transacted our business. I need them; you don't, as you once were kind enough to inform me. But what's the row?"

With perhaps more profanity than was necessary, Anderson explained how Joicey's sapphire sphere upon being mounted in gold according to the Maharajah's orders, had gradually dimmed, until in fourteen months its brilliancy had vanished, the gold mounting had turned to copper, and the supposed sapphire to gray sandstone. The Maharajah naturally had demanded his money back, and the courts, with indecent haste, had enforced the demand. Anderson forgot to mention how much he had been obliged to disgorge. But as he looked quite pale and a bit puffy under the eyes, it probably was not less than everything the Maharajah possessed.

Joicey followed the account with absorbed attention. "Deuced interesting," he remarked when Anderson had finished. "Do you know," he said, "if I had had just a little more faith in human nature I should never have sold you that stone." Anderson gaped at him, and Joicey continued. "For then I should have believed at least some of the things which the old gentleman who had the stone before I took it told me. When I sold you the stone, Anderson, I had not the faintest idea that it would have any effect upon any metal whatsoever. If I had even dreamed that it could turn gold into copper I should not have sold it to you for a thousand million. For it's a clue."

"It's a thwindle! I'll—"

"No, you won't, Lem," Ford broke in good-humoredly. "Does Lemuel Anderson, the shrewdest man at a bargain in all Europe and Asia, long to advertise that he was done brown by a perfect fool of a young Englishman? You haven't a legal leg to stand on, and you know it. Otherwise you should have had us in jail twenty minutes ago. Forget it. What about my sapphire disc?"

"I couldn't thell the rotten thing after the other."

"I'll give you fifty thousand pounds for it," Joicey snapped.

"Fifty-five thousand?" Anderson haggled.

"Done!"

THE END

If you've enjoyed this book, you will not want to miss these terrific titles...

ARMCHAIR LOST WORLD-LOST RACE CLASSICS, $12.95 each

B-5   ATLANTIDA
by Pierre Benoit

B-6   FORGOTTEN WORLDS
by Howard Browne

B-7   THE LOST WORLD
by Arthur Conan Doyle

B-8   THE CITADEL OF FEAR
by Francis Stevens

B-9   A STRANGE MANUSCRIPT FOUND IN A COPPER CYLINDER
by James De Mille

B-24   THE PURPLE SAPPHIRE
by John Taine

B-25   THE METAL MONSTER
by A. Merritt

B-26   THE YELLOW GOD
by H. Rider Haggard

B-27   UNDER THE ANDES
by Rex Stout

Made in the USA
Middletown, DE
28 October 2023

41521600R00130